中英文双语版短篇小说选

Selected Stories:

An English-Chinese Collection

严力 著

易文出版社

中英文双语版短篇小说选

Selected Stories:

An English-Chinese Collection

by Yan Li

严力 著

责任编辑：邱辛晔
封面插图：严 力
美编设计：王昌华
出版： 易文出版社·纽约
版次： 2021 年 4 月第一版，第一次印刷
字数： 100 千字
定价： $25 美元

ISBN： 978-1-940742-60-1
Published by I Wing Press, New York
Iwingpress@gmail.com

关于作者

严力，北京人，祖籍浙江宁海。朦胧诗诗人、旅美画家、纽约一行诗社社长。

于1973年开始诗歌创作，1979年开始从事绘画。星星画会成员。1985年夏留学美国纽约，1987年在纽约成立一行诗社，担任社长，出版一行杂志，并创作小说。著作包括《这首诗可能还不错》《黄昏制造者》《纽约不是天堂》《带母语回家》等诗集、小说选集十多种。现为法拉盛诗歌节主任委员、纽约华文作家笔会会长，纽约一行杂志主编。

YAN LI (painter, poet, fiction writer, China; b. 1954, Beijing) is a member of a group of artists known as The Stars; as a poet, he is identified with the Misty Poets; as a fiction writer, he is known to be the O. Henry of China. In 1987, he founded Yi-Hang in New York; the publication is a quarterly journal that features the works of contemporary Chinese poets as well as translations of American poems. His poems have been translated into French, Italian, English, Swedish, Korean and German. He has held many exhibitions and published numerous books, the most recent a novel, *Meet with 9.11* (Literature & Art Press, Shanghai, 2002).He is living in both Shanghai and New York now.

e-mail: yanli777@gmail.com

Contents

Dial Heaven

The tale I'm going to tell may not strike you at first. The experience of photography is too commonplace to need a new portrait. Which is why I've never used it as a subject. Until this Sunday afternoon, that is.

The morning sun had breathed a bit of life into a long winter of much too much snow. The last three Sundays just didn't have the right feel. After lunch I took the camera to be imprinted. But when I got there, the sun was gone and the chilled had returned. I thought of turning back after a few minutes. I thought of turning back after a few minutes. But not before a few shots. I used the tele and snapped a few of the freezing pedestrians. Suddenly, an outburst of laughter rang out from across the street. A homeless person was staring at a garbage can. Treasures spotted, judging from his delight. He put his hand into it. My lens was trained on him, shutter release cocked. Old clothes, it flashed across my mind.

As the shutter release went down I saw it was an old white telephone he was pulling out. What's the big deal? Another mentally ill, I thought. He turned out to be not entirely without sanity. He put the phone on top of another garbage can. "Hello!" SO loud everyone heard him on this side of the street. A few more people stopped to watch. "Yeah. Smith here. Haven't heard from you in a long time! Must be living the good life up there. Hey, I can only envy you…God, the clouds are thicker than my blankets." He was wearing a worn black felt hat. His blackness and his black clothes seemed New York enough. I hadn't thought so much of the sensitive stuff. Technical aspects of man eat man, historically destined existentialism, and cultural factors. "Ha ha," he seemed to have heard some good news, "guess you know nothing about rent. I tell you, my name's Smith. I live in New York…What? You don't know New York? How tragic, you must be kidding, you make me sad! But you must know New York because you know my number." A line to God, I thought. His logic and associations weren't bad." Unemployment benefits?" He lifted up his head, "So you have heard about unemployment benefits! Great, looks like I wasn't well-educated enough. I just didn't expect you to know about unemployment benefits. Must be in the textbooks. If I had known, I wouldn't have dropped out to work! … Who cares about tomorrow or no tomorrow, let's talk about unemployment benefits. How much a month can I get?… Do you pay tax? US? Canadian? To Clinton?" He paused to laugh at what he had just said, punctuated by a few diseased coughs, "Poverty is my God. Poverty, God. Poverty, God…yes, call more often." He noticed us across the street and rambled on merrily," I have friends. Many! They all say hello to you. Come visit when you have time…Clothes? Got no need, they must be expensive up there, just bring a few angels when you get down here…Of course I like girls! I will buy you a drink when I get married. Come to think of it. I've never had your champagne, and you've never had ours...It's OK, I'll stay sober...Alright, take care of yourself. "He hung up, smiled, lowered his head in thought, then dialed a number. "Son? It's me. Me! Of course I'm your dad, who else?...Cut it out, my woman is next to me!" He held out the receiver to us, "Say, that's my son, he wants to speak to my wife. What a joke, he doesn't even know who I am! Tell him about me. He who doesn't know me is my son, cause I don't know who my woman is!" While he was ranting on, I lowered my camera. I didn't want to get him raved up by being seen taking pictures of all this. "You!" He pointed at me, "You get me here! Hurry up, hurry!" Trouble, I thought. Better cut out. The crowd was thinning out. "Don't' go! Give me a smoke. I will let you take a photo." I hesitated. I guess I wanted his performance to continue. I dragged myself over, gave him a cigarette and lit it for him. His stench was strong, but his expression relaxed me a little. It was a face with humor, and that's the truth. He said to me, "This way you smoke one less, and your lungs get polluted by one less." I said to him, "You are a performance artist." I had meant it. "Yeah, should've charged you admission. Say, can you spare a buck?" I knew I had made a faux-pas. I didn't want to refuse and get hassled, so I gave him a dollar and retreated back across the street. Better stay away a little. I looked at him. A fleeting expression on his face seemed to have said, "The rich are afraid of the poor." That moment the Culture Revolution came back to me.

He had thought of God, then his son. Clues to his like. If I were a western psychologist, I would sure be able to analyze him for you. But as a new Chinese immigrant, I probably have different views on religion and procreation. I mean he must have been born to a religious and male-dominated family. Even more, his last hopes rest on these two premises. But I can also try to imagine he did have a son, only he's dead and the death drove him to madness. His son would call him from heaven, or he would call there to take to him. Just what's God's number? Suddenly, a friend's joke came back to me and I laughed. A professor, a very serious fellow who taught philosophy, one day ran into an old student of his and invited him for a cup of coffee. They had a good discussion and exchanged phone numbers before leaving. The young man insisted on paying for the coffees and told him it would be his turn next. The next day the professor thought of some more philosophical problems he wanted to discuss and called the number he was given. He hung up immediately after hearing the greeting. He thought he had dialed the wrong number and tried again. The same greeting, but this time he listened for a moment longer before hanging up, livid. But then he shrugged it off. The student had given him the number of a sex hotline. He liked to think he understood the young man and remembered they had talked about Freud and sexuality. Perhaps the young man was trying to make a point with the practical joke. Or perhaps it wasn't premeditated. Business leaving no stone unturned, and even cum can get through the line, he thought ruefully.

Smith started to dial again. My mind wandered off a bit. I wondered whether in his mind the line was hooked up to Africa or was there simply for his own interest. In the United Nations called America, the individual is probably more important than race, Personal problems come first. I continued my watch. He held the receiver under his chin and listened hard. Ten long minutes. I took a few more shots and suddenly felt the cold. I looked at him. He wasn't wearing much but did not shiver. Mentally ill. He finally hung up. And who would know what he had heard? I wanted to know, but didn't have the guts to ask him. He seemed to have noticed the other garbage can and was obviously no longer upset by the last call. I laid aside the camera and started to scout for another object.

When he busted out laughing again, I was curious what he came up with this time. It was a red hat. A woman's. He took off his black hat, gave it no thought and tossed it into the garbage can. He put on the red one, but not before making sure of its orientation and dusting it a bit. Well, he appeared brighter and stood out more, I snapped a few more shots. God some good stuff, I told myself. Something off the beaten track, for a change. But the joy was tempered by with something a bit uncomfortable. An afterthought perhaps. An easily forgivable fakeness. We photographers and visual artists often are suckers for destroyed things. Burnt houses, a recent battlefield, and slums. More contrast and photogenic, they are preferred over more perfect things. Minutes ago when I was taking the photos, I spent most of the time fussing over technical details like shutter speed and aperture, savoring the pleasures of my labor. I had not only taken a close-up of him, I had also taken some wide-angled views of his surroundings. I didn't forget either to take a close-up of the receiver with the broken cord. After he had put on the red hat, the color stood out even better. Just the thought of developing the roll gave me pleasure and stamina to withstand the cold. But it hadn't been perfect. I should have brought the camcorder. It would have made good TV viewing. If only I had caught him on video.

Once again he dialed a number. He shook his head, tried another time and shook his head again. The line was busy, I guessed. The third try got through. "Hey, Marianne," he said, "It's me, come over here...I don't know the name of the street! Well, I am not going anywhere, so you some. I'll take you out, nothing to worry, sweetheart...Hey. You are still sleeping with that son of a bitch! Fuck!" He slammed down the phone. Wrath for an old love. Some toy, this phone. He recovered quickly though and made another call. Got through. He pulled over an old man who happened to have walked by and dropped the receiver in his hands, "Your call again!" The old man replaced the receiver on the phone, shook his head and continued on his way. Yes, it's true, New Yorkers have long known how to deal with the likes of him. Keep quiet and get away as soon as possible. The old man's smoothness aroused in me a certain disrespectful kind of respect for the City.

I was sure he would continue like this forever, and it was time to go. But I still wanted to see what he would do with the phone, so I gave myself a few more minutes. All of a sudden, he raised his head, saw me watching him from across the street and made an obscene gesture at me. But I didn't care. To reciprocate, I took out my pack of cigarettes and waved it at him. He waved back. I crossed the street, gave him a smoke and crossed back.

He signaled a motion of taking a picture. He's letting me take more. Letting himself be an actor. He's into it alright, but it's not what I wanted. I pretended to walk off. I still wanted to see what he would do with the phone. He just tossed it back into the garbage can, turned the corner and disappeared with his red hat.

Tr. By John Chow. 1984

A Vacation

There are ocean, sky, beaches, and an isolated little house; behind the house are scrub trees shorter than a person and some rolling hills. Nothing else is seen. The first night upon arrival, I think of Mr. S, who would make the three-hour drive from New York on a weekend to stay here alone for two days. Of course I figure that Mr. S. is a rich man; otherwise he couldn't afford this piece of property along the Atlantic Ocean.

Mr. S. is one of my best friends in New York. Although he has other Chinese friends, it was our appreciation of music that brought us together. We often go out and listen to music, and our personalities are very similar. Thus, we both enjoy the same kind of life rhythm. He gave me the keys to this vacation house, which he bought five years ago, so that I can come here when I am free. He has left New York for Hong Kong, where he will be working for eight months.

Passion through Holland Tunnel from New York City, I drive onto the Garden State Parkway. I do 60 miles an hour through the woods. Pulling my car into a private driveway, I stop the engine, put my swimsuit on, and dip into the ocean. Coming back to the little house, I put away the food I brought and sit on a sofa near the window. Ocean and sky join together far beyond the bay window. I view the scene and quickly fall asleep.

I didn't dream much, and did not wake up till dusk. The setting sun of mid-August, blocked by a few clouds, generates a bright red sky. I remember I saw a purple halo in my dream: the halo could be touched by hand and looked like plastic. I come here for a date with myself and I didn't tell anyone before I came. I don't want to call anyone from here; I really want to enjoy myself. The fast-paced life in New York City had me looking forward to this trip.

When nothing can be seen outside the bay window, I turn on the lights and look for some food in the refrigerator. I carefully prepare two dishes, then start to sip wine while slowly chewing and swallowing. I imagine the meals extraterrestrials eat; perhaps they drink a kind of fuel. I am thinking like this, because I am imagining what is going on out in the cosmos while I stare at the scene where sea and sky converge outside the bay window. I also think that the sun might have been created by extraterrestrials as a satellite, in order to keep the terrestrials alive. The unseen extra-terrestrials might have created more advanced creatures in other places, and maybe they have given up on the preliminary product-the terrestrials, when the sun, a satellite, exhausts its energy, terrestrials will be done for. Thus, we terrestrials should make every effort to create another sun as a light source before the sun disappears.

I pour a fortifying portion of wine, as if these thoughts were true. I quickly finish the remaining food and put on a coat to walk to the beach. The dark sky covers the beach; I pick a rock to sit on. I find that the moonlight is actually very bright and the surf pounds loudly. I don't know where I picked up this habit of thought, perhaps from some book, but I start to miss China, my homeland, which I've left for six years. I cannot find a homeland.

I recall a scene of visiting the Great Wall in Beijing. Then I was also alone after losing in love. I walked a long way along the Great Wall, leaving a group of travelers behind. Sitting on the Wall and looking at the green rolling mountains and gray sections of Wall, I felt that sitting there was something certain. It was not like having a girlfriend, with the kind of emotion that can't avoid changes and pressures from society and family; sometimes it can't even avoid influence from one's occupation and bodily health. I found the real reason for the break-up. As society changed, she found a new way out of China. She returned to her original boyfriend who had many relatives in Hong Kong. He could take her to Hong Kong as his wife. She was a hope-one that could be taken away by someone else. She didn't have to sit on this remote Great Wall to experience the pain of breaking up, because she was active. After less than half an hour of sitting on the Great Wall, I found that I was active too; no matter how great the wall is, it cannot move, whereas I can move any time at my discretion.

I sat at the Great Wall for more than two hours, so that I could let the Great Wall take a look at me as I put out my cigarette and withdrew back into the crowd. When I withdrew, I sensed that I was doing it aggressively. Soon afterward, I found someone in the crowd of life who would help me to go abroad to study. What am I learning on this beach? It has been six years: for the first time, I have come to occupy a place on the earth alone. Within a radius of about one mile, I am the only one here. I know Mr. S. has this place to himself or he wouldn't have bought it, how many pieces of private land like this on the earth belong to people? First, we have different continents and countries, and then we have different nationalities, families, and individuals. These are all properties. The globe is a big property. Whom does it belong to? It could be human beings or extra-terrestrials, but it looks as if it belongs to mankind. Even if it belongs to the extra-terrestrials, they already gave it up. Human beings enjoy being masters of themselves; some of them aren't satisfied with themselves and others like them; therefore, they turn toward God or Buddha. Now this global property has been divided by God and Buddha/

I sense the sound of the surf is getting strong. If I were a fish, I would be able to hear the ocean's opinion about God and the Buddha. I can only guess now. I guess the water is trying to get onto the seashore, but it is not able to get over the high water line. The high water line is the limit of the ocean's brain power. Everything the ocean thinks is below the line. Only divers can hear the truth, but most divers are there for purposes of war or petroleum, or they are looking for treasure. They are not interested to hear what the ocean says.

I am tired; when the ocean wind blows strong, I walk back to the little house and hope to meet the beach and sunrise tomorrow morning.

Meeting with morning is not very ideal. It is a very cloudy day. The dark clouds seem ready to reach down and wet my head. I remember turning the corner of a lane to avoid a shower one day near the Bund in Shanghai; so did a beautiful girl. But someone ported a full washbowl of water from upstairs, wetting both of us all over. So what if a young man and young woman were together in one place: we were soaked and we walked out separate ways in the rain. I am hoping the cloud will pour out its wash water, the sooner the better. I really want to walk on the streets in Shanghai. The cloud does not care what I'm thinking; the wash water just doesn't come. The cloud may have forgotten to wash its face today. The cloud overhead remains until noon but no rain falls. It keeps me from going to Shanghai in my thoughts; instead I go to New York.

I forget many umbrellas in the New York subway. When I get out of the station, I find that my umbrella has gone with the train. Once a kind person reminded me of the weather, but when I left the station I found the rain had stopped. I don't know if that means I am lucky or not.

I rented a top floor in a cheap and leaky house when I just arrived in New York City. The landlord had someone fix the roof after I complained. But it still leaked. The landlord told me that good things were never cheap; he didn't want to spend more money to fix it. Afterward he put the house up for sale and had me move out. The landlord also said he had heavy clouds over his head because he was laid off. He was selling his house to survive.

Many more things are clouds overhead. The heaviest one is something that happened. It was in fall, just when I finished my English studies at a language school. I thought language was not a big problem anymore. I should be able to demonstrate my true ability now. I took alone some of my designs and rushed into an advertising company. The boss was from Hong Kong and spoke fluent English and Cantonese, but not Mandarin. We conducted our conversation in English; he seemed more interested in my English then in my designs. He said not many people from Mainland could speak so well.

He hired me on three months' probation. In addition, I had to produce at least five satisfactory commercial designs. The first design was for a ham company. I designed a picture of a deep hoof print of a pig next to a lighter shoe print, with a subtitle: "Delicious taste gives muscle to your appetite!" My boss liked it. He patted me at least three times on my back for each of my following designs.

My colleague, Miss Chang, a commercial design graduate from Pratt Institute in New York, was very jealous of my design ability. She was not getting good jobs, because my boss liked me. She was assigned to design a commercial for an athletic shoe manufacturer. Because it was an urgent task, she called me at home to see if I could help her. I am the kind of person who won't take hard tactics, but I can't refuse soft ones. Though I felt she had not been nice to me, I could not deny her begging. I stayed up all night and designed a shoe for her the following day at a coffee shop outside the company. Of course she received praise from the boss. But I was called into the boss' office and given a pink slip the following day. The reason was a very simple-recession. My company had to reduce the workforce, and one of the four designs had to go. I was the last one hired (only five months before); thus, I had to go first.

On the same night, one of the designers called me and told me why I was let go. The boss had seen us, Miss Chang and me, at the coffee shop and what's more he had seen Miss. Chang kissed my lips in thanks when we left the shop. We didn't see the boss. This designer knew that the boss and Miss. Chang were lovers, but he wasn't close enough with me to tell the company's secret. I was in the dark. The designer told me he overheard the boss questioning Miss Chang in the company's basement. Miss Chang not only didn't speak up for me, but complained that I was trying to seduce her. After hanging up the phone, I called my boss and angrily told him my side of the story. He did not believe me and he had to confirm with Miss. Chang. Of course, she denied what I had done for her. This made me look even worse. The words of the lover are true, as long as the boss needs her.

I've learned something from this lesson-not just the feeling of clouds over my head, but a general principle. Although this country is democratic, every private company can be a dictator's kingdom, and the boss is the king. He can do whatever he wishes and his dictatorship is protected by the country's democratic laws. The clouds of human nature come between human beings below and the sun above. The sunlight represents democracy and clouds represent evils. Bosses are those who can control the clouds and those who can establish their own dictatorship.

After a few drops of rain around noon, the clouds move away. Maybe they are taking a vacation somewhere. I am lying down on the beach and enjoying the shower of sunlight. A black dog pops up from nowhere. He stares at me strangely, or should I say I look at him questioningly, because this is, after all, my turf. The dog stops at a distance of twenty meters from me, He sits on his haunches looking alternately at me and the ocean. With his glossy body, well-bred and well-kept, he must be a neighbor's dog. He is definitely not a wild dog. Maybe he wants to see me swimming, and I want to swim. Pointing to the ocean, I run into the water, turning my head to look at the dog from time to time. I swim for about ten minutes and see the dog climbing onto my deck chair and sitting there with the same posture.

I start to like him. After another ten minutes swimming, I walk back onto the beach; the dog still sits on my deck chair. As I approach him. He agilely jumps out of my deck chair and runs about tens meters and sits down there again. He looks at me while I am rubbing my body with a towel and lying down on my deck chair. I wave my hand and he runs into the woods behind the beach. Dogs don't bother people's privacy here, I think. The dog may have been brought here by its master for a vacation. The dog's master may be lying on the beach somewhere like me, while his dog can intrude on someone else's turf freely, so long as he does not bark ill-naturedly.

But this dog makes me happy; his presence enhances my

sense of being on vacation. The reason is simply that he is the only audience I have for my vacation. If there were some food here, he might stay with me a little longer. A friend of mine brought some inexpensive cans from a supermarket. He enjoyed the taste and even told another friend, who figured out right away that they were dog food. My friend stopped eating the food in the can, but he did not feel embarrassed; he always tells his new friends from mainland China that he once ate dog food. He tells them to be careful when buying canned food. This guy is very honest and likeable. Later he found a girlfriend; she said he is so honest he is even proud of eating dog food. She decided to marry him. I wonder if I should eat a can of dog food when I am his best man.

I dreamed of seeing that dog, but he was with me only in the dream. This has nothing to do with cans of dog food. Marriage is marriage; imaginary marriage has other shapes. I would like to see the dog again, because he has a personality. But I never see him again; the dog may realize that this is not his master's turf, or his master already has taken him back to the city.

I started to like this kind of American-style vacation. I thought it was rather dull to face beaches for several days. By contrast, we Chinese believe that people should be more tired than usual; the more tired, the happier we are with a vacation. We have to see more on a vacation: that is what we call getting a good harvest. But I suppose we have no vacations like this because there is no private land in China. Once land can be traded, I believe there will be a lot of private keys to the beaches on Qingdao Island. I swam in the ocean along the Qingdao coast before. It was so crowded that people couldn't do anything there during summer time. People were cooking in water like dumplings in a boiler. That kind of environment is, of course, a happy place. But one should taste an environment where one person occupies the whole empty beach. What flavor of stuffing does this lonely dumpling have?

Tr. By Kevin Dong and Denis Mair. 1992

Dog Knows

My neighbor in New York suddenly won a big lottery: five thousand dollars and two airplane tickets between Hong Kong and New York, round trip, plus a week's free hotels. His name was David. David planned to enjoy the trip with his girlfriend Anne. He left me his only burden-Apple, a male mongrel but stronger and fiercer than a pure dog. David told me to walk him twice a day, half an hour each time. He mentioned some payment. I told him to forget about it, just leave me the car keys so I could take Apple to the suburb for a drive sometimes. David gave me the keys to the car and to the apartment and left.

That night (David left in the morning), I took Apple to the street. He seemed to be extremely happy to walk with a new friend. He went aggressively ahead of me as if he were walking me. This was my first time walking a dog since I came to the United States three years ago. A relaxing feeling flowed from my fingers to my heart. The power on each end of leash, between the dog and me, made life seem easy. Apple suddenly slowed down and dragged me across the street. On the other side of the street there was a dog looking at us. I pulled the leash and walked forward. Apple looked up at me, but I ignored him. It was just something between male and female.

I used to see Americans walking their dogs, but I had never given them too much thought about such a common scene. Now that I because one among them, and had experienced the relation between dogs and human beings, I swore to myself that I would never eat dogs again. I had eaten dog meat several times in China. I was thinking of driving Apple around the rich areas on Long Island on the weekend. During my three years in America, I hadn't gotten around much. I didn't have a car. Now I suddenly owned two things at the same time: a dog and a car. I have to take some pictures: driving a car with a dog, in my best clothes. My friends in China would think I had become a millionaire when they saw the pictures. I fell asleep to my own fantasies,

The next morning I opened a can of dog food for Apple, of which he ate only half,. I took him outside and chose a different route. Apple seemed to know the street. I realized the dog had been walked by David thousands of time, and must know every street around here. Apple stopped at a liquor store to look at the liquor bottles. I loved drinking, so I stopped to look at them too. I had never tasted some of the brands. One of them was in a small bottle of dark blue porcelain. The price was eighty something. I had never tasted that, either. The reason was simple: I was a poor student and couldn't afford it. There was another kind I hadn't tasted-"XO". At a private party, I once saw a bottle of XO in the cabinet. I gathered my courage to ask for a glass. The person in charge of pouring drinks told me that the bottle had sentimental meaning to the host, and was not to be opened by anyone. It was not till the end of the party that I leaned the "XO" had been in the bureau for more than ten years, the only property left to the host by his uncle, who died of alcoholism at the age of thirty-two. Apple and I had been standing before the liquor store for quite a while. Apple didn't bark to leave. He was looking more carefully at the bottles lined artistically in the window than I was. I wondered if Apple could read some of the words on the bottles.

I went to school after we got back to the apartment, came back from the school, did homework, and ate my supper. Then I took Apple out for another walk. Apple had a better manner than any other dog when he did his duty. Before he took a leak, he would look around. If there was someone around, he would wait until they passed by. If he wanted to shit, he would make a special noise as a warning so I could put a newspaper under him. When he was done, I wrapped it and put it in the garbage can. If I didn't do this, I would be fined by the police. Apple would not shit unless there was a piece of paper under him. He was such a clean and law-abiding dog. Before I went to bed, I had a small drink over TV while Apple hunkered nearby, looking at me gently. When I put it down, Apple sniffed at the glass and licked it. I grabbed the glass and gave him a bowl of water in the kitchen. He smelled it and left without touching it. I suddenly remembered the way he looked at the liquor store window. I poured some vodka into the water. Apple drank it up in a second, then looked up at me asking for more. I laughed. David must have given liquor to the dog. Would he get drunk? Would he bite when he was drunk? I took the liquor away and resumed my TV-watching.

But I didn't notice that I had left the bottle uncovered in the kitchen after I poured the liquor into the water for Apple. When I went back to the kitchen after the show, Apple had laid down the bottle. I say "laid down" because I didn't hear the sound of a falling bottle. Apple had been licking the spot. I touched the floor. The liquor was almost gone. Apple didn't pay any attention to me. I grabbed the bottle and turned it upside down. There had been a quarter bottle of liquor left in the bottle and now it was empty. I looked at Apple in fear. He seemed quite normal and followed me into the living room. I watched him. He walked near the telephone as if I were expecting him to, took the receiver in his mouth, and reached his left paw to press the buttons. I watched intently. He pressed seven buttons and gave me the phone. The phone rang but no one answered. Suddenly the answering machine was on. It sounded like David's girlfriend Anne. To make sure, I hung up and found Anne's telephone number. Did David train him Did David know Apple loved drinking? I thought of the stories about Chinese poets who drank and write poetry. I wondered if Apple's mind became sharper from the liquor. I put down the phone and let Apple do it again. He pressed another seven buttons which I thought must Anne's. I took up the phone. A man answered. I asked him if he was David's friend. He said he was David's brother. I understood and explained what had happened. He wouldn't believe it and said that he had never heard of it from David. I put down the phone and sat on the couch, pondering. Apple looked up at me intelligently. I really loved him, I went into the kitchen to find a hotdog for him. Apple licked the spilt spot again. I felt it and found there was a little liquor left. He quickly licked it clean and went back to the living room to call again. This time he was pressing Anne's number, 8735326. I was going to leave a message on the machine that I had a secret for her when she came back from Hong Kong with David. Suddenly Anne was on the phone. I asked her, in astonishment, when she had come back from Hong Kong. Anne said she had never gone with David. I realized that David had gone to Hong Kong with another girl. I muttered a few words to Anne. The secret was revealed. It was not my fault. David had not told me to cover it up. He told me he went with Anne. I was sure Anne was his girlfriend, though I had seen her only twice. Why did it turn out this way? Apple revealed the truth. Smart Apple. How stupid of me! I should have asked Anne if she knew the dog could make phone calls. I called her back and asked. Anne said she had never heard of it. I asked her if she knew the dog like to drink. She said she didn't know about that either. She asked me what else David said when he left. I said nothing else, Anne said angrily that David is deceitful.

I was not really too curious to find out if David was a deceiver. Such things happened almost every day. But wasn't it amazing that a dog loved drinking and could make phone calls after drinking? Wasn't it line the Chinese poet Li Po who drank and wrote poetry? I wouldn't say the results were the same thing, but liquor certainly could stimulate inspired thoughts. I would let David know who revealed the secret.

David shrugged his shoulders on hearing the news and told me he had decided to be engaged with his new girlfriend during the trip. As for Anne, it was over. David didn't believe Apple could make calls. Nor did he know Apple loved drinking. So Apple's talent had unexpectedly been inspired by liquor. TO prove it, I called Apple to the phone, but he made no response. I gave him some vodka in the kitchen; he actually pressed the buttons and makes the calls. David was shocked. Apple knew only two numbers, one for Anne, the other for David's brother Jim. I said Apple must have watched David make the calls many times and learned it by heart. The modern telephones were press buttons and easy to imitate. If it had been a dial phone, Apple couldn't have done it no matter how much he drank. His body structure limits him. But he must know in his mind. I told David it might be more complicated. Maybe Apple liked Anne. When knew David went to Hong Kong with another girl friend, he thought of this idea to reveal the secret. David wouldn't believe a word I said. He shook his head and took Apple for their first walk since he'd come back from his vacation.

Tr. By Ping Wang and Denis Mair. 1989

When Firecrackers Went Off

Having moved into a loft on the lower East Side, I worked doubly hard to cover expenses. The magnetism of Manhattan compels artists, especially those starting out, to feel they can only have a stimulating life after personally experiencing an artistic earthquake. In the fall, having sold a few sculptures, I was finally able to breathe, create and live more easily. I still had to work a few days each week just for money.

One day I realized that firecrackers were occasionally being set off from the building across the street. Five or six at a time, never more. Three or four times a day. Even late at night. I wondered which kid liked to do it so much, yet would only let go a few at a time. Like the habit of an alcoholic, smoker or drug addict. From then on, I often looked out of my window at the building and sidewalk across the street hoping to figure it out.

I liked firecrackers. Every New Year's day when I was living in Shanghai, I would spend the luck money I collected from adults on all kinds of fireworks. Unlike the person across the street, however, I only enjoyed the setting them off all at once-I had always been impulsive. I had really liked exploding them in tin cans; watching the cans take off, then crash on the concrete after a muffled explosion. One time I got careless and blew a fissure in my palm but I keep on playing. I don't think anything is left of that passion, my lifestyle has changed. My age also keeps me from such activity.

I finally discovered the person was a middle-aged woman on the third floor. She would light the fuse with her cigarette on the ledge, throw the firecracker out and then disappear into her apartment. I also realized there was no set time for the explosions. I thought she just one of the crazies of New York. After I bought a small pair of binocular, I found that her face was expressionless while doing it as if it were a matter of routine. I wondered whether she was doing it for emotional or historic reason, like commemorating a lost one, even though firecrackers are usually associated with evil-repellence, feasts or other joyous occasions. I was certain she had her reasons, at least a neurosis.

She looked about forty, with light brown hair that was probably dyed. She had a tall nose, big grey eyes and skin color between Caucasian and Latin, I came from China three years ago and I'm not very good at telling where people come from,. With so many people from so many places, plus mixed-race people, I'll just call her a New Yorker. Her manner indifferently lighting the fuse and then disappearing haunted me. Whenever firecrackers went off, I thought of her.

Then I saw her with a man. Or, more accurately, a white man stood besides her watching her ritual. Like her, he too was expressionless, and seemed to know what she was doing, disappearing with him and leaving me vexed across with street.

I made up hypotheses but couldn't confirm them.

When I was small, in village of Shanghai, I had seen farmer's children tie a link of firecrackers to a dog's tail. After the ignition, the dog would run like crazy in the field, driven by fear of the explosions. They also tried the trick on a pig, but the pig seemed to understand things a lot better. Once the explosions started, it would just shake its body, then roll on the ground to extinguish the firecrackers. Just like an adult who know what children were up to. Back then, the pig was far too serious for me.

Ever since I saw her with the man, she had become much less mysterious. The image of her own mysterious world no longer existed only in my imagination, because at least the man share the secret of her daily rituals. I had a few fantasies, influenced by literature, no doubt. One is less elaborate and more commonplace: she left with her newlywed husband the day after the wedding for a honeymoon in Asia but returned by herself. Her husband had become entranced by Indian religion and stayed behind. He had promised to come in two months but never did. She had returned to India but failed to find him. Afterwards, she grew mentally infirm, tossing off firecrackers because her husband had done the same on their wedding day. The other fantasy is convoluted and bizarre. An idealist and loner, she is extremely angry at the injustices of the world. A doctor at Harvard, she did research on the structure of societies and national consciousness, but then endless invasions, aggression and civil filled her heart with conflict, every time there was something or someone she hated in a newspaper or novel she was reading, she would run to the window and toss off a few of firecrackers. They were gunshots aimed at those she hated.

Of course, I knew that all the fantasies reflected my own experience and world-view. Gradually the explosions set off my moods for fantasies and strengthened my own imagination. After nearly a month, I had much more confidence in myself as an artist than before. I often laughed at my own preposterous yet literally logical hypotheses. I even thought of paying her a visit but put it out of my mind thinking she wouldn't let someone else get involved with a neurosis that was a big part of her world and a support for mind.

There is more to the story. After all, I am not just saying that this strange city has a lot of crazy people in it. I hadn't told many people about these discoveries. The first person I told the story to was a neighbor who had been a hard-working painter for over twenty years and who teaches art history at a university. He said he had heard the firecrackers too but never wondered about them. We were drinking that day and for two hours and nothing went off, but just as he stood up to leave we heard them. I took him to the window and pointed to the third floor window, then at the man standing at the corner waiting. We stuck our heads out and saw a man and coming out of my building. The two met and walked away. We went downstairs, tailed the men, and from far away saw them talking at corner in alert manner. My friend immediately understood what they were doing when he saw the quick contact of hands and their abrupt parting. He asked whether it was like this every time. I said ye.

He said drug dealers and buyers have their own precautions. He was sure the buyer would first call the woman who would then signal to the dealer in our building for the sale. He was curious how I discovered this, I had noticed it for more than a month and one time met briefly on the staircase the man at the window. My friend warned me severely to mind my own business and not to let them figure out I had been watching them. He put his index finger to his lips. From then on, I never tried to imagine more.

Tr, by John Chow

Abstract Taste

A painter who relies on selling his paintings to make a living always has a couple of incidents from his marketing experience which are more memorable than the others, I have had over ten years' experience of making my living by selling my paintings, and so of course I have a number of such stories to tell. Many people will have heard of the business of someone buying his or her own paintings, and I myself know more than one example. One of them happened like this: there was a painter who, at an exhibition of his work, in order to show that his paintings were not only capable of forming an exhibition on their own but also sold well, got one of his brothers to pretend to be a buyer and negotiate with the gallery, and have "reserved stickers" below some of the paintings he fancied. After the exhibition was over there was of course a phone call telling the gallery that he had changed his mind. I've also heard of a gallery which, hoping to get some business, selected a couple highly unsalable paintings from an exhibition that they had organized and stuck sold signs on them. All in all, the market place is a battleground. In every move you can see something out of Sun Tzu's Art of War. The instance I came across is not in the least exceptional, as you will see from what I am about to relate.

In China, the custom of giving away paintings is quite firmly entrenched. If a friend asks me for a painting, it shows how good a friend he is, and I will happily give him a painting. But in America, in fact in the West generally, this custom is much less current. According to the Western view, all labor should be paid for, a painting is the product of labor, and so it should not give away, or at least should not be given away lightly. During the third year I spent in New York I met an American called Tom, We became friend, and within a year we had become extremely close. He ran an import-export business dealing with China, but due to bad luck and various other circumstances he wasn't really making any money. So he occasionally helped me with the sale of my paintings, and we came to an agreement that he would receive a ten-percent commission on any painting that he helped me to sell. He was not a particularly good salesman: in over a year he had helped me to sell only one and a half paintings. The half-painting was one that was sold to an uncle of his who only paid half the money at the time, and later decided not to buy it. This was because shortly after buying the painting the uncle got divorced, because he'd fallen in love with a young girl and, since he wanted to get his divorce as quickly as possible, he'd distributed most of her belongings amongst his wife and children. In the circumstances, he wasn't inclined to pay the other half of the money. So he brought the painting back to exchange it for any painting that I considered to be worth half as much, and I ended up choosing another painting to give to Tom's uncle. This is not one of particularly memorable.

One day Tom rang to say that a friend or his had seen an exhibition of mind and was very impressed. He'd just bought himself a new house, and was preparing to acquire one or two paintings to hang in it. He was thinking of having a look at my paintings, as he felt that the tone of my work would tune very well with the character of his house. Actually, it's true that my abstract paintings have a lot in common with modern buildings. I always put my signature, which risks being distinctly meaningful in some way, on the back of the painting, so that the language of the painting comes over as completely and utterly abstract. On the day we had arranged for him to view the paintings I suddenly had a call from a friend of mine who was in hospital, so I told Tom to take the pictures that I had prepared for sale over to his friend's place. In the meantime I rushed off to the hospital to visit my sick friend, who was on the point of leaving this world as a result of sudden illness. Perhaps it was AIDS, or maybe alcoholic poisoning; if not, it would be as unsuccessful suicide attempt.

This friend of Tom's was called Burns. He chose one painting and Tom brought the rest them back. I gave Tom one tenth of the asking price and also treated him to a Greek meal, because Greek food was his favorite (he was half Greek), and also because Tom had doubled the price of my painting, I asked him if Burns had a lot of money. Tom said that, during the past year, Burns had been amazingly percipient about the stock exchange, and had made a lot of money in some big deals.

Two weeks later Tom told me that Burns had asked us both over to his house. The decoration of the new house was already finished. Tom and I arrived at the duly appointed time. Burns led me humorously into his study to look at my painting. As soon as I saw it I knew that he'd hung it the wrong way -not upside down, but on its side, Out of politeness, I didn't say anything just then, and anyway my paintings are abstract color paintings which can be hung any way up, as long as the owner feels comfortable with it. Burns had also invited a few other friends, among them one man who knew that I had painted the picture, and began to chat to me there in the study. The others went into the lounge and the bedrooms to get a taste of Burns' sumptuous house. The man who was chatting to me was called David. He asked me about the position of Chinese painters in New York, and began to express an opinion on the painting on the wall. He tilted his head to one side to look at it and said that it seemed to him as though the painting would look better hung vertically. At that stage, I still wasn't inclined to reveal that the painting was originally meant to be hung vertically, so I just said that abstract paintings could be looked at any way up, whereas figurative pictures could only be looked at one way. Thus, in certain respects, abstract paintings allowed artists more freedom. At this moment Burns came in, and David immediately began to tell him that if the painting were hung vertically it might give it a different feel, and asked Burns if he had tried it that way. He replied cunningly that the way he had hung it accorded best with his understanding of material structure, and added that a bank note was still money whichever way you looked at it. We all laughed.

As well as being a humorous man, Burns was also careful.

After a few minutes, he quietly drew me aside and asked me which way up the picture should really be hung, or in other words, which way up had I painted it. Following his train of thought I said that I had painted it my way up, but that if someone else hung it his way up, there would be no contradiction. Laughing, he said he would like to know which way up my world was. I felt obliged to tell him that I had painted it vertically. When I had finished speaking I noticed that, contrary to my expectations, he seemed a little bit unhappy. However, he soon became even more jolly and humorous. He grabbed Tom who was standing drinking nearby, and told him that I had done some divination for him and reckoned that his eyes were different from other people's, and that, as a result, he'd have much better luck in business than an ordinary man. Tom looked at me completely baffled, but I began laughing, in a knowing way, along with Burns. Burns abruptly changed the subject and said he must thank Tom because the picture he had recommended particularly suited his tastes.

It wasn't long before Burns again called me to one side and asked me wasn't the signature on the back of the painting and if so, which way up was it signed? I said I had signed it in the vertical position. He then dragged me back into the study (the other people at this point were all in the lounge listening to the music and drinking coffee), shut the study door, took the picture down, and asked me to sign it horizontally as well, which I did. Before he re-opened the study door he suddenly thought of something else, plucked the picture back off the wall and asked me to sign it in the other two directions. That way there'd be a signature in all four directions.

Before we left that day Burns gave Tom an envelope to pass on to me. I opened it in front of Tom and inside was a hundred dollar bill, and on the envelope was Burns' signature, signed in all four directions. Tom was bewildered and asked me what it was all about, so I told him what had happened, and also pulled out a ten dollar bill and gave it to him, in line with our agreement. Tom didn't want to take it so I forcibly stuffed it into his pocket, saying that money was also abstract, depending on how you used it. The sale of the painting was thus concluded. To begin with Burns had paid $1,500, added to that this $100 made $1,600 altogether. Perhaps Burns saw it as having bought four paintings. This is not most people's idea of humor, or perhaps Burns has his own and different form of logic; I'm really not too sure.

Tr. By Deborah Mills

A Pigeon Story

Not far from the curb, behind a black fence, there are a few apparently healthy trees on a patch of glass. Behind them is a solemn church, its doors made of good wood that makes me recall the texture of leather skirts and jackets, not those worn by girls or young boys but by mannequins in shop windows. On the glass a flock of pigeons are feeding on whatever they consider food. They take easy strides, too lazy to fly, their feathers shiny and clean.

I am standing at the street corner, beside the fence, waiting for her who may become my girlfriend. She is late, I may have even more time to look at the pigeons.

A small fountain lies at the corner of the church yard, its water blue reflecting from the sky. A pigeon pecks at this piece of sky, then leaps in, playing with the water that reaches its waist. Silver lights flicker in the blue sky. On the grass a male pigeon makes a guttural sound, running after a female who is small but has a confident stride. She is small only in comparison to him. I think of the supple body and full frame of my date and cannot help laughing, as I am too small in comparison.

There are eleven pigeons. Three I can tell are males, five

females, and three younger ones I can't determine. I look up. The street sign says Twelfth Street. I say to myself: "Twelfth, eleven pigeons and myself. What does Twelfth signify? Twelfth? Oh, not I'm supposed to meet her on Eleventh". I look from the corner of Twelfth to the corner of Eleventh. She is not there. I stroll back to Twelfth, only to once again look at the peaceful picture composed of grass, church and pigeons.

A woman in her forties comes out of the church with a paper bag, walks straight to the center of the yard and empties its contents on the grass. Then, without turning around, she goes back into the church. A few pigeons slowly stroll over for some food-yellow grains, probably wheat-but most seem full and uninterested; I turn around and walk towards Eleventh.

She is still not there. I don't know why but I am thinking, "Perhaps she is late because her boss asked her to buy grain to feed the pigeons on the company's steps". She works for a big accounting firm in midtown, with many steps and pigeons.

The corner of Eleventh is dirty, unlike Twelfth with its church. There are two telephone booths. One has the cord pulled out and the receiver gone, the other is in use.

All of a sudden I notice, there at the corner, another flock of pigeons, much dirtier than those on twelfth. Some are thin and weak; two in particular appear ill, limping reluctantly as if too tired to fly. They are also pecking around, but on the concrete there does not seem to be any particles of food. Neither are there any guttural sounds. Could they all be females? Of course not.

Why don't' they go to the patch of grass on Twelfth? Why

not? It is only one block away.

I can't help but wonder back to Twelfth. I count the pigeons, each dirty and thin, still pecking at the concrete, as if the act of feeding was itself satiating or gave their stomachs the illusion of eating. Why don't they go to Twelfth? I try to chase them-towards Twelfth, of course-but they seem to know something about that direction and just won't go. I am very curious. I almost want to ask them: "Are you citizens of Eleventh Street? Do you have to live here? There is plenty of food on the grass by the church on Twelfth, you know. Hurry, idiots!"

Once again I come to twelfth. I lift my head, look at the church spire, and then the grass. Those well-to-do pigeons now make me think of the woman that feeds them. Is she really proud of feeding only eleven pigeons? Does she know that, only some ten yards away, there is another flock of dirty hungry pigeons, unaware that there is food here? Perhaps pigeons cannot be notified without a communication network. In any case, this incident torments me. Perhaps pigeons have races and tribes too, even different sponsors, like the tens of thousands of companies bug and small in New York City.

Tr. By John Chow

My Hooker and I

This story takes place at Waikiki Beach on Honolulu Island. Hawaii. There are many hotels at Hawaii Beach, one of which I lived in for five days, relaxing from the tension of New York City. In the meantime I wanted the experience some new creative feelings in this new setting. There were many Japanese travelers. Aside from Hawaii's tropical climate and a taste of foreign exotic atmosphere, this may have been due to convenient, direct flights that came here from Japan.

I didn't write a single word in Hawaii, but comfortably enjoyed the sun and ocean. It was February: New York City in February is chilly. I called some friends in Beijing from the hotel, telling them I was getting visas ahead of time so they could visit New York this spring. They were very envious.

Five days passed more quickly than I thought, and I was packing up for New York. I still didn't have anything to write, little did I d=know that two months afterward, one incident would resolve out of memory and gradually assume larger proportions. I knew I would feel sorry for myself if I did not write anything about it.

When night falls on Waikiki beach, the streets become even

busier. People who lie on beaches during the day crowd onto the streets, in restaurants, and in bars and pubs. I did not feel lonely walking along the streets, but regretted I had no girlfriend with me. A few hookers were stopping two Japanese male travelers and discussing business. I heard one Caucasian hooker talking in fluent Japanese when I passed by. UI thought there were very professional.

Two hookers were heading my way, and one of them winked at me. I found she was a very charming white girl, not more than twenty years' old. She didn't dress like the other hookers, who were halfway stripped. As I stared blankly, she wound her arm around my arm and spoke a phrase to me in Japanese. I shook my head and said I didn't understand Japanese. She changed to English and asked me if I wanted a date. I stared at her beautiful face which had very little make-up on and shook my head unwillingly. I saw some other passers by looking at her and me. They probably were watching for us to wrap up the deal and go somewhere to finish up.

I moved her arm away inexpertly and gave her a definite shake of my head. I left her behind and firmly walked straight ahead. But I turned back after several feet, walked across the street, and then walked toward her, because I wanted to see if anyone became her customer. I especially wanted to see what kind of person she would grab hold of.

I kept to the shadows and watched her talking to a Japanese. This time they talked a little longer. One of the Japanese seemed interested because he even put his hand on her shoulder as he talked. I thought he must be a veteran, he acted as naturally. I blamed myself for being so tense. I could have talked to her easily and maybe discovered material worth writing about. I also thought about AIDS, but thought they might have a way to prevent it. The longer she talked with them, the more courage I built up. I thought if she couldn't get this customer, I would go over and grasp her arm and then take her to a quiet restaurant for dinner. I hadn't had dinner yet.

As I was approaching them, the two Japanese left her. She shook her head, combed her hand through her hair, pouted her lips and walked away. All right! It's my turn. I encouraged myself to cross the street, walking toward her. She suddenly turned and saw me. She was really pretty. But her eyes noncommittal slid aside. She didn't recognize me, or she knew I had refused her before. I believe she must have recognized me. She was certain that she couldn't get anything from me. That's why she did not care to see me again. Suddenly my courage was entirely gone.

I stood there and lit a cigarette. She was walking ahead again. I was quite willing to follow slowly behind her. I was looking for every reason to convince myself to build up courage again. I had lived for more than thirty years and never touched a prostitute. Their existence had never had an effect on me. But this time it seemed different. I thought about expression of sympathy for prostitutes in literary works. Yet those descriptions don't come from prostitutes themselves. What is their own conception? I believe that among the prostitutes of the Eighteenth, Nineteenth and Twentieth Centuries, many must have held common ideas of liberty and sexual freedom. I was approaching her again, wondering why twenty minutes had passed with no one wanting to take such a young, beautiful girl off the street to enjoy the night somewhere. I passed by her again and still didn't say a word. I felt very hungry and gave up the idea pf taking her with me.

I walked back to a quiet restaurant. When the waitress asked me how many would be at my table, I forgot myself momentarily and said two people. I was ushered to a tale for two. She left two sets for silverware. Thoughtlessly I ordered a bottle of wine with two glasses. Of course, I started to sip the wine alone and read the menu.

I began to assume that she was sitting across from me. I stared at her eyes. Not only were they transparent and dazzlingly blue in color; they were also somewhat artificial. The waitress came over and asked me again if I wanted to order first. I said OK and explained that my friend would come a little late. I filled up the other glass and took turns with both of them.

I thought the first thing I should ask was if she had another job. She said she was still going to college, a student at the University of Hawaii. I was very embarrassed to ask how long she has been working like this. She said it had been two years already.. She had been going to school during the day and worked about three or four nights every week. I drank a lot of wine from what was supposed to be her glass. I saw her carefully taking offer her brown wig after looking around the other table. Having revealed a full head of short-cut blond hair, she looked much more like a student.

After taking off her wig, she naturally began to ask things about me; I answered one question after another. She said she hadn't encountered any Chinese. She mentioned the events that occurred in China on June 4th, 1989 and the changes that had taken place in East Europe. Her ancestors had come from Poland.

The waitress brought over my food and very sympathetically looked at the empty seat, I looked at the entrance of the restaurant and helplessly shrugged my shoulders to the waitress. I emptied the remaining wine in her glass and filled it up right away. I asked why she wanted to work like this. She said she had to pay her tuition and living expenses. I asked if she had tried any other jobs; she said she had tried, but all these part-time jobs not only never paid well but were very tiring.

I told her that many of my American friends received college loans and would return them gradually after graduation. She said she had the freedom to choose her way to make money. She said she was gifted and very well suited for this type of job; she often made her customers feel satisfied.

I was very reluctant to mention AIDS. She said she took steps to protect herself from getting it. In addition, she preferred Asians because very few Asians have AIDS. She added that any job had its advantages and disadvantages. This professor was not different from others. She sounded as if prostitution was one of those decent professions. Because of her self-confidence, I couldn't help but ask her if she had a lover or a boyfriend. She said none right now, but she had one about half a year ago. She left him because he had demonstrated contempt when they were talking about prostitution, even though she hadn't told him what she had been doing secretly. I asked if she had fallen in love with any clients. She nodded, but added that almost none of her clients fell in love with her. The truth was, as she explained, no one would like to marry a hooker after the deal is over. I said such things happened, not only in China but also in Europe and the United States. She said she would never hope for such luck. In fact, she said that men were used to sleeping with any woman without love: thus, women could sleep with any men without love; the money compensated for the historical inequity.

I asked for another bottle of wine. The waitress seemed more sympathetic when she stared at the empty sear. I asked if she experienced any difference between making love with someone she loved or with someone she didn't love. She almost refused to answer this, saying that it was a man's question. She said that she treated this job as a temporary real job and a way to find a boyfriend. She asked me if I had a girlfriend. I let her guess and she said I should have one. I asked if she would have a different way of thinking about men after having worked, even temporarily, at this kind of job. She replied that this kind of thinking would be more realistic. I have thought about her answer many times since. How do we really answer this question? Which would have a more accurate understanding about a man-an ordinary woman or a hooker? Which man reveals more about his innate character?

I asked what kind of impression she had of me. She said so far I had been objective, perceptive, and rational, but I might change after a few more glasses of wine. I laughed, and asked if the cops on the street interfered with girls like her, since it was obvious they were soliciting customers on the street. She said cops are doing their jobs according to their rules. I asked what kind of rules prostitutes had; she said they were making an effort to earn a living. I asked her if she would call this also an effort. She nodded and added that she believed this was a job. Many people might disagree with her and worry that she couldn't have a normal family and love life after. But this was her life. No one should worry for her. She could balance and differentiate sex and love quite well.

She was giving me quite a lesson, but I didn't want to give up yet. I asked if she thought that the desire to make love is natural, just as the ears are fond of melody, the mouth is greedy for food, and eyes are lured to vivid colors. I asked if it was the same for both men and women. She replied that they were almost the same, but the existence of prostitutes satisfied the desire of men, while it wasn't important for the prostitutes to have sex or not. Men had to pay for it and everyone was happy.

She was suddenly interested to talk about women's fatal attractions-love beyond marriage. She said that once these women had outside love, their lovemaking with their husbands was just like providing free prostitution. What a remark! That caused me to finish most of my wine as well as the wine in her glass. I asked if she thought that men were biased against prostitution. She nodded. Then, I asked how women thought about prostitution. She said no matter how they looked at it, only women could be prostitutes. This job was a woman's privilege. If women were against prostitution, they were actually against men thinking of women as prostitutes. Many men look for girlfriends, but in their hearts they know they will dump them later. This is a prostitute-hunting mentality. After all, men usually think that hookers are too easy to get and therefore not as precious as the girls they had chased a long time. This is not to say that all men treat women as their hunting objects, likewise, not every women was a hooker, and not every man is looking for a hooker. She saw I had drunk too much; so she put on her wig quietly. She asked me where I was staying. I said I knew how to get back there. We went back onto the street. The street was still crowded with men and women passing by. I found that I was actually alone and crawled sottishly back to my hotel, where I fell asleep instantly.

Tr. By Kevin Dong and Denis Mair

The Price of Love

Finish reading a Chinese newspaper in New York, and you'll find your hands all covered with sooty "news". It is said there is no hope of solving this problem of printer's ink in this century. But Young Wang was a Chinese student just two months in America. He blackened his hands leafing through the papers, but not to find out the news. A friend-of-a-friend had given him a place to stay, and for two carefree months he had kicked off his shoes and settled in without paying rent or electricity. Now the friend-of-a-friend wanted him to move within three days because another friend of the friend-of-a - friend was coming from Mainland China to study abroad. Young Wang's friend back in Mainland China was like a general deploying his troops. It was impressive, the way he made international arrangements for his friends' accommodations.

On the first say of the three-day limit, Young Wang found that the friend-of-a-friend had packed the door to the small living room where the phone was. Young Wang got some quarters and went to a pay phone at the street corner to start apartment-hunting. He made dozens of calls to places listed in the Chinese newspaper, trying to find a room near the school he would attend, at the cheapest possible rate. At last he found a place that seemed to fit the bill. The landlord was from Taiwan, an amiable person who had married an attractive overseas student from Mainland China. The wife had stopped her studies and now stayed home cooking and caring for their baby. When Wang told the friend-of-a-friend he had found a place and wrote out the address, the friend-of-a-friend was amazed: the pretty wife had once been *his* girlfriend, but had ended up getting married to a green card from Taiwan.

Young Wang gave it no more thought, After Wang moved into the new room, the friend-of-a-friend called frequently, and often brought the conversation around to questions about the wife. When Wang told him the wife was making eyes at him, the friend-of-a-friend strongly urged Wang to make advances. He claimed the young wife surely did not love her Taiwanese husband. Actually, Young Wang had only been joking with him.

A few days later, the friend-of-a-friend called Young Wang and blurted out that he had told the Taiwanese husband what was going on between Wang and the wife. This gave Wang a fright, but soon he figured that the friend-of-a-friend was disrupting the wife's married life in revenge for being dropped.

Young Wang waited for a chance to talk with the wife while the Taiwanese husband was out. The wife said her husband had not questioned her about this. Perhaps her husband was keeping it to himself so he could observe them. All in all, the wife felt her ex-boyfriend was pretty shameless, to trap Wang with this false rumor. Young Wang patted his chest and said he would not be hounded out by such a thing; he should keep living there unashamedly. If the Taiwanese husband demanded an answer, he had the truth on his side and was not afraid.

Over a month went by, and one day after returning from class Young Wang blackened his hands looking through the Chinese paper. Again he was not reading news from home, but was trying to find a job and get some money. Although it was illegal for an oversea student to work in America, there were jobs to be found in Chinese restaurants and such, even if the pay was low. Young Wang tried a few places, but turned down each time. Then coming out from a Chinese restaurant, he saw a Chinese baby-sitter service. He jostled in, thinking he could earn a good hourly rate by babysitting for a rich family. He was ill-prepared for what he saw when he went in: the Taiwanese husband was there chatting with the friend-of-a-friend. Young Wang ducked sideways in alarm; luckily several jobseekers were there waiting. Young Wang secretly observed the two of them. Obviously they both worked for this company, being seated at end-to-end desks. The friend-of-a friend was nodding deferentially to the Taiwanese husband, making it clear to Young Wang that the Taiwanese husband was the boss, and the friend-of-a-friend was working for the Taiwanese husbands.

Young Wang's heart kept pounding after he snuck out of the waiting room. Turning things over in his mind, he realized what was behind all of this. Based on his own experience, he surmised that the story went something like this: The wife and the friend-of-a-friend were both overseas students from the Mainland. They were in their early thirties, which is not young, so studying for an MA or PhD. Was a tough proposition. Also, they were hurting financially. As Taiwanese husband had money, so the friend-of-a-friend and the wife conceived a plan to get a green card by paper marriage. Of course the Taiwanese husband did not know of this. Once she was married the wife introduced the friend-of-a-friend to work at the Taiwanese husband's company. The Taiwanese husband was kept in the dark the whole time. But later the wife had a child with the Taiwanese husband, and the friend-of-a-friend was not sure who the child's the friend-of-a-friend began to have all sorts of suspicions. His nerves were a tough distraught.

The questionable outcome from all this made Young Wang's own story hard to foresee. Young Wang paced slowly down the avenue, wondering what goal to set in life and how to create conditions for it. But it was all a big unknown. This incident made Young Wang feel uneasy, because his predicament put him close to the friend-of-a-friend and the wife, since they had all gotten out of the Mainland and were in their early thirties.

A few months passed, and Young Wang gradually stopped thinking of this, because he was facing plenty of problems getting himself established in America. He found a job as night watchman in a warehouse, where the boss said there was no worry about the immigration Service coming at a late hour to check for unregistered workers. If by any chances they did check, he would just be a friend who was staying overnight in the warehouse. They would have no way to catch him. But the wages were extremely low. On this particular day Young Wang didn't get up early. He had gone out drinking with his boss from the warehouse, so he did not go to class. He could hear the friend-of-a-friend and the wife talking in the next room. The friend-of-a-friend was saying what a paragon the Taiwanese husband was-a veritable Lei Feng. Never in his life would he forget such helpfulness, such spirit of sacrifice. He said this because the Taiwanese husband had agreed to go to Mainland China, marry the friend-of -a-friend's sister and bring her back to America. The friend-of-a-friend admired the Taiwanese husband so much for never sleeping with the wife that he felt like throwing himself at the husband's feet. What was more, the husband was going to let the friend-of-a-friend marry the wife right after the divorce, so the friend-of-a-friend could get a green card. Overhasty would ruin everything, so they were dragging the process out. A few more months should do it. The present situation was like this: the Taiwanese husband had gotten married on paper to the wife and would soon get divorced, after which he was prepared to marry the friend-of-a-friend's sister. As for the friend-of-a-friend, after a few months he would marry the wife, who had a green card. The child was the issue of the friend-of-a-friend and the wife, because the Taiwanese husband was only trying to help and had never slept with the wife. The friend-of-a-friend had tried to frighten Young Wang into moving out, but later he saw Young Wang was not making trouble, so he let it be.

This was a true eye-opener for Young Wang. He was moved to reflect on the relative superiority of two social systems, but he found his knowledge was not equal to the question. Nevertheless he had a sneaked sense that neither side was all that wonderful. He felt that both were not natural enough; they were too mechanical.

(At this point let me tell the circumstances of this story. My name is Yan Li, and I am a self-supporting overseas student from Mainland. I got to know Young Wang at a party one night. Knowing that I write things now and then, he told me of this incident. He felt this was worth writing about; it was perfectly suited to being a short story. I patted myself on the chest and assured him I would write it within three days. Just as I was writing the conclusion, Young Wang came to see me with an agitated look on his face. He told me of new developments in the story).

Young Wang's friend in Mainland China wrote a letter, saying he did not know Young Wang's new address, so he had mailed a dictionary for Wang to the friend-of-a-friend's apartment. So Young Wang went to the friend-of-a-friend's place to pick it up. He happened to be passing through the neighborhood that day, so he did not call ahead of time. He knocked on the door and nobody answered. Young Wang had a key with him. He had not been able to find it when he left, and later when he found it he did not return it. Anyway, he hardly ever saw the friend-of-a-friend, so he decided he would open the door and check inside for letters. He would pick them up and leave a note, then be on his way. So he opened the door and went int. What he saw shocked him: the Taiwanese husband and the friend-of-a-friend were lying naked in a bed. The friend-of-a-friend spoke to him severely, making a single demand: Young Wang was not to tell the wife of this under any circumstances. The friend-of-a-friend took the key from Young Wang and pushes him out the door. Then, through the door, he spoke these words softly: "Love has a price".

Tr. By Denis C. Mair

Blood Behavior

Bamboo Li was labeled as a landlord at the end of 1966. When the rebel faction ransacked the house of a local landowner named Noble Fang, they found evidence that Bamboo Li's grandfather had sold a large property to the Fang family forty years ago, before the Li family turned poor. That is to say, before selling that piece of land, Bamboo Li's family had been landowners of a sort. The failure to discover this in the Fifties must have been an oversight, or perhaps there was a hidden reason. So investigating this hidden reason became a full-time job for several young men in the rebel faction. They locked Bamboo Li up in the local primary school, where no classes were being held. Bamboo Li knew that his family had been well-off forty years ago, but this did not justify making him a target of denunciation. So he defended himself firmly, maintaining that his family was now dirt-poor. How could something insubstantial like "class background" prove that he was an oppressor? Whether or not he could accept this reality, half a year of captivity took away his courage to defend himself. As an "exposed landlord," there were struggle sessions and labor reform in store for him. For the next five years he and his family suffered grueling treatment in the town. In 1972 Bamboo Li's distant cousin became a township cadre, and due to this connection he was finally classified as a reformed landlord; he became an ordinary citizen of the town. But the strain had traumatized him. He felt his landlord background made him vulnerable, and he could be denounced at any time. He still carried the pressure of his family background with him; he felt that landlord blood ran in his veins. This corresponded with two statements the rebel leader had drilled into him during his captivity in the school building: "You will never get rid of your grandfather's landlord blood." "We rebels will always possess the blood of lower peasants; we are completely different from people like you."

Precisely because of Bamboo Li's mental problems, his son Forward Li seized on a chance to become a barefoot doctor. With behind-the-scenes help from the same distant relative, his son took classes for two years in the city. Forward Li was an only son, and his two sisters married men in other towns, so he took responsibility for his father. Forward Li's wife kept Bamboo Lee well-fed and clothed. Bamboo Lee's mental condition was tolerable most of the time, but at times it would flare up, and he would disappear from home for days. Sometimes his family had to look for him in the mountains and bring him back. After Forward Li became a barefoot doctor, he gave his father considerable help. Besides, demand for his medical skills helped the family's relations with the townspeople. As overall conditions improved, Bamboo Li's mental state changed for the better. On top of this a grandson was born, giving him someone to talk to. Although the grandson could not keep up a conversation, at least Bamboo Li could speak what was on his mind, and this was an outlet he needed.

In 1986 Bamboo Li's grandson Victor Li finished junior high, and was admitted to a high school in the neighboring city. Of course this was because Victor Li's father was by now assistant director of the town's only hospital. Forward Li hoped to send his son to study abroad someday, so he made sure the boy got into a good school. Bamboo Li could not accept the boy going away to school, and he had a few outbursts. Forward Li's tried to console him, but it did little good: Bamboo Li hardly touched his food for two weeks after the boy's departure. Finally, Forward Li persuaded the old man by mentioning his detention as a landlord. Forward Li said the boy could only break loose from his landlord ties by going abroad, and going abroad required study at a good school. But their town's high school had a poor lineup of teachers. This time Forward Li's urgings had the desired effect, which showed how traumatized Bamboo Li still was by his "landlord" label.

From then on, each time the boy came home on vacation, Forward Li would hear Bamboo Lee instructing the boy that study overseas would free him from any taint of landlord ties. Of course, everyone knew this was a sign of Bamboo Li's illness. Though it was pathological, it showed how badly the rebel faction had mistreated him years ago. His face grew livid whenever he spoke of being locked up for six months in the school building, and years of labor reform after that. Such agitation was bad for his health, and each time Forward Li noticed it, he would interrupt his father and change the subject. Forward Li understood his father's illness perfectly.

In 1992 Victor Li tested into a university in Shanghai. In his second year of college, his grandfather fell ill with blood poisoning--a disease treatable only by frequent blood replacements. Luckily, Forward Li was hospital director by now, so the treatment did not ruin them financially. As Bamboo Li lay on his sickbed, he told Forward Li this was finally a chance to purge his landlord blood and replace it with peasant blood. "Make sure you find peasant blood to replace it; don't overlook this." Forward Li came to supervise each blood replacement, not because the other doctors might make a mistake, but for fear his father would remind them to use peasant blood. Such a thing would not be seemly. So Forward Li was at his father's side during each blood replacement, saying "Don't worry, father, this is peasant's blood."

Soon Victor Li came home for summer vacation. Bamboo Li lay on his sickbed and revealed his reason for happiness to the boy: Finally all the landlord blood in his veins would be replaced. He also said that if he had known about blood replacements earlier, he would have gotten it done in 1966 and saved himself a great deal of suffering. He suggested that if Victor's application for foreign study did not work out, it would be best to have his blood replaced. Victor knew that his grandfather was raving, but he answered that the times were different now: if he could get a blood replacement he would get capitalist blood instead of peasant blood. The idea of getting capitalist blood brought a shout to Bamboo Li's lips: "Oh no!

That won't do! You'll be making trouble for yourself. Don't do it. It has to be peasant blood!" Victor Li could only calm him by saying, "You're right, you're right. I will insist on peasant blood." When his grandson said this, Bamboo Li drew an easy breath. He went on to say, "I only need two more treatments for the replacement to be complete. Up to now I've had eighteen treatments, and your dad says it takes twenty times to replace all of my landlord blood." Victor Li went along with him and tried to say things that would not agitate him. He and his father both knew that treatment was normally abandoned in such a cases, if this were not the director's father. Even so, the outlook was not positive: Forward Li quietly told Victor that the old man had two more weeks to live.

As it turned out, Bamboo Li's 75-year life ended five days later. Just before his death, as Forward Li performed the twentieth treatment, he contentedly told his son: "You ought to consider getting your blood replaced too. You are the director here: getting a blood replacement should be easy. But of course you have to avoid publicity. If everyone got blood replacements, there would be no differences of degree, and everybody could become a hospital director. So don't give blood replacements to too many people. To keep your position secure, you shouldn't give replacements to other people. I don't have any regrets. I just hope little Victor has no trouble going abroad. Give him a replacement of peasant blood before he goes abroad: that way nothing can go wrong." Forward Li could only nod in reply. His father was a sick man, a sick man on the point of leaving this world. Forward Li wept, remembering the years of humiliation he and his father had suffered under the Red Guards. His father's sickness was an after-effect of that humiliation.

Victor Li was with his mother the last time he saw his grandfather alive, just before the twentieth transfusion. Bamboo Li took held his grandson's hand and said, "Everyone has to die. If a wish can come true before death, then things don't seem so unjust. My sufferings left a mark on me that can't be erased. But now that I think of it, they helped me understand the importance of blood replacements. I feel good about going to the other world now, because I'll go with the identity of a peasant. Of course I won't act like the peasants who persecuted me years ago. I won't persecute rich peasants and landlords. I am not interested in that. I think that bloodlines are important, but having a good bloodline doesn't mean a person should persecute others. With a good bloodline, a person should do something good. You just wait to hear from me: when I get to the other world I'm going to do good things. In this world my bloodline kept me from doing good things, because they wouldn't allow us. Only people of good background got the chance to be officials and do good things." He looked Victor in the eye and said, "Your mother did some admirable things. She was born a peasant, but she was treated as a landlord along with our family. She did not resent us, and even helped us out of tight spots with her peasant background. I've told you all about that. Whatever happens, be good to your father and mother. If you have a chance to go abroad, take them to another country someday. I've heard that everything is fine overseas. But no matter what, I hope you all have peasant blood when you come to join me in the other world. Little Victor, once you get a blood replacement, your children will have a peasant background too. That will never change." With these words he fainted away. The last time he awoke was for his twentieth transfusion.

Victor Li had been close to his grandfather, and he went through a moody period after returning to school. He knew there was no basis to the idea of blood replacements, but his grandfather had died in contentment because of the procedure. Victor did not remember any sufferings from the Cultural Revolution, because he was born in 1974. But his grandfather's sickness gave him a taste of the terror of those times. He experienced the Cultural Revolution through his grandfather's lingering illness. This was what made him different from other students. Sometimes he felt hollow inside, and he felt his grandfather's fate casting a shadow over him. At such times he lapsed into utter silence, and buried himself in his studies. In this state he plunged into his homework with great concentration. As time went by, when doing difficult homework, he would remember his grandfather without intending to, and then go back to his studious mode.

Victor graduated with honors in 1996, and received a passing TOEFL score. He was debating whether to enter an M.A. program in China or try for a scholarship abroad when a relative of a hospital patient offered to help Victor go overseas. The relative, who had just come from America, did this in gratitude to Victor's father. Before Victor went abroad, Forward Li said to him, "You should count yourself lucky not to have been thrown off course by the Cultural Revolution. People five or ten years older than you missed chances because of the Cultural Revolution. Do the best you can at your studies. Someday your mother and I would like to go overseas for a look. After you get a degree find a job overseas, and then find a wife. I am sure you will be happy. We'll be fine here, so don't worry. Computers are the wave of the future now, so if you keep working hard, there will be economic benefits for you. China will have places where you can use your ability too. The future should be pretty good to you, wherever you decide to make a career." Victor's mother added, "It's best to find a Chinese wife. I hear that foreign women are too fancy-free. They are not so stable." Forward Li cut in and said, "You don't have a girlfriend yet, do you. How about finding one before you leave. That would put our minds at ease." To this Victor said, "What's the point of finding one for a short time? Wouldn't that be more trouble than it's worth? It would be foolish to tie myself down when I'm about to leave." What he said made sense, so his parents did not bring up the subject again.

New York first appeared before Victor's eyes at nighttime, through the window of an airplane. The lights looked magnificent, but told himself he must be ready for tough times. He knew a somber life was about to begin for him, from all the things he had learned about New York while still in China. But he knew that the rules here were fairly straightforward. As long as one chose a sought-after field at a fairly famous university, one could find decent-paying work. After that, one went about "enjoying" a peaceful life day after day. Of course, this scenario did not include matters of the heart, for these could not be predicted. No matter how rich a person was, there were no guarantees against emotional suffering. Thinking of this, he laughed aloud. Still, without question money was the crucial thing. First, he wanted to get on his feet financially.

His life at school soon began. English did not give him any trouble. He felt he had a talent for language, and he could accomplish anything if he made an effort. Actually, things did not go as smoothly as he expected, because he got caught up in a relationship. The object of his affections was an American-born Chinese. Differences of culture and experience showed up from their first contact. This was his first love, but life had been smooth at college in China; now he was getting his first taste of frustration. Although this did not involve his coursework, it happened at school. The first time he made love with Jenny, he could tell she was an old hand at this. Both of them were 23 years old, but she taught him to make love. He was not her first lover, but this did not disappoint him. Instead, he rejoiced to himself, because he supposed that there would be no regrets later if he broke up with her. But when Jenny showed less concern about this than himself, he felt frustrated. Jenny went on dates with an American classmate, maintaining that "more than one flower blooms during youth." She meant she wanted to be involved with more than one man at a time; several flowers could bloom at once. No matter how modern Victor Li was, no matter how much he had learned about America, he could not accept this. So he began to take a stand. First he demanded several times that she save her affections for him alone. Of course she did not take this seriously. Then he stopped going to see her, and he would not accept her invitations. Two months later she came to his room; he claimed he had an errand to do and quickly walked out. Jenny yelled at him from behind, "If you have any balls, let me see you get an American girl."

Sure enough, Victor found a pretty American classmate and took her to a party where Jenny happened to be. Looking pleased with himself, he chatted and guffawed with the new girl Nancy. Naturally Jenny knew what game he was playing. She walked up to him, put her hand on his shoulder, and said, "I agree to your demands." He gave her a blank look, not expecting this move, but he quickly realized she was getting revenge on him. This was a spur-of-the-moment thing, not something she really meant. So he lightly removed her hand from his shoulder and said, "I don't know what you're talking about, but I'd like to introduce you to my girlfriend Nancy." Jenny looked at Nancy's extended hand, saying: "I thought I was the only woman you could find. At last here is someone who will get me free of you! So let me show my gratitude." With this she gave Nancy a nod and walked away. Victor knew that he had won this round, and the satisfaction prompted him to take a few extra drinks. As a result, upon leaving the party he fell drunkenly onto a strip of grass. Nancy was a timid girl, and did not know how to handle someone keeled over beside the road. Deciding to leave him there to regain his senses, she went home and went to bed. After all, she had not known him long, and there had not been time for them to be involved sexually.

When he sobered up and went home, he found Jenny sitting on the steps at his dormitory. It was already past two o'clock; he felt a familiar stirring at the sight of her. "It looks like you used up all your energy on Nancy," she said. "Did you imagine me while you were making out with her? If you did, I forgive you." This time he did not refuse her entry. He went to the bathroom, and found she had poured him a glass of soda when he came out. As he gulped it down in silence, a strange thought came to him: What kind of blood ran in her veins? Could an American have peasant blood? Or was hers the blood of a purebred filly? No mistake, she exerted a powerful attraction. Regrettably, he had not been involved with other women, so there were no grounds for comparison.

They made ravishing love. He had never done it so well, he felt, and attributed it to the unusual passion she had shown. Afterwards she asked, "You stayed out pretty late with that American girl. Don't tell me you didn't do anything?" He said, "Do you think I could do it more than once?" She said, "Men have a physical limitation. You can't always do it when you want to. It looks like you couldn't get your hands on her." He said, "So you were my outlet of release, is that it?" She laughed and said, "Let's not talk in circles. We two care about each other. I can't say what it is about you that attracts me. Anyway, from now on I won't let another man ruin the feelings between us." He let out a belly laugh, then suddenly stopped and said, "When my grandpa was sick he had no idea of blood types, so he wanted a transfusion of peasant blood." Jenny could not make out his meaning and asked him to say that again. But instead he went on to a new thought and asked, "If you could get a blood replacement, what kind of blood would you want?" Without a pause she said she wanted the blood of Madonna, the pop star. She asked him what sort he would like. He said, "I want to have gasoline instead of blood." She asked, "What did you just say about your grandpa?" "Oh, it's nothing," he said. "It's just that my grandpa wanted to be someone without any wealth." She shook her head at the thought that anyone in this world would wish poverty on himself. He said, "You people in America don't know how the power of idealism, when it is twisted, can give human nature a pretext for doing many evil things. A poor person is someone with the freedom not to worry about what he might lose. Such freedom feels contempt for all property, and this leads it to destroy property. It boils down to the natural joy of one animal in combat with another. This is something that existing civilization doesn't dare imagine." To her this was as clear as mud, but she knew it had to do with previous events in China. She was Chinese by blood, but her mother tongue was English. Her language and personal history were Western. The background she expressed in her speech was Western.

Victor Li's financial situation was no different from most Chinese students studying in America. He worked part-time in at a dry cleaners under an American boss. At the same time, he helped a professor of Chinese Studies do some translation into English. As for Jenny, she was attending school on loans, which she would pay back slowly after graduation. She earned spending money by working weekends in a department store.

Victor met an American named David who played the stock market, and under his influence bought some low-demand stocks, hoping to make a killing. Regrettably, within a few months he took a loss. Victor realized he must plunge into the market if he wanted to get a feel for its pulse. A classmate's father agreed to teach him, so Victor worked without pay for his mentor two afternoons a week. He wanted to learn the ropes, so he could open his own brokerage office and speculate with other people's money.

One day Jenny came by with some marijuana; they settled back and had a long talk as they smoked. This was the first time he smoked it, and Jenny watched his reaction closely. He ended up having long, sad recollections of his childhood. "You don't understand the first thing about China," he said. "Anyway you can't be considered a Chinese. Your native language is English, which makes you an Anglo, but you can't be considered an American either. Why is that? Because you have a Chinese environment at home. You're just a second generation immigrant: you're still on the way to becoming American. When I was small my grandpa said I had a landlord background. I was only five then. I said a landlord is someone who owns land. My grandpa said no, and do you know why? Because they were checking into people who had owned land in the past. It could have been 50 or 100 years ago, but such people were called landlords. Even if you didn't own land, you were accountable for the lives of your ancestors. I did not understand such things then. All I knew was that Grandpa wouldn't let me hit back when I got into scrapes with the neighbor kids. Our family had a landlord background, and the neighbors were peasants all the way back. People with peasant backgrounds were allowed to hit people with landlord backgrounds, which made me think peasants must be relatives of the emperor. On the other hand, they didn't look very special. One time the pent-up anger was too much for me. When the neighbor boy kept throwing garbage near our doorway, I gave him a beating. He was a few months older, but shorter than I was. After beating him up I felt pleased with myself, because he hadn't dared to make a noise. But, unbelievably, he held it back until his father came home from work. That is to say, four hours after I beat him up, he suddenly burst out crying in front of his father. My grandpa was called over to hear of my terrible crime. The plain truth was, the neighbor kids thought they could get away with throwing garbage at our doorway, because of our landlord background. But that was already 1979. My stupid grandpa turned around and gave me a beating. Of course I gritted my teeth and didn't make a sound. The more I refused to cry, the harder my grandpa beat me. As he walloped me he said, 'Listen, little fellow, go ahead and cry out loud. Just let the neighbors hear that I'm punishing you, alright?' But I wouldn't make a peep, and that touched off Grandpa's temper. He picked up a hardcover book of Chairman Mao's quotations and pounded it on my hand that was gripping the leg of the desk. I did not loosen my grip, and he slammed it down again. My whole body shuddered, and I broke out in a sweat. My hand pressed itself against my chest. Still I would not cry. I fled out the door, feeling a sense of victory, because the neighbors didn't hear my grandpa punishing me! I ran to the house my friendly uncle, wanting to hide there for a while. That was when I noticed my hand was swelling, and my uncle knew grandpa had been beating me. He took me to the hospital; my father examined my hand and found a bone fracture. I had my hand wrapped in a cast, like a casualty of war. I could tell from my father's manner that he supported me. He felt it was wrong for the neighbor kids to throw garbage at our door. But he said to me, 'I am on your side, but you must not cry. Your grandpa's nerves are under a strain. Don't make him feel guilty. Most of all, don't call attention to your injury.' When Father and I got home, grandpa was still angry. I raised my plaster cast twice, and tears blurred my vision, but remembering my father's warning, I forced myself not to cry. Grandpa asked what had happened to my hand. Father said, 'You hit him a bit too hard, but it's no big thing. A child's bones grow quickly, so we'll remove that cast in a week.' I felt triumphant to see Grandpa's astonished look, because he knew he had done wrong. But the way he admitted guilt was excessive: he took my hand and knelt down in front of me. Mother had to pull him to his feet. At this point I was just like the neighbor kid: I couldn't hold back the sobs any longer."

Jenny held Victor close to her, because this story coupled with the marijuana had cast a pall over them. Jenny said, "I don't know what truly happened in China, but from what I've heard, China and Russia were pushed over the brink by ideals that turned sour. But whatever happened, it seems to be over now." Victor drowsily pillowed his head on her chest and entered a half-awake state.

Smoking marijuana was something they often did together. One time they got into a discussion about the meaning of attending college. Jenny said it was a rule of the game in modern society: everyone has to learn a skill and use it to earn a living. Ultimately one exchanges skill, time, and physical effort for money. And then one uses money to buy commodities that have a price attached. "Is there anything that doesn't have a price?" she wondered. "I don't. There is no price attached to me," Victor burst out with his answer. "You're on your way to getting a price attached to you," she said. "As soon as you get a degree in America, you'll find a job that pays a salary. That salary is your price." "Well what about creative works and inventions?" asked Victor. "Those things always have a price put on them when they are completed," she said. To this Victor replied, "Suppose a college graduate gets a job that pays $50,000 and he works at it for forty years. If his income jumps to $60,000 the last twenty years, he will make a total of $2,200,000. But people who deal in real estate or stocks make this much in two or three years. This is too big a difference." She said, "Only a tiny number of people can be that lucky." Victor said, "Well, since the purpose of going to college is to get a job, why don't we start a company for ourselves? Starting from now, there is no need to go to college." Jenny said, "If your own company goes out of business, you're left with nothing. That is the difference between being the boss and having a boss. Those big companies have built up plenty of capital, so they can weather a recession. Little companies are different: if a breeze of recession comes along, it might blow them over. A large company gives better job security in the long run." He said, "The way you put it, the world is always going to be under control of large corporations." "That's usually how things are: it's the way of the world," she said. "I don't want to go to college. I'm starting my own company tomorrow," he said. "It sounds exciting," said Jenny, "but where will you find money to start a company?" He said, "I don't need much money, because I'll pool investments. I'll use other people's money to play the market. I've learned a few ins and outs. I'm serious. Since all roads point toward money, I don't think one method is more valid than another. I don't see any problem with quitting college." She said, "But you are in this country under a student visa. You don't have a work permit." He said, "What's so difficult about that? The company where I'm learning securities can get me an employment visa, or we two can file for a marriage certificate." She asked, "Do you really want to drop out?" He said, "I've been thinking about it for a long time. So what's it going to be? Will we file for a marriage certificate, or should I have the company file for my employment visa?" She said, "I'll have to think about it."

Failure. Within half a year Victor Li failed. After quitting school he worked hard and pooled some investment money. But the tricky currents of the market and the jumpiness of his investors defeated him. He hung on for a while, until he knew no upturn was in store for him. The only choice was to try a different line of work. He told Jenny what he had learned the past half year, and that prompted him to tell another story that happened in China. In 1992 there was a classmate of his named Lu, whose family had been capitalists before 1949. In 1992 the government returned all the family's confiscated wealth. Suddenly, Lu became a rich man. Many people envied him, but his family had suffered several attacks in the Cultural Revolution for its capitalist background. Three people in his family had died. Two of them committed suicide after being tortured, and one was beaten to death by Red Guards. This was the price they paid. Yet when those deaths happened, the family had no property, and there was no way of knowing the government would return their property in 1992. Past wealth was the only reason for those deaths. That was why his family felt that wealth was both a good thing and a terrible thing. From another angle, one could say that wealth always takes a toll. Jenny said, "That was in China, and it happened during an abnormal period. Now we are in America. What are you getting at?" "I'm not getting at anything," he said. "It's just that my idea of wealth is related somehow to my grandpa's landlord background. My grandpa's grandpa became poor after he sold his land. That's going a long way back, but my grandpa's class background was still landlord. Strangely enough, in 1980 my grandpa was reclassified as having a rich peasant background. It's because you can't change all at once from landlord to peasant. You have to be a rich peasant first. Rich peasants are somewhat better off than peasants. Actually, before 1949 my grandpa's circumstances were no different from a peasant's. So what I'm trying to say is, the most reliable way to stir up struggles between people is to use differences in wealth. You can even do it by pointing to a concept like class background. I have heard that some big corporations in America are not run very well, but based on their reputation they get infusions of capital that keep them alive. This sort of corporation has a 'background' as a large corporation, not as a small company. We're talking about the 'largeness' of a landlord and the 'smallness' of a peasant."

"Don't talk in circles," said Jenny. "What are you going to do from here on out?"

"Haven't I already begun?" said Victor. "I'm involved in a trading company that will do business with China. I am handling liaisons with businesses in China. I have found a college classmate whose business in China is doing well. I think the prospects are good."

"What is it you like about me?" Jenny had asked this question several times, but he had not given a definite answer. This time he was ready to answer carefully. He put his thoughts in order and said, "First I'll say that in America, no, in New York there are all these Chinese people. To me their features indicate a tie of blood or family. There is no question that the rules of the game among Americans include elements of their own culture, so there is a gulf. When I face an American girl, I'm facing a world of differences, from appearance to habits. But put me face to face with someone from China, and there are scars that affect the way I see her. I'll think how it's impossible for her to get what she wants from me. Perhaps because we are both from China, we bring the same things, and we offer no solution to each other's problems. New York is like a farmers' market. We have brought the same goods, expecting to

71

exchange them for U.S. dollars. There is no exchange to be made between us. Maybe I'm putting this too bluntly, but that's the only way to make it clear. I end up thinking a Chinese born in America is suitable for me. Appearance-wise, there is a sense of blood ties. Inwardly, there are none of those scars from having lived in China. Although you can't write Chinese well, you can speak it. English is your first language, and Chinese is your second. For me it's the other way around. This shows that our relationship is complementary in some ways. Also, you taught me to make love, and you've taught me a lot about English. For my part, I've taught you some things about the Chinese language. Of course, I find your good looks irresistible as well." Jenny nodded her head in satisfaction.

"Really, I don't like doing this kind of logical analysis," he said. "It sounds like a business deal. It lacks romance. Didn't it sound to you like I was reporting on company performance at a stockholders' meeting?"

"I understand you better from hearing your report," she said. "You have a talent for putting things in perspective. I've seen you do it in other areas, but now I am sure of it. Do you want to know what I like about you?"

"You like my bold ambition," he said.

"No, I like you because all the suffering in China did not make you feel inferior about who you are. I have seen many people from China who feel inferior about being Chinese. Some tell me they hardly associate with Chinese here, because Chinese people are unworthy. Some of these people consciously avoid speaking Chinese. They think that if nothing but English comes from their lips, they are released from their Chinese background. And some use almost any occasion to show disdain for Chinese people. They are simply too shallow for words. But you are different. You have shed that baggage, and that makes a non-Chinese Chinese person like me feel fairly treated."

"Is there anything else?" he asked.

"Of course," she said. "You have a style that makes American girls friendly toward you. I must say, normally they wouldn't consider a Chinese man, but they like you. This makes me jealous. Another thing, you never have me invest money in your business ventures. You say it's because I would lose faith in you if you lose the money. But I think you have other considerations. You don't want to play upon my feelings just to get this little bit of money. You're someone who thinks things through. Since you have been with me, you have considered your steps with two people's future in mind. Am I right?"

He nodded quietly and said, "If the company doesn't vouch for me to get a visa, would you marry me so I can get the papers to do business?"

"I think I would," she said. "Really, it wouldn't be any different from the way we're living now." Another year passed quickly. There was no upturn in Victor's business. He was cheated by his classmate back in China. Victor shipped a large batch of goods, but his classmate in China never made good on the unpaid half of the money. Victor found the phone was disconnected at his classmate's company in China. He said to

Jenny, "That guy doesn't have much ambition. For $100,000 he closed down his company. If he had waited half a year, I would have tied more money up in this, and he could have made off with it. I had to scrape together $100,000 to make good on the unpaid half. Now I'm starting from zero again." "It's not that simple," said Jenny. "This has put a bad mark on your record at that American company. Word will spread in your sector of business. Your reputation will suffer. And another thing, you put too high a value on honor. Business should not be lubricated by personal feelings: it's all about rules and contracts. Those things have to be made clear before a transaction. Anyway, you're not professional enough. Maybe it's because of your Chinese background. You've got to change your ways."

Yet he failed at the next project he tried.

Marijuana was not the solution. Though Jenny smoked it with him, she reminded him he had to pull himself together. He took another drag, held in the smoke with tightly closed lips, and let out a long breath from his belly. He said, "My grandpa got his blood replaced with peasant blood. I wonder if that has jinxed me." She said, "Your grandpa didn't really have all his blood replaced. That was just a wishful way of speaking." He said, "Grandpa wanted my blood to be replaced too. If I do get it replaced, I will insist on blood from a millionaire." She said, "You are a warm-hearted person. You can do something besides business." "But I quit school to do business," he said. "How can I stop now?" She said, "Well it won't do any good to replace your blood with alcohol. A person's behavior is determined by blood and personality." He stood up and poured whisky for himself and her. He rolled another fat joint, then sat silently, sipping and smoking. Jenny realized she was also depressed over his business failures of the past two years. But she could not help him because she was still a year from graduation. So she traded nonsensical remarks with him. She told him she was born in America because her father, while studying in England, had dreamt his future wife would be an American Chinese. The wife had appeared in the dream, saying that her blood background was made up of cheese and potatoes. Also, she confided that her fondest wish was to sleep with her arms around the Empire State Building. Victor interrupted, "That's a sexual delusion. She was hoping she could get pregnant with a skyscraper, so she could give birth and solve her housing problems in New York." He poured their glasses full again, then leaned against the wall unsteadily and said, "I've got to solve my blood replacement problem. My grandpa's subconscious wish must have been a command from higher realms. My grandpa said he'd wait for us in the other world, but we must get our blood replaced before we go, or else we'll be mistreated." She said, "Don't you think this marijuana is stronger than before?" "I don't feel anything," he said. "I just feel that I'm connected with information from a distant source. Most of all, I can have a conversation with my grandpa's inner mind. I always thought he was a crazy person, so I didn't pay heed to what he did or said. But now I am having a realization: there was really something there. In Chinese we have the phrase 'hard-won foolishness,' and maybe that's the condition we're talking about." She said, "Connecting with information like that won't help your business. You should access information selectively. Maybe those wealthy businessmen have some kind of paranormal power. But I don't seem to have it. When we smoke marijuana, you get into the mood better than I do." He said, "Not necessarily. Maybe the realizations that slip by now will appear in your mind two or three days later. I really feel good now. I can feel my grandpa breathing. I sense the meaning behind what he said when he covered me at night: 'A warm body keeps the nightmares away.' I can feel his wish that I get a replacement of peasant blood. But times are different now. I want a replacement with millionaire's blood, or a genius' blood, not peasant blood." She said, "Where are you going to find a millionaire's blood? When I was little I dreamed of living on Long Island, in a place with a storybook atmosphere. It was in a house standing by itself, with woods around it. Especially around Christmastime, that atmosphere stayed around me like a cloud." He said, "That was a dream of growing up, not about getting rich." She said, "With those possessions, doesn't that prove I would already be rich?" He said, "We want the ability to get rich, because we want to enjoy the experience of getting rich!" She said, "Look at Bill Gates. Within a few years his company became the largest software company in the world. That didn't happen through blind luck." He said, "Well, Coca Cola used a one-page formula to become the largest company in the world. Almost everyone drinks Coca Cola. Everyone's blood has Coca Cola in it. That's it! To succeed as a businessman, Coca Cola has to flow in your veins like blood. Hardly any company can compare with Coca Cola! That's right! My grandpa would approve of replacing my blood with Coca Cola, don't you think?" No answer came from Jenny, and he knew she had fallen asleep. He talked to himself excitedly: "Coca Cola, I've finally found you. Once you are flowing in my veins, I'll be able to do any kind of business. No more honor and ties of feeling. From now on I'll have smooth sailing in my business." He reeled to the refrigerator, opened it, and found a one-liter bottle of Coke. He let out a burst of loud laughter, but Jenny did not awake. He placed the Coke bottle against his chest and sat on the sofa, wondering how to get the Coke flowing through his veins. He remembered his father using needles for blood transfusions. But this was Coke; it should be poured in a glass. Then how could he get it into his veins. He laughed, because he heard his grandpa whisper in his ear, "Go ahead and use a needle." He knew the pharmacy next door sold disposable needles. He ran out and bought two of them, one to draw blood and one to inject Coca Cola. He hesitated as he picked up the needle, then inserted it without feeling any pain. He happily realized that his grandpa was guiding his hand. He drew out three syringes full of blood, then smoothly injected three syringes of Coca Cola. He said to himself, "That will be enough for today. I want Jenny to be a part of this memorable moment." He tried to rouse Jenny, who opened one eye halfway and said, "My head is dizzy. Let me sleep a little more." He lay her back down and told himself not to be impatient. Doing the replacement over a week's time would be fast enough. His grandpa's blood replacement had taken twenty transfusions.

He was roused by Jenny, who yelled that there was something black in the sink. "That's my blood," he said. Blood turns black when it's cold." She said, "Why is your blood here?" He said, "Didn't we talk about replacing my blood with Coca Cola? This way I'll will be undefeated in the business world." She screamed, "Did you really inject Coke into your veins?" He said, "Would I lie to you about this?" He rolled up his sleeve to show the needle marks. She was at a loss for words, because there was nothing unusual in his appearance, and he was in good spirits. But still she had to ask: "How much cola did you inject?" He said, "Three syringes full. If I inject several syringes a day, I estimate that two weeks will be enough. Then you'll see how I ride the winds in the world of business. Your dream about Long Island won't be any trouble."

That evening, he said to her: "You don't have to study. Spend the next two weeks with me; watch me until my blood is replaced." He was cleaning the syringes as he spoke. She said, "Go buy a couple of new ones." He said, "No need. If I wash them they'll be fine. Besides, we don't have very much money." She said, "I'm really afraid. This is like being in a dream." He said, "You are not in a dream, you are on the threshold of a new era. Don't you realize, my grandpa has entered my soul to give me help? Don't you worry. My grandpa did not enjoy blessings in his lifetime, and neither did my father. Now it's my chance. Chinese people say 'Blessings from past lifetimes come around in this one.'" As he did the injection, Jenny closed her eyes. He shouted, "I'm telling you, keep your eyes open!" She opened her eyes, and was convinced of the facts in front of her: she saw the blood drawn out, and then watched as the cola went into the vein.

When two weeks had passed Jenny said, "How do you intend to get your business started?" He said, "First I need some capital." An impact had been made on her soul by two weeks of watching him replace his blood. By now she was convinced Victor Li would succeed. Several days ago she had withdrawn her money from the bank-all $1325 of it. Now she pushed the money into his hands. "I'm going to start with stocks," he said. He picked up the phone and called the friends who had played the market with him earlier. "Would you tell me which two stocks on the Hong Kong market have the highest rate of fluctuation?" "Tell me which American stocks are going on the market today." "What stocks from Chongqing City are ready to go on the market?" "I'll call back soon about this." When he phoned again, it was to invest all his money in B-stocks offered by Chongqing City Telephone Company. He told Jenny, "We won't know what happens for a month or two. Now let's go sell my old car. We can use the money to decorate the coffee shop your uncle opened downtown. That will be our investment.

Jenny's uncle had no confidence in his coffee shop, so it had been limping along half-alive for ten years. He uncle was moved when they went to him with $2500 they got from selling the car. He said, "Are you really willing to make this coffee shop a going concern?" Victor said, "Of course. I know you named this place after your late wife. We want to make it work, so we feel it needs refurbishing. We are ready to buy materials, and we'll do the remodeling ourselves. I will probably take a week or two. Our condition is that we get 20% of the profit." Jenny's uncle laughed, "If it makes a profit, I can give you 50%. For the past five years I've kept this place open, but the money is not worth it. I do it as a memorial to my deceased wife. I made a vow to keep this place running until I die. If you are willing to take over, I'm willing to come two days a week. You take care of it the rest of the time. As long as you don't ask me for money, you can keep all you earn." This was like manna from heaven to Jenny and Victor; they were overjoyed. "Alright," they said. "We'll start the remodeling tomorrow."

They were struck by a realization: this chance had been there for the taking. Why hadn't they thought of it? Why did they think of it after Victor did his "blood replacement"? It could only be explained by the effect of the cola. Jenny said to him, "I'm really afraid you'll grow apart from your loved ones. You can grow apart from other people, but what is between us should not be just for profit, like cola." Victor said, "Don't worry about that. I thought about the possibility of such a side effect, so before the transfusions I drew up a plan for distribution of all assets. Half of them will be yours. There is a clause saying the document cannot be revised without your signature. You can ask Jimmy the lawyer about this. But so far, I feel plenty of confidence about us. It seems the cola's effects are only in the business domain. I hope it will stay this way."

The coffee shop was remodeled to look like a cafeteria in an American prison movies. Of course this idea grew out of Victor's cola blood. And he thought of an advertising slogan:

"If you've been in jail, relive old times; if you haven't, get a taste of it." He used large pots and ladles to serve simple food. Of course this was a publicity coup in the restaurant trade, especially for tourists. A week after the re-opening, they had to reserve tables, and before long they were booked solid for two months.

Within half a year, Chongqing Telephone stocks soared to thirty times their original price. The coffee shop absorbed the furniture store next door; it became one of the largest coffee shops in New York, with business of $10,000 per day. Features and reports on it appeared in various newspapers and magazines; television stations did special segments on it. Ex-convicts were eager to bring their friends and reminisce about life on the inside. The ex-cons made suggestions that helped the coffee shop have a more authentic feel. People from various walks of life regarded the place highly, and restaurants in other cities asked to open under their name. Victor and Jenny made several million dollars on franchises, and this was just the beginning, for soon a percentage of earnings would start rolling in. They signed contracts for use of their name in 60 cities: almost every state in America had one of their franchises. Small wonder that a New York Times reporter wrote in his article: "...It has the energetic hum of a fast food restaurant, but with much higher style and quality. It can be called a significant feature of fin de siècle American culture."

At this point someone came to them with a plan to write their success story. They refused, for a simple reason: they feared it would stir up a global craze for Coca Cola blood replacements. Jenny felt they should authorize the biography, but keep the blood replacements secret. But Victor disagreed, feeling it would offend his grandpa who had given them inspiration. Victor's grandpa had never concealed his wish for a blood replacement, so Victor should not conceal it. Right now it was best not to say anything.

One day Victor was invited to a ribbon-cutting at a new cultural center. Of course, the aim was to get a donation from him. With a flourish of his pen he wrote a check for $50,000. Afterwards there was a program of literary entertainment. One poet read a piece that touched him deeply: it was a poem called "New York," and it included these two lines: "New York washes blood at the heart of the world, / Blood washed into Coca Cola flows around the globe." He imprinted these lines in his memory, and kept the poet's name in mind. He went home and recited the lines to Jenny, who thought he had composed them. When told they were someone else's, she said, "It seems that other people are coming to the same realization. This world needs something cold and neutral to keep functioning." He said, "I didn't write that $50,000 check on an impulse today. I feel there are strange people in those cultural groups. Those people are not committed to money, but they are committed to uncovering themselves and others. There is no need for their views, except in the other world. Take that poet for example: he seemed pretty confident in himself, but he pointed out the power of money in this world. Since he knows that power, why does he go on writing poetry? It would be more sensible to go make money. Is he trying to criticize this phenomenon of money? Could this world ever get rid of the function of money? Money is the best standard for the circulation of value. I can't think of anything to take money's place for measuring value of labor. I want to print these two lines on our restaurant's flier. What do you think?" Jenny thought it over and said, "Maybe it's not a good idea, because it sounds like you're doing publicity for Coca Cola. Besides, what does it have to do with your restaurant?" Victor said, "The connection is simple: it's my personal wish. It has to do with the cola in my veins. Besides, the uncanny way I met him proves that somehow he is like me." She said, "You can use the lines he wrote, but first you need his permission." Victor said, "Of course. I'll have my secretary get in touch with him."

The poet's name was Will Chinn. At the moment he walked into Victor's office, Victor had a notion of playing a game with him. Victor said to him, "I'm thinking of printing your lines about washing blood on some advertisements, but I don't know how much to pay you." Will Chinn shrugged and said, "See how it goes. This has never happened to me; I don't know how it's done." Victor put on a straight face and said, "I can give you fifty dollars." With no change of expression Will Chinn said, "Alright. Anyway, poems are written to be read. It doesn't matter if you keep the $50, because I never expected to make money off poems." Victor asked curiously: "How do you support yourself?" The poet said, "I work at a copy shop and write poetry in my spare time. I only do the job so I can keep writing. If I had money I would write poetry full time. I've been writing for over ten years." Victor asked, "Have you published

a book of your poems?" The poet said, "I've put out two books."
"Can you make money selling poetry books?" The poet replied,
"Like I say, it's impossible to make money writing poetry. I do
it to express my view of the world and society." "Well, can you
explain what you meant by saying New York washes blood at
the heart of the world?" With a gleam of excitement in his eyes,
the poet said, "Business is not about feelings, it's about
products. Products are objects that have no feeling. If they do
have feeling in them, it's imputed to them by people. For
instance, you might have feelings for a floor lamp at home,
because you've had it for years and gotten used to it. A new one
would be hard to get used to. In our world, more and more
behavior revolves around business, and this affects how much
behavior revolves around feelings. Blood produces feelings, but
if we can replace it with Coca Cola, people would make less
trouble for themselves." The word replace gave Victor a jolt,
and he said to himself, 'So this poet thought of the same thing.'
He said to Will Chinn: "Well, tell me if it's possible to replace
blood with Coca Cola." The poet laughed, "Do you think it's
doable?" Victor said, "I think it's worth trying." Still laughing,
Will Chinn said, "You could be a poet!" Victor said, "I am a
poet, a poet of action." Changing the subject, he said, "You said
I can use your lines without paying you money. Will you sign
a contract to that effect?" Will Chinn shrugged and said "O.K.,"
as he took a pen from his pocket. Victor went to the next room
and told his secretary to draw up a contract. Coming back he
said, "It's unlike me not to pay. Tell you what, you can have ten
percent of my company's profits next month, just for a month,

however much that is. My secretary will notify you to come and pick up a check. Besides that, I'm willing to be your friend. Every Friday evening I'll be eating at my restaurant off Broadway. You can come any time to have a meal and chat with me." The poet said, "If you don't turn a profit next month, but lose money instead, do I have to pay ten percent of your loss?" Victor laughed out loud and said, "Don't you know how good my business has been lately? Haven't you seen the write-ups in the papers?" The poet shook his head and said, "I really didn't know." Victor sighed, "You really are a poet. Poetry lets people hold onto non-mainstream things. That's why a poet can't get popular." Will Chinn said, "Aren't you going to publicize two of my lines? I'm afraid they will affect your business." Victor said, "I am a businessman, I don't go in for losing propositions. Who says I can't use a poem to help my business? The poet said, "Poetry is a hard thing for business to take advantage of. For the most part, art and literature are being used by business. I don't think that is a bad thing. But businessmen are stymied when it comes to poetry, and so are the poets themselves. It isn't that poets don't like money, but for some reason, you can't sell poems for money. Even so, many people insist that human beings can't do without the poetic spirit. Look at the Nobel prizes for literature: over half of them have gone to poets." Victor said, "I'm going to try. At least these two lines are going to be tied up with my business." The secretary came in and gave him the contract. He read it, signed the duplicate, and then handed them to the poet. The poet signed them without even looking at them. Victor gave one copy to Will Chinn, kept one for himself, and then gave him a parting handshake.

Victor narrated this encounter to Jenny, who listened absorbedly. She said, "Poets are an obsessive breed. They treat writing poetry like raising a child. Any money they earn goes to 'raising' this child." Victor said, "From what I can tell, poetry is a kind of literary religion. Otherwise, why would the Nobel Prize be given to something people don't care about?" Jenny said, "Right, I wonder about that too. Is it a religion?" Vincent said, "Will Chinn was able to conceive of replacing blood with cola; this proves that something called to him from an unseen realm, just like my grandpa called to me. Do I qualify as a businessman? I simply used a method others don't know about to unlock my mind. That lets me discover business openings. I'm not under emotional influence from my blood. I'm an innovator, not a businessman." Jenny laughed, "You're neither a businessman nor an innovator. You're a poet!" He said, "But I can't write poetry." She said, "You can write it through your actions. The act of replacing your blood was like Will Chinn writing those lines of poetry. Your actions are poetry." He said, "That may be so, but poems don't earn money." She said, "But didn't you let Will Chinn earn at least $80,000 from two lines of poetry? Last month our profits were close to $800,000, but next month they will be more, maybe even $1,000,000, because we'll have three new franchises. More royalties will be credited to us. Will Chinn may get $100,000." He said, "So Will Chinn is going to become a full-time poet. He told me if he had money, he wouldn't do anything else: he would write poetry full time. I'll be glad to have a friend like him." She said, "You should make friends with him. Who else could imagine replacing blood with cola? You two must have a blood tie." He said, "If so, I think I should ask him to write our biography. He would make it come alive, because he conceives of things the way I do. What do you think?" She said, "It's worth considering. But after it's published, all kinds of people will try replacing their blood. The world will be a mess." He said, "What has already happened is bound to be exposed sometime. The question is, how soon? I have an urge to see how people react: it will be something to watch for sure. I can already imagine the media frenzy this will whip up." She said, "You'd better think it over awhile. You don't have to decide right away."

Two weeks later Victor decided to meet with Will Chinn. He asked the poet, "Are you interested in writing my biography?" Will Chinn said, "Not very much, because there are plenty of writers who specialize in biography. Why come to me?" Victor said, "You're right, there are professional writers, but I'm not sure they could do it well. There is a crucial reason. If I tell you something amazing, will you agree to write it?" The poet said, "That depends on how amazing it is. Does this world still have something to get amazed about?" Victor said, "Usually there wouldn't be anything to get amazed about. Everything that could happen has happened. But what happened to me is different. It is something that has never happened before, I can guarantee that." The poet said, "Well then, let me hear it." Victor said, "Sorry for beating around the bush. You see, I really want you to write it, and I believe only you can do this subject justice. Alright, I'll tell you. I am the first person ever to replace his blood with Coca Cola. I have Coca Cola flowing in my veins!" The poet shook his head dubiously. Victor led Will Chinn into a secret room. Before the poet's eyes, Victor drew from his arm a syringe-full of fluid, not exactly the color of blood, and injected the same amount of cola. Victor explained, "I still draw out a few hundred c.c. of blood every week and shoot in cola..." The poet broke in amazedly, "Are you saying you got the inspiration to do this from my poem?" Victor said, "I did this a long time before I heard your poem. But you are the first person who thought of this besides me. Now you know why I decided to have you write my story. Do you feel like writing it now?" The poet nodded and said, "Are you telling me that after the cola-change, everything you wished for in business came true?" Victor triumphantly said, "Within a short time I have made ten million dollars, and before long I'll have a hundred million."

Will Chinn spent two weeks writing a 200,000-word biography. After Victor and Jenny read it, they corrected only a few small errors, then had it published. It created a huge stir, but many reviewers were skeptical. Most upset of all were research directors from two medical schools and a social critic, who filed a joint suit against Victor Li and Will Chinn, claiming their sensationalism would cause young people who lacked independent judgement to replace their own blood, which would lead to deaths. Victor and Will Chinn defended themselves in a television interview: "We don't claim that everyone can replace their blood. Perhaps only a small proportion of people are physically capable of this. At least it was proved in Victor Li's case. It was not rejected. At this point he is still replacing a few hundred c.c. per week. If necessary, he can do this openly, to be witnessed by the public. In addition, we'd like to read this paragraph from the book:

> *Victor Li's grandfather believed that blood type should not be a criterion in blood replacements. In 1992 he had to receive massive transfusions due to blood poisoning. During a long course of treatments and blood replacements, his consciousness was able to change the landlord blood in his veins into peasant blood. This was because he had faith in the power of consciousness to do so. This power, clearly, was then transmitted to his grandson Victor Li. Of course, it is possible that he helped his grandson from the other world, to further Victor's wish for an effective blood replacement.*

"We are speaking of something that has already happened. Of course, research needs to be done on this, but Victor should not be confined in a hospital without his own approval. Otherwise, this would be a violation of human rights." Here Vincent Li interjected that he would not give approval, and that he intended to enjoy his own life.

At this point Victor Li was willing to do a blood replacement in front of television cameras. But this did not come about, due to fear of a copycat effect. Within a week after the book was published, dozens of people had to be rushed to the hospital after trying to replace their own blood. The court had no choice but to have a hospital analyze the composition of Victor Li's blood. A government investigation team determined that all findings should be kept out of the media. The book was to be suppressed for the time being, and sales would be stopped. Victor Li, Jenny, and Will Chinn were taken by the investigators to a secret clinic, where everyone awaited the results of the blood analysis with grave faces. Only Jenny and Victor chatted casually about company matters. Finally the lab technician handed the test results to the head investigator, shaking his head and saying: "The composition includes a significant amount of Coca Cola."

The government investigation made ruled as follows on the test results: An agreement would be drawn up with Victor Li and others privy to this case, to observe strict secrecy for five years. This would give the government time to do medical research on the Victor Li Anomaly. After five years, the agreement could be extended for a number of years. Meanwhile, the book could be promoted and sold only as science fiction.

But Victor Li hired a lawyer to defend himself. This agreement would make him look like a charlatan; it would do irreparable damage to his reputation. Newspapers and television had done major reports on this incident: suppressing it was not going to be all that easy. So how to handle this thorn in the government's side? Officials on the case racked their brains for a solution, but could not think of an ideal proposal. Finally, only one plan seemed feasible: the federal officials went to talk with Will Chinn alone.

The officials said, "There is no other way--you must take the outcome upon yourself. Here is what we will say: After writing those two lines of poetry, you had delusive hopes that they would turn into reality. You found Victor Li, a man who enjoyed sudden success in business, and used him to prove your delusions could come true. You played upon Victor's wish to stand out from the crowd and wrote a biography about him; you also persuaded him to accept the story you concocted, because this would make his biography different from any previous success story."

Will Chinn asked, "What will happen if I agree?" The official said, "You will give interviews to reporters, in which you will admit to this 'fact.' We can assure you that if anyone presses charges against you, we will allow you to plead insanity and avoid any criminal penalties. As for your finances, a company will buy all the rights to your book." Will Chinn said, "If it's done that way, my reputation will be damaged." The official said, "So what are you asking for?" Will Chinn said, "I want the government to lease a huge billboard on Times Square, and display my two lines about washing blood. I want the lease to last for a year." The official said, "That won't do. You don't have that much money. It would cause speculation and complicate matters further." The poet said, "If Victor Li comes up with the money, will the government interfere?" The official said, "Give us two more days: we'll discuss this further then."

Will Chinn told everything to Victor Li, who said, "It looks like there's no other way. Since the government has stuck its hand into this, and is even considering our position, there's nothing else we can do. What's more, this whole incident has been uncanny. Common sense says the public will probably not believe us. Obviously, most people will be on the government's side. As for the billboard rental, I can certainly pay it, but I don't think the government will agree to it. So what can we do to keep from getting a raw deal?" The poet said, "The fact is the book influenced some teenagers to try replacing their blood, and they were taken to emergency rooms. I am responsible for that. So I might as well give in. As the saying goes, a poet is society's conscience. On the other hand, what happened to you is true. Between telling the truth and saving people, my conscience tells me to save people. What is true will still be true after ten years."

The government official said, "The billboard is unfeasible, because your lines of poetry may lead to a lawsuit by Coca Cola. They would think you are slandering their product with the words 'New York washes blood at the heart of the world; Blood washed into Coca Cola flows around the globe.' There is no telling who would win, but it would cause unnecessary trouble and financial burdens. Is there anything else you have in mind?" The poet was already fed up: "Just let me keep writing poetry. I don't have anything else in mind." The officials shook his hand delightedly, for they considered that this wrapped up the case.

March 1997

Manhattan

Tr. Denis Mair

One Hundred Dollars

To perform on the street would attract the attention of passers-by. Occasionally, there can be several persons who appear interested in the performance. In this scenario, the first thing coming to most people's minds is supposed to be money; some even say that the pay is good enough to be envied by a lot of employees who work from nine to five routinely. To be frank, the reason why I performed on the streets was completely driven by the motivation of Chang, my roommate.

Just like me, Chang was also a student from China. We shared the same apartment. In addition to flute playing, I almost had no other habits. Therefore, during my school years in America, the flute I brought from China became the main source of entertainment. Besides, the flute was the reason Chang made fun of me every day of his life. He said that if I had guts to play the flute on the street like some American did, I should have to pay the pedestrians rather than asking for money owing to my awful performance.

It was my street debut. Before moving to the corner where I was supposed to be later on, I stood at the other corner for a while, staring at my target location, and imagining how I would appear. Would it be like a careless musician, ignoring all the passing cars and even treating them as strolling cows and sheep? I was a little worried that Americans wouldn't understand what kind of musical instrument it was. As far as I was concerned, no one in America would assume it was some sort of musical instrument for a real musician. I put down my old backpack, took out my flute, and fell into meditation. I was going to make my own history; I was going to make a brand-new start. I tapped my own shoulder and encouraged myself, "Buddy! Let's go!"

Finally, I moved toward that corner. It was 5:00 pm. Chang told me that he would be there at 6:00 pm. to watch me give money to the audience.

I felt like that I had stood firmly on the corner of this street, one of thousands of corners in the Broadway area. I sighed with relief. I moved one step to the right and another step to the left. Finally, I was sure that I had positioned myself.

For some reason, I failed to start my performance immediately. Rather, similar scenarios came to my mind, in which I watched other performers playing musical instruments on the street. Most of the performers were Americans. They liked to put their old hats or boxes in front of themselves, and there were always some coins inside. From time to time, there were also several bills. What I had that day was a box which I had made with a flyer advertising of American Citibank. It looked artistic like what I had observed from American life.

It was 5:20 pm. To put it more exactly, it was 5:20 pm, July first of 1988. I was ready. I leaned my lips close to the flute.

However, I was so nervous. During the rush hour in the Broadway area, countless of people flooded into the streets, and countless of cars rushed to and fro. I couldn't overlook them, not to mention just treating them as strolling cows and sheep. I had no choice but to face the fact: all I need was bravery. I was confused whether it had anything to do with losing face which bothered me a lot in the beginning. There were a number of performers everywhere in the world playing music on the streets. Besides, some were pretty enjoying themselves without caring about people around them at all. Why was I so nervous?

My lips were too dry to move, so I licked them over and over again. It was 5:23 pm. Nothing came out after my lips had stayed on the flute for three minutes. I tried several notes with my eyes closed. At the same time, I stretched my fingers to rejuvenate them. I opened my eyes a little bit and found several passers-by were standing in front of me, staring at me, and waiting for me to play. I closed my eyes responsively and started playing my specialty, "The Full Moon" followed by "The Deep Deep Sea" and "The Great Socialism." Toward the ending of "The Full Moon", my eyes were wide open. However, I didn't focus on my audience. I raised my head and watched the clear sky. By accident, a helicopter flew across the sky. An idea came across my mind: the pilot threw out a coin and it exactly fell into my paper box.

When I moved along to "The Great Socialism", I had been completely relaxed, and even my toes started counting the beats unconsciously. However, my entire face was socked with sweat. So, I kept wiping my face and wiping my flute. I took a deep breath and came up with more songs. All at once, I found that I myself and my music were in harmony, and all the chaos and nervousness had already gone away. Several coins came to my paper box and contributed to a nice sound which was even more beautiful than my music. I imagined that Chang also heard that sound.

One person came closer and chatted with me. Not until he found that my grammar was weird did he stop talking to me. Yet, he fumbled a five-dollar bill and held it high for a while to show his appreciation and support. Then the bill fell into my paper box. Suddenly, I found there were some words in my box, "It is your bank. . . Citibank!" I was secretly happy: there was some money in the box! It was 5:45 pm, and Chang hadn't appeared yet.

"It is your bank. . . Citibank!" I was thinking to myself, "If I could also translate it into Chinese, it would be more fantastic." I repeated the songs I had previously played, since a new group audience had replaced the old one. Chang arrived at 6:04 pm. He was standing with the audience, smiling at me. The smile implied that he had lost the game. There was money in the box beside my feet; I didn't pay the pedestrians.

I earned around forty dollars at my debut. To put it more exactly, I spent less than three hours earning thirty-nine dollars and eighty-five cents at my debut. I collected my paper box and left the corner at 8:07 pm. I treated Chang to Kentucky Fried Chicken. Both of us felt that the fried chicken tasted extraordinarily good that day.

Ever since then, I performed on the street three to four times every week. Nothing special happened except for one thing. I have to tell this story as my ending; otherwise, it made no sense to choose the topic of this article.

It was during my seventh performance. After I had finished several songs, a member of my first audience chatted with me feverishly. He looked like he was in forty's with the typical dress of a businessman: a tidy and neat suit in a light color, a tie in oblique stripes, and a suitcase. There was even a light smell coming from him. He took out a one-hundred bill and handed it to me instead of putting it in the box. He pointed at my paper box made of the flyer and commented that it was a great idea. He said that he liked it. In addition, he also took out some one-dollar bills and threw them into my paper box. He seemed to greatly appreciate the way money was kept in the paper box. He mentioned nothing about my music.

Before he left, he handed me a business card and said that he hoped I would always use the paper box during my performance. I was touched and moved. When he went away, I read his business card. He was the Vice President of the Citibank.

Tr. Cindy Hsueh

Wedding

It was an invitation card for a wedding, and the location of the wedding would be in the gallery. The groom, Lu, was a painter from China; the bride was Su, also a Chinese painter. Lu and I knew each other in New York City. We were acquaintances, but I never heard that he had such a close girlfriend who was going to become his wife. The only thing I heard from him was that his mother would come to visit him soon. The last time

they were together was six years ago in China.

I was really shocked. It was just last week that we were having fun together. It was unbelievable that Lu's wedding would be held in two weeks. When I received the invitation card, what came to my mind were Lu's witty and quick eyes from which you knew that this person always had wild ideas.

Lu is a weird person. He worked on abstract paintings when he was in China. After coming to America, he has focused on the conceptual arts instead. One of his well-known works is a daily newspaper from a particular day in which he changed the date. He attached the date of a typical day last year to the paper this year. So, all the news on the paper became history.

What impressed me most was the news that some elders had died of coldness, while, in fact, it is summer. Some of his works really make him look like an odd avant-garde artist. However, when he is painting portraits on the street, he appears very serious.

I called him and asked him about his fiancée. He laughed a lot and said all was God's arrangement. He met Su in a café when she came here from China two months ago. It was love at first sight. Then, everything just happened naturally. I explored more and had a nice impression of Su. She is twenty-three, fourteen years younger than Lu. Before she came to America one year ago, she had heard of Lu. Therefore, when meeting each other in America, they became close very soon. I recalled that Lu had been chasing a dancer long time ago. They broke up after being together for two years.

Some other friends also showed their curiosity and shock about the romance and the wedding. So, I told them what I was really thinking. Lu never had a real girlfriend over the past six years in New York. He is thirty-seven, and it is time for him to get married. With his understanding of New York, coupled with his fluent English, his fiancée might have been attracted to him very much. Besides, Lu is nice-looking, not to mention that he has a fashionable car. All of these contribute to his fantastic love story. By the way, the reason why the wedding would be held in the gallery was that he was going to give a painting exhibition simultaneously. All was too good to be true, wasn't it?

I envy Lu. What a lovely event the wedding would be. If

things like this happened to me, I would be grateful for the rest of my life. In comparison with Lu, I am miserable. I married twice and divorced twice, and neither of the marriages lasted for more than two years. Now I raise a son with my first wife. As to my painting career, never have I been given the chance to give any exhibition. I support myself by painting portraits on the street. Well, it is hard to say if this kind of event wouldn't happen to me. I am four years younger than Lu. I still have chances to be a lucky person like Lu. However, I don't want to get married again. Marriage scares me. I doubt if I really understand women, despite the fact that I married twice.

The wedding started at 5:00 pm. Being Lu's good friend, I arrived at the gallery earlier around 4:15 pm. Lu and the gallery staff had finished all the decoration by then. As a place for an exhibition as well as a wedding, the gallery appeared artistic and romantic. I found that all the works had something to do with love. In the regard, Lu really manifested himself as a creative artist.

There were some fantastic enlarged photos from his travels with Su. Interestingly, the dates on the photos ranged from three years ago to three months ago. Lu said that he set the false dates on purpose, so that people would assume that he had been with Su for a long time. He also framed some of their love letters. As always, the dates were not genuine. It went without saying that the content was also made-up. For example, he said in the letter that he was very impressed by the bike riders in New York. So, he bought one mountain bike for Su to ride in Peking. In the other two letters, Su mentioned the way she wanted to educate their children in the future. She emphasized the importance of bilingual education, and insisted that their babies speak Chinese at home and English outside. Lu's idea was for children to speak both Chinese and English for each sentence. He then commented that it could be troublesome, but was worth giving it a try.

At that moment, Su came in, and Lu introduced his bride to me. She was not cute, but smart. She pointed at the works and said almost all of them were derived via Lu's inspiration. I asked her if she had decided to give birth to a couple of children. She nodded without thinking twice. Then, Lu's mother came to the gallery, as well. At the glance of her jeans, I immediately speculated that it was Lu's idea. I was wrong. It was Su who went shopping with her mother-in-law and suggested that she buy jeans. What struck me more was that Su made her own wedding dress with table clothes, colorful and flowery. Lu and Su were virtually a couple by nature of their talents in arts.

The guests arrived gradually. The wedding began at 5:00 pm as scheduled. The owner of the gallery gave a short speech at the opening of the ceremony. He said he couldn't be more excited by the combination of the paint exhibition and the wedding. He emphasized that it was the best paradigm as a mixture of fine arts and the real life. Finally he appreciated that two TV programs--one Chinese and the other, English—were sponsoring the wedding and were videotaping the whole event. When Lu and Su exchanged their wedding rings, all the audience joyfully clapped for several minutes. They put on and took off the rings from each other's fingers over and over again, till they were both confused which ring belonged to whom. The guests couldn't stop laughing.

Some people asked them to kiss each other, but they didn't do that. Instead, they took out a piece of paper from each of their pocket separately and it was read on the paper, "NO AIDS!" Su put the two pieces of paper into a huge envelope which they prepared beforehand. The mailing address was the moon, and the stamp was a picture of a couple flying to the moon. Su sealed the envelope with her red lips and then nailed it onto the wall. Another awesome work was done.

When some VIPs were introduced, most of the guests started enjoying the champagne. Some were reading their correspondences, and others were talking about the paintings. Obviously it was a special and successful wedding. I went to chat with Lu's mother. She said that her happiness was beyond words. With the participation of so many celebrities and even the TV programs, she was proud of her son. I praised her son for his gift in the conceptual arts. She asked me what the conceptual arts was. I explained briefly that the gist of this type of art was to inspire people's thoughts rather than offer visual image only.

The staff of the TV program would like to interview Lu's mother, and she accepted the invitation happily. She said that she hadn't known anything about the wedding before coming to America. She just wanted to visit her son whom she hadn't seen for six years. All that had happened was unexpected and she was so excited about that. She also said that she liked Su, young but mature. When being asked how many grandchildren she hoped to have, she suggested that they ask the newlyweds directly.

At that moment, I noticed that two people put a box of letters at the front door of the gallery. Curious and concerned, I went forward to take a look. They asked me if I would like to leave immediately. I said I would like to stay for a while. They said that the letters would be given to guests when they were ready to leave. They also stated that only after we left the gallery for half an hour would we be expected to read the letter. I was wondering what kind of trick it was. In terms of Lu's extra ordinary character, you would never know what would happen next.

The party came to an end at 9:00 pm. I was given the letter and couldn't wait to open it as soon as I caught the subway. The letter said,

My dear friend, this wedding was designed for the wedding itself; it was a piece of our work. There will be no history and no future for the bride and groom. All starts in the gallery and ends over there. There will be no extension at all in the real life. That was our performance from 5:00 pm to 9:00 pm. Thanks for coming.

Lu and Su in New York, July of 1992.

I called Lu two days later. He repeated that everything was over. I asked him if he would consider marrying Su. He said it was impossible, because Su had been married. It was an agreement that they cooperate to give this exhibition. I asked further if his mother had already known the whole project beforehand. He said that she had no idea about that until she read the letter at the last moment. In the beginning, she was shocked and irritated. Later on, she seemed to be a little joyful, since she kind of realized what the conceptual arts was. I asked to chat with his mother for a while. It sounded like she had overcome the shock. She said that this kind of story could only happen in America. She commented that his son, Su, and the owner of the gallery were really crazy; however, the wedding was really touching and nice.

Since the wedding, I have been noticing the way the TV programs and the paper have reported this event. To be frank, I think their analyses were neither appropriate nor correct. However, I myself have failed to give a sound analysis. Here I would like invite you, my readers, to imagine that scenario. Probably some of you will come up with some points which I can't portray in words. If you are interested in that, we may talk or even make an appointment with Lu and Su to share our thoughts.

Tr. Cindy Hsueh

A Story of Stone Status

One's earliest dreams are always the clearest. I dreamed my first dream a long time ago. Since then I have been reviewing it all the time in my mind. Colors are added to the picture and the dream never fades away. Glancing back through the historical events, I find that dream of mine quite plain: I dreamed of a camera.

Actually, the key point of the dream is not the camera but why I longed for one --- for otherwise the idea of a camera would have never come to my mind. In the winter of 1965 I was too young to feel premonitions, let alone political premonitions. Therefore, I was in no position to describe how the Culture Revolution broke out. I was then living in a small squatty building in Shanghai with a big courtyard. There were two stone statues in the yard, one near the gate and the other near the building. They looked the same except that they were of different sexes. Since there are only two sexes in the world, we had only two of them, one male, and the other female. If there were four or five sexes, then perhaps we might have had four or five statues. Anyway, two make the story much simpler. In fact, two have already made things complicated: thousands of stories have been written on them; yet new ones pop up every day.

One morning, it was so cold that the yard seemed contracted when I peeped out of the window. The door also looked smaller in the cold, though its frame remained the same. The wind wriggled in through the crack like a man, first the head then the body. Bt then I laughed at the image because the wind was actually climbing right in over the walls. Soon I remembered that I left my scarf on the neck of the male statue when my uncle took photos of me last night. My uncle was happy to do so because he wanted to send the photos to my parents. They were working in another city for their ideals and salary --- something easy to understand. But why couldn't they realize their ideals and get paid here in Shanghai? Well, there is always somebody who determines who can work and live where. That is the best answer to the question. That's what we call "power" and my parents didn't have the "power" to make decisions for themselves. Were they born without the power or did they lose it later? I didn't ask questions like there at that time and now these questions are no longer questions, for two small parts in the same machine won't ask each other why you are there while I am here. When I went out for my scarf, it was on the neck of the female statue near the building. But I knew I had put it on the neck of the male statue. I was still young and had a good memory. But perhaps it had just been my imagination? Still I imagine that someone else moved it away. Everyone in the building was asked. But no one seemed to have ever seen my scarf. Anyone who had seen it would have simply taken it anyway --- so said Uncle. Nobody would take it from one statue and put it on the other. That's the simple logic.

That night, Grandma said that it would be colder tomorrow and I would need to put more clothes when I went to school the next morning. Before going to bed, I thought about the "scarf incident" again. I began to fancy that the male statue put the scarf on the female statue. But how could he walk all the way to the back of the yard? After all, he was inanimate. I wouldn't let it go without an explanation. So I went out into the yard, wrapped the male statue with my scarf and returned to bed. The next morning, the scarf was again on the neck of the female statue. I knew that I had discovered a miracle. But I said nothing to Grandma or Uncle. I decided to keep vigil that night and find out how it happened.

I was very excited that night. Having turned off the light, I sat by the window and gazed at the man. The yard was lit by a nearby streetlamp. So I could clearly see what was happening there. Two hours later, I fell asleep and woke up to find the woman with the scarf. I went to bed reluctantly and dreamed a dream. In the dream Grandma told me that boys should always be manly. If there is only one scarf, you should give it to the girl. Boys are stronger than girls.

After I woke up, I began to imagine how the man walked to the woman and handed her the scarf. But can a statue walk? I'd never seen a walking statue. When I sat by the window that night, I tried hard not to fall asleep and pricked my finger with a track from time to time. Finally, I saw the man start walking. Amazingly, the woman walked too. They moved somewhat like the robots that I saw many years later in the United States. They stood face to face in the center of the yard. He took off the scarf and offered it to her. She pushed back his hands, seemingly asking him to put it on. The scarf flapped in the cold west wind. I began to worry that it might drop to the ground. Fortunately, he managed to put the scarf around her neck despite her reluctance. Then she walked to the gate and gestured him to go to the back of the yard. I thought that I knew what she meant: Now warm from the scarf, she would stand in the front of the yard where the wind blew more bitterly. I hoped that he wouldn't agree with her, for otherwise, the other family members would soon discover the secret. I didn't know what would happen if they knew it. Just as I wished, he drew her back. She then took off the scarf. Clearly she meant that since the wind was cutting by the gate, he should put it on. Then I was reminded that I had another scarf. So tomorrow whey would be spared the heartbreaking dilemma. I also told myself that I needed to take the scarf away tomorrow morning and put scarves on them before I went to bed at night so that nobody would notice.

The next evening, I gave each of them a scarf and thought that they would not have to walk that night. But in fact, they did walk. The scarf on the woman was longer and thicker. So she insisted that he should take that one since the wind was more biting there. In the following nights, they also walked together and murmured something that I couldn't hear. So soon I came up with an idea.

I asked Grandma and Uncle if we could put the two statues side by side. Grandma then explained to me how they protected our house: The man statue was the first line of defense against

Evil, while the woman statue was the second. I said it didn't make any sense. If Evil could defeat the stone man, it would be easier for him to defeat the woman, for men are always stronger than women. But if we put them side by side, they would combine with a greater strength. Grandma stuck with her answer, but Uncle said that it sounded like a good idea. So he put them side by side. I was most enthusiastic when Uncle moved the woman statue to the gate. I glanced at the statues from time to time, expecting to find smiles of taciturn understanding on their faces. But I spotted no change. Nevertheless, I was content that Grandma and Uncle and the rest of the family were happy with the idea. Yet I soon felt regretful that night --- standing side by side, they wouldn't walk any more. I couldn't ask Uncle to move her back because it was my idea and my education forbade me oppose my own idea, especially when it was regarded as a good one. I suffered in the dilemma when I leaned out of the window and looked at them standing there quite still. But I soon realized that I had done the right thing when I thought of my parents in another city. The reason why they had to work there and leave me here remained unknown to me. Grandma said that their work needed them to be there. The need was a cruel need to me. So I reunited him and her. If there were a little statue, I would certainly put it together with them.

Unfortunately, the happy reunion did not last long. In the summer of 1966, a mob of Red Guards broke into my home and rummaged about in the house. They struck the heads off the statues and said that they were superstitious idols and should be destroyed, that all superstitious idols in the world should be destroyed. The photos that I took with the statues as well as the plates were burnt in the yard. After the Red Guards left, I tried to put the heads back on the statues. The head of the man was broken into dozens of pieces. I recalled the bandage that Uncle used when he broke his leg. So I bandaged the head and put it back on the shoulders of the statue. After that, I went to Uncle and told him that the photos were burnt but we could take more with the statues. Pulling a long face, Uncle said I should take a look at the camera. I went into the next room and found that the camera was in no better shape than the statues, or even worse, since even a bandage couldn't help it --- its lens had broken into pieces. It was lying next to Uncle's pillow. Obviously, Uncle had already mourned over it. The Red Guards smashed it because it was made in the Soviet Union, Uncle said. But how I wished I could take a photo with the wounded statues. I was hesitating over whether I should tell Uncle what I found about the statues when he dashed into the yard as if something of extreme importance had suddenly occurred to him. I followed him out. He took off the bandaged heads from the statues and said that I oughtn't to do that, it would court disaster for the whole family.

Trans. Haihong Yang

Starboy and I

I know that people have the right to fictionalize in various ways about the future, for instance, by the year 2010 we can vacation on the moon or hold a wedding on Mars. These scenarios may only be extrapolations, but we can also write them in books as if they were accomplished fact. However, it is more popular to fictionalize about the past, at least in China, such as the endless stream of novels and TV series full of romances and intrigues set in imperial palaces. The closest thing to this in America would be fictions about heroes set in the western cowboy era. Clearly the length of history makes a difference. China has a huge amount of history to fictionalize about, but America only has a couple hundred years, and most of that is documented in detail. Documentation gets to be pretty important, when you think how many versions of history China has had during those same couple hundred years, which have given Chinese writers all the more room for fictionalizing. So a foreigner who observes Chinese history from the outside must feel bewildered. And not just foreigners: even Chinese people are losing interest in their history, for one simple reason. A lot of history is treated vaguely, with big words covering up a great many details, and when you lose the details the fascination of history is gone. I am not attempting to write a serious, in-depth analysis. I am just writing about a friend of mine, about his background and his talent for fictionalizing which I greatly appreciate.

His name is Starboy. I am told that three days after his father's wedding in 1949, someone gave his father a boat ticket to Hong Kong. Because he could not find a second ticket, he gave up on Hong Kong and stayed on the Mainland, where he and his wife raised three children including Starboy. After the Cultural Revolution, the common fiction in China was to say: 'If my grandfather or parents or whoever had left the Mainland in 1949, it would have been a different story.'

From there switch to Shanghai in 1981, when Starboy was 31 years old. By then I had known him for over ten years, but never once had I heard him fictionalize his parents in that manner. He made up a different story, saying, "I just pretend my father returned from Hong Kong to the Motherland in 1950." That is the way he is, someone who thinks like a writer but does not write. Maybe I should not say he thinks like a writer, because so many writers approach writing as a way of making money. In 1981 Starboy got a chance to go to Hong Kong. His superiors in his work unit wanted to broaden his training, so they put him down for one of three openings on a fact-finding trip. Starboy said that the trip was actually a bonus, to give him a glimpse of the outside world and make him more obedient to his superiors when he got back. But around that time he was thinking of quitting his job. If he took the trip to Hong Kong, it would be hard to bring up quitting. Another possibility would be to play the turncoat and stay in Hong Kong. He thought it over for two days and asked his leader: "If I like it in Hong Kong, can I stay there?" His leader said, "That would be terrible. If you don't come back, my position will be in jeopardy. Are you really considering such a thing?" Starboy said, "I'm being frank because you treat me decently." So the leader gave the tour opening to someone else. Later the leader said to him in private: "You really did the right thing. If you had taken that trip and stayed in Hong Kong, I would have been forced to give up my own position." So Starboy jumped right in and said, "I've been wanting to quit, so how about giving your approval, considering how considerate I was!"

In 1981 it was almost unheard of to resign from one's position, especially at a large downtown agency. The leader was taken aback and asked, "On what grounds?" Starboy replied with perfect casualness: "To go into business. People are going into business for themselves now, and I'd like to give it a try." The leader said, "There's no precedent for this. Let me make inquiries, and I'll get back to you."

Later he became the first person from his work unit to quit and 'go to sea.' He said, "That trip I took to Hong Kong made me a different person. It taught me about the free market, and I'm ready to strike out on my own." I asked him what he was preparing to do. He said, "I'll open a restaurant. For ordinary folks, food is a little taste of heaven, so I'm sure I can make money." Back then my thinking was not yet in step with his, and I thought he was romanticizing.

Before the year was out, the restaurant he opened in partnership with a neighborhood women's association made a sizeable profit. However, a tree that grows tall is exposed to the wind, and he was pressured several times by sanitation enforcers. Although he managed to keep the place open, he lost interest in day-to-day operations, so he transferred his share to someone else. I remember the day in 1983 when I sat drinking in his restaurant, on his last day as boss. He said he did not regret quitting his job, because now he had ten thousand *yuan* in cash. How many people could lay claim to that? At an average monthly salary of 100 yuan, that was 100 months of salary. Compared to most people, he was Hong-Kong-in-the-flesh. But on the other hand, if he had stayed on while the agency groomed him for a leadership position, he might have become an office director or even a department head. Power is another form of money!

I told Starboy: "You are your own person. Back then you wanted to quit, but your parents were against it. You said that once you became your own boss, you could quit whenever you want. Now that statement has come true. So what do you plan to do?" Starboy said, "To tell the truth, I just want to enjoy myself. At most I'll buy a color TV for my parents and sister. With the rest of it, you and I will party with our buddies a couple times a week, and I'll pay the bill."

When 1985 came around, Starboy had been reading avidly for two years. He read mostly literary works, but he had come to this conclusion: "Literature is too much fun. Things that take years and years to happen can be compressed into one book, or even into a few lines." I asked if he felt like writing something too. He shook his head, saying, "It would be more romantic if we could make life unfold like a novel."

In 1986 I told him I was thinking of going abroad. He said, "Don't think about it, and just make the effort to go. But you've got to pass through Hong Kong in place of me." Sure enough, when I went to study in America, I made a point of passing through Hong Kong for him. When I wrote to him from America in 1987, I mentioned that while in Hong Kong it occurred me that if he had stayed decided to stay there, he and I could have gotten together. In his return letter he wrote, "If you had found that person named Starboy in Hong Kong, he would have been a different person from me. You two would have had a superficial dinner, and chatted for a little while. So this is what history does: it gives us an environment to solidify our friendship. As for people who belong to different environments, I always have my doubts."

Starboy made a good point in that letter. I was changed by my environment in America, so the question was whether I, being changed, could still be his friend. This question was in my mind the first time I returned from abroad in 1994.

Starboy came to meet me at the airport with a bouquet of flowers in his hands. I said, "We don't stand on ceremonies, do we?" He said, "I couldn't figure which direction you might change in, and anyway, elaborate manners are better than no manners." Starboy had a job as a planner at a trading company then, so he was carrying a cellular phone with him. I said,

"You're making yourself another bundle. Do you still have a hundred months' salary for treating people to dinner?" He laughed and shook his head: "If I did, wouldn't that make a new returnee like you feel unworthy? In order to save face for people like you, I have cut down on my savings. Right now I have one month's salary for treating America to dinner."

"The whole country of America? You've really made a bundle," I said. He said, "America has representatives. You're enough of a representative for America. When you go back and write a report, just say that I gave you a reception fit for the American president." He knew I was working for a magazine in America, so he made a play upon that. I told him I had missed him. He played off of that too, saying: "It looks like you learned about homosexuality in America also. Not bad. Your hometown elders are waiting to hear your report."

On this first trip back home, my two-week vacation was over in a flash, but I got together with Starboy several times. I have especially fond memories of one time, when we went to his new house in the new Xinchuang Residential Development. He invited a few friends I did not know; we chatted and drank liquor while enjoying his collection of avant-garde artworks. Judging from surface characteristics, these Chinese artworks were fairly similar to Western ones. But there were differences in subject matter. Another difference was that most of the four dozen pieces in his collection were gifts from the artists. I said that in the West this would be impossible. Starboy said, "This goes to show Chinese people are not good at business yet, but it also proves there are lots of 'customers' like me in China.

Thanks for reminding me. From now on I'll pay for their work, even if it's only a little money." Later the conversation turned to movies. Starboy qualified a friend's comments on the vulgarity of the movie industry by saying: "The point is not the vulgarity, it's that intelligent people are using vulgar means to make money. Money is what they're after. The crux of the problem is not money or vulgarity, it's what human intelligence applies itself to. We've gotten into a worldwide vicious cycle in our ways of using human intelligence to make money! Why do I call it a vicious cycle? Because money lets us invent new ways of knowing and turn them into reality." He took a swig of wine and went on, "All forms of knowledge are being used as money-earning knowledge. That is an insult to knowledge, but now that we're running on these rails, the smartest course is pretending not to see it."

He spoke so seriously that his gathered friends felt a moment of pressure. But he laughed out loud, saying: "Don't get nervous. I'm just fictionalizing that I'm addressing American imperialism right now: I can see myself making a speech at Harvard University." Hearing this everyone pointed their fingers at me, as if I were there to represent America. I started laughing too and said, "Starboy is getting more and more Chinese. This shows that people keep their inner reserves if they don't go abroad. They don't turn into bastardized specimens." Starboy poured me another glass and said, "Your going to America is like being sent down to a production brigade during the Cultural Revolution, except this time you were placed somewhere that is wealthier than here. Isn't it the same--the way you've been pulled out from your original environment, causing an interruption in all your regular thought processes and modes of behavior? Maybe you can comfort yourself with material abundance, but you are solitary! You can't be young again in your new environment."

What he said touched a sensitive spot. I said, "It sounds like you were the one who went overseas instead of me. How could you know how it feels?" Starboy said, "We've been together these past few days, so I've gotten a chance to fictionalize myself into your predicament. Being in your shoes these few days, even fictionally, has not been a pleasant experience." Saying this, he mimed a tear-wiping gesture. I laughed and said, "You can live in a fiction, and so can I. While I'm in America I fictionalize the life in China." To this Starboy said, "You're wrong! Fictionalizing is supposed to have a conclusion: it's not a solution for real life. My point was very clear, that is, I want you to come back here. When you're missing, something feels wrong."

His last statement came as a shock, and with all the wine we'd had, I broke out crying. But he ended up crying ever harder than I.

Does the center of our life really shift about so easily? Although Starboy and I practically shared the same skin, I went back to America without planning when I would return to China. Still, I knew clearly the time would come for me to return.

In late December of 1999 I did return, to usher in the new

millennium on New Year's Eve, and of course to spend some time with Starboy. Not until February did I go back to America. After returning to America, I wrote two short pieces, which I sent to him by fax. Before long he faxed his answer: "Long live fictionalizing! But the written word cannot be fictionalized, and you were using Chinese characters. Aside from this, what is the conclusion of your two pieces?" I faxed him back: "If you and I could be fictionalized into a single person that would be a truly powerful fiction. So tell me, is that single person now in Shanghai or New York?" He faxed a one-line answer: "In the Chinese language!"

What follows are the two pieces I wrote.

I

"Tomorrow evening there will be a ceremony for the wine god, and you don't want to miss it." While my friend Starboy was saying this over the phone, I sensed a charged-up feeling in his voice, as if he could hardly wait for tomorrow. "This must have to do with tomorrow being the 31st," I hazarded. He said, "You're right. It's time to bring in a new century, so it deserves a ceremony!" I joshed with him a little, asking "Are you sure you haven't made a mistake? Maybe those people are holding some kind of cult activity." "No way," he said. "This will be far more artistic than what those religions are up to." It's in a large space, and the host loves drinking. There will also be artworks on the theme of wine. It will start after dinner. You can show up at 10:00; it will be lively by then. You've just gotten back from

America, so you don't know things are on fire here in Shanghai too. We have conceptual art to rival what you'll see in America."

At ten in the evening of the 31st, I went to the address Starboy gave me. A sizeable group was already there, with plenty of room to spare. Artworks were set out in the fifty-square-meter living room, and I could see a table full of food and liquor and some chairs. I was introduced to the host, a man named Dabao who was creator of the artworks. "Have a look around," he told me.

An old mattress was resting on four wine bottles, and on top of it were lying all kinds of bottle opening devices. Another piece was a copy of Marx's *Das Kapital*, with the pages hollowed out, and a half-empty bottle of sorghum liquor placed in the bottle-shaped hole. As Starboy stood beside this piece he said, "In this era it should be a bottle of French X.O. brandy." I said, "We ought to add a book by Nietzsche next to it, with a bottle of Coca Cola inside. It would be a study in contrasts between the two books and the two bottles." The last piece consisted of two computer-altered photographs, one showing the Statue of Liberty in New York with a liquor bottle instead of a torch in her hand. The other showed Shanghai's Pearl of the Orient television tower, with a goblet at the tip of the tower. People were conducting discussions around the pieces while sampling all kinds of and of liquor and wine.

With a trace of disappointment, I asked Starboy: "Will there be any other pieces?" Starboy said that Dabao was more of an abstract painter, and had done these pieces in a spirit of fun, just to liven up the New Year. Dabao approached and urged us to drink up; he said he needed more bottles for a piece he would make one the spot, so we should do our best to empty a few.

Finally there was a lull that let me talk with Starboy, whom I had been separated from for five years. So far on this trip back, I had only eaten dinner once with him and some friends who met me at the airport. I asked, "I couldn't find you the last few days. Where were you?" He said, "I was busy making money-- what else do you think?" I asked, "You're still living a single life. Haven't you found someone right for you?" He said, "In times like this it's easier being single. I do have a girl-friend, but neither of us have the urge to marry, so we've been dragging it out." I asked him: "Have you ever been apart on an important day like today?" He wrinkled his brows and said, "She went off to play mahjong. A lot of people are using mahjong as mental opium. She told me she would come, but it looks like she can't get away. Bringing in the Twenty-First Century at the mahjong table is an observance too." Laughingly I said, "You're pretty tolerant. It's a good attitude to have, but actually it shows you two don't have much passion." He said, "What does passion have to do with it? Every bit of passion has gone off in the direction of money. These days money is the motivating force." I said, "You don't have much money, but aren't you having a good life?" He said, "I haven't been able to earn big money; I can't help being like this." At this point a new group of people came in, forty minutes before midnight, and one of them was someone I knew. So I talked with him for a while, and then I was pulled away to meet some new friends. I switched from group to group this way, drinking and greeting people.

Dabao took over a corner of the room, where he started to line empty bottles up in rows. People handed him bottles that had been scattered around the room, and many people watched from the side to figure out what he was doing. In serious tones Dabao said, "God of wine, god of wine, Li Bai is China's god of wine. It is said that after drinking he had more poems than piss." Everyone continued to watch uncomprehendingly. He lined up the bottles in rows, until there were no empty bottles left. "Still not enough," he said, so he added all sorts of half-full bottles to his rows. Then patting his hands and stretching his arms he pointed to the first line, counting off bottles and saying: "This is the title: 'A Sonnet to Piss off Li Bai'."(1) Everyone counted and found there were exactly fourteen lines. Someone said, "You can't beat that." Someone else counted the total bottles and said, "There are a hundred bottles; that makes one hundred words including the title. The last line has only one word. What would that one word be?" At least four or five people yelled out at the same time: "Fuck!" Then everyone in the room burst out laughing.

Ten seconds before midnight, the roomful of people counted down from ten, and when they got to "one," a large number of them yelled out "fuck." That is how I welcomed in the 21st Century with a group of artists in a certain Beijing apartment. I thought of Starboy's girlfriend, and what a thrill it would be if she picked up her tiles at the stroke of midnight and a shout of "free draw" escaped her lips! I told Starboy of this notion, and though he chuckled, his eyes showed a hint of melancholy in his eyes, so I did not pursue the topic any further. Then everyone pulled the mattress and bottles out of the way and commenced dancing.

It was almost two o'clock when Starboy and I walked out on the street. Quite a few people were still out on the street, many of them waiting for taxis. A grinning foreigner walked by, holding a Chinese girl in his arms. Starboy said, "There are limits to his stamina; he can't hold onto her for very long." I said, "You're a fine one for making jokes." He said, "He may have a grin on his face, but Shanghai girls can chew up foreigners and spit them out. You know something: as a man, I can't help feeling sorry for him." I asked, "What do you mean by that?" He said, "It's no longer unusual to see someone courting his own misery. But when there are good times to be had, the guy always pays the bill."

I quietly surmised what Starboy's state of mind must be: in these times how would it feel to be a Chinese male on the threshold of middle age? Starboy seemed to know what I was thinking about, for he asked, "What are you thinking about?" I answered, "I'm thinking about you." He said, "What is there to think about? You use up your life in exchange for money, then you use the money to keep yourself alive. Isn't that how it is for Americans, along with everyone else in the world?" There was nothing I could say to that. When you put things in blunt terms that is how things are. The context of his fatalistic remarks was a fiercely competitive society, set against a backdrop of global population growth and depleted resources. He changed the subject and said, "So how do you feel about America? You've been there for seven or eight years; do you still think of coming back here to live?" I said, "That's a good question. There are advantages and drawbacks on both sides, so I'm still hesitating." He said, "It's better if you come back. As one writer who went overseas put it, the mother tongue is an irreplaceable source of nutrition. Isn't it a delight just to speak your mother tongue? When we got to the last line a little while ago, didn't you notice how everyone hit on the same word? And why was it a sonnet of fourteen lines, instead of a verse in five-character or seven-character lines? It shows the overall trend. Human culture is enjoyed in unison, and there are things that don't translate: they only emerge upon impact." It was intoxicating to hear him expanding on this argument. While in America, I hadn't heard anyone confide in me at such length for a long time. My mother tongue was calling to me, and Starboy seemed to be its representative, because I had grown up in my mother tongue with him.

Before parting we spoke again of art dedicated to the god of wine. Starboy said, "There's something you don't know. That place Dabao used tonight was rented for 500 *yuan*. He didn't have any money, but to make his friends happy and stir up an artistic happening, he and I came up with the money. We worked from December 25th to the 30th to earn it, assembling palace lanterns and washing display windows for a department store. We spent 500 *yuan* to rent the space, and five hundred to buy liquor. We know the manager at the department store, so that's why we could do a little moonlighting there." What

Starboy said brought back wonderful times we had in the past, when amount of wealth counted for nothing and open-heartedness meant everything. I could see that Starboy had not changed. And what about me? In a few days I would be returning to America. *Fuck!*

II

"Time sure passes quickly. Before we know it, we'll be pushing fifty." As Starboy said this, his eyes gleamed with the fire of someone in his twenties. Clearly, his thoughts had gone back to twenty years ago.

So I took my time swigging wine from my glass, then asked him, "Come on, tell me what you're thinking."

"Look at the lavish furnishings in this restaurant," he said. "Places like this only used to exist in books and movies. We used to be bursting with energy, and we did a lot of drinking. Now we can't handle much liquor." Hearing this, I guessed he was thinking of the time when money was tight, and we sat in a restaurant sprinkling black pepper in glasses of liquor to give it more kick. He laughed and said, "No, it wasn't that. I was thinking of when we first found out about disco. You used to practice at home in front of the mirror. You had the stamina then to practice an hour at a time."

I said, "First you say the restaurants are furnished lavishly, now you say I had good stamina. What are you getting at?"

Starboy said, "Don't you get it? Everything was plain and

bare then, but we had our strength. Now everything is plush, but our strength is declining. Here's an example: remember when you kept lookout while Little Yan and I made love in that grove in the suburbs? That was in 1978, and things were pretty tight in China then. We did it in broad daylight for the thrill. You were at the edge of the woods smoking, maybe for forty minutes, and I shot my wad at least three times. It may be the 21st Century now, but the romance is gone."

"Have you seen Little Yan since your breakup?" I asked.

"You know I haven't seen her since we broke up in 1985. After you went abroad in 1990, I heard that she did well in business. Looking back now I realize she was on the cutting edge. She was such a good disco dancer in the early 80s, and hardly anyone could dance then."

"That wasn't what you were getting at. Go ahead and speak your mind," I said.

Starboy had a young laugh—a contagious laugh that piqued my interest in what he had to say. Several girls had fallen for him because of that same laugh. "I'll be honest with you," he said. "In these days' girls aren't as romantic as they used to be. That's why I'm still single—I just don't get that feeling I used to get. Half a year ago I had a relationship with a girl. Well, I wouldn't call it a relationship, we were just looking for that feeling. She would only look for it in ritzy places. So we rented hotel rooms a few times. Once we went to Hangzhou. We were in a woods at Beigao Peak, and I remembered that time with Little Yan, so I kissed her and wanted to do it right in the woods.

But she said the place was dirty; she wouldn't hear of it. She could only get the feeling after we went back to the hotel, and then she said I was not passionate. She said I must be getting too old. But to me it was because she wasn't being romantic." Then Starboy summed up his thoughts: "People play out their lives on a materialistic stage these days. They can't live without material displays. Without material displays, they can't get the feeling. Don't you think it's tiresome?"

"Don't make too big a thing over it. How old was she?" I asked.

"Twenty-six years old," he said.

"If she's twenty-six, then she was born in 1974. Her generation's experience is completely different from ours. They don't need spiritual fantasies to know pleasure: they can find expression through material means. That's their experience."

"Our relationship has tapered off over the past half year," said Starboy. "She thought I could get rich in the real estate business, but it hasn't been doing well. She was hoping I would fund her study overseas, but if I sent her overseas, there is little chance she'd stay with me. We were both trying to squeeze what we could from the other person, but we are ready to jump at a better opportunity. So it's probably better to stay single. It's too much trouble getting married just to get divorced."

"Maybe you can find a woman closer to you in age," I said to Starboy.

"Is it possible?" he asked. "How many women over forty

are childless? If she has a kid, would she care all that much for me? Besides, I'd have to learn to love a kid that wasn't mine, and I can't take on such a burden. Even if she doesn't have a kid, a woman around forty is bound to have emotional scars. That makes it hard to get in a romantic mood."

"Your problem is that you're still seeking romance, at your age," I said. "I wonder about you. Sure, you have good looks and a good personality, with a great sense of humor. But face it, the younger generation has more standing in the marriage market." Starboy gave one of those laughs that has a story behind it, as I know only too well.

"Do you really want to know?" he asked. "Let me tell you what I did in the first week of the 21st Century. I got married, but only as a job. I earned $5000 dollars, which converts to more than forty thousand *yuan!*"

"Really? That is quite a big surprise," I said. "I've heard of Chinese people paying over ten thousand bucks to get an American green card. Don't tell me someone wants to get a Chinese 'green card' by marrying a Chinese citizen like you!"

"It's something else entirely," said Starboy. "A Frenchman had the idea to film the process of two Chinese couples getting married and divorced at the beginning of the new century. One couple got married, and one got divorced. He filmed the process, without constructing any kind of plot; it was a record of the procedures that Chinese people go through to get married and divorced. That Frenchman found my friend Dabao. Remember, we rang in the new century at Dabao's place! I didn't let it out then, because I feared unexpected consequences. You know how things are in China. Dabao was married, so he and his wife got a divorce. I was single, so I found a collaborator to get married with. First I went to the neighborhood committee and got a certificate of single status. Then we went through the whole process of filling out marriage forms and submitting them, all in front of a video camera. We spent a whole week doing it. The only hitch came during Dabao's divorce, because his wife's friend reminded her that maybe Dabao would take this game seriously. Finally the Frenchman showed up and explained everything. Luckily the Frenchman was a guy, otherwise maybe Dabao's wife wouldn't have gone along! To make a long story short, the Frenchman had funding from an American foundation. He got a grant to cover his budget, but he only needed five thousand for expenses. So he divided the rest of the money among us—five thousand per person. That was a once-in-a-lifetime thing, don't you think?"

"I don't think anyone would spend that much money to record marriage and divorce procedures in 21st Century China," I said. "There must have been more of a rationale for that grant than what you've said."

"I can tell you've been in America for ten years," said Starboy. "You understand how Americans think. You're right. The Frenchman's project had to do with conceptual art. The point was to film people who were willing to get married or divorced for money. Before the filming started, he posed a question: 'Would you do this if there were no money in it?' We all said, 'No, we wouldn't!'"

"Is that Frenchman a conceptual artist?" I asked.

"Yes, a successful one. While he filmed us, he was having similar footage shot in America, Africa, Europe, and Australia. He picked one country from each of the five major continents."

I turned it over in my mind awhile and said, "There is an angle to this—it's as if to say that real marriage and divorce are for money too!? What an intriguing project. But can a newly married person get divorced right away? Or are you going to wait awhile before getting a divorce? In the eye of the law you're a husband now."

"I like to think of it as performance art," said Starboy. "Just now you grasped some meaning in it. I had the same idea after the videotaping was done. As for my marriage, I'll wait awhile to file for divorce. I don't need to worry about aftereffects with my collaborator; she's an avant-garde artist in her own right."

"Will that Frenchman show the movie publicly?" I asked.

"Of course he will. This is real, it's the present condition of our society, don't you think? But maybe we won't get to see it. Maybe it will only be shown in America. Anyway, we'll get a copy of the video."

I nodded and said, "Conceptual art and installations are still popular in New York. There are foundations that support conceptual art projects. Actually it was popular in Europe during the late Eighties, but America was in a recession then. Over a hundred art galleries had to shut down in the SoHo area alone. Not until the mid-90s, when the American economy turned around, did those art forms come back into favor. You can see that modern art needs the economy to flourish. This is another example of what money can do!"

Starboy went along with my line of thought and said, "It's all money. But at least the Americans spent some money to leave a record on film. Here in China we gobble up the money going to dinners and karaoke bars. I don't know if it's culture or national character, but people here sure know how to make money from other countries."

"Do you have any more stories?" I asked.

"I can't think of any right now," he shook his head and said. "But there are stories everywhere in China. Come back and get in touch: I can guarantee you a rich harvest." Finally, in a tone of summing up, he said, "Every person and every society have their own value systems. Living means putting your own value system in practice. That's why I say that life is performance art. According to my values, many things in life cannot be bought with money—romance for instance."

January 2000

Tr. Denis Mair

1. *Qi-si li bai de shi-si-hang-shi*—literally means "A Sonnet to Make Li Bai Die of Anger." (Tr.)

打电话

　　摄影这个行当的乐趣和苦恼已经被讲得太多了，重复肯定是对着初学者讲的，而面对读者，我才想起要讲的东西并不容易引人入胜，所以多年来我从来不讲有关摄影的事请，直到今天（1994 年 1 月 30 日，星期天）下午，我到纽约曼哈顿（MANHATTAN）的苏荷（SOHO）画廊区转悠的时候，才遇到了可以与摄影联系起来讲的故事。

　　上午有太阳，使冬天的感觉突然有了一些生机，更因为今年纽约的雪特别多，已经有三个星期天没有星期天的感觉了。所以，吃完午饭，我带着相机出了门，直奔苏荷，我曾在那个地区住过一年多，了解不少有趣的画廊和街角，有不少可以进入底片的景象。但当我到了那里时天气却开始阴了下来，冷风把我很好的情绪吹得做出了再转五分钟就回家的念头，我多少有点不甘心地想按几下照相机的快门，于是很随便地用长镜头把一些冻出姿势的行人摄入底片，就在这个时候，街对面有人大笑，是一个无可归者看着一个垃圾桶笑，他笑得那么开心，一定是里面有什么东西是他认为的宝物，他的手伸进垃圾桶，我的长镜头也已经把他对准，我右手的食指在快门上等待，我很快地闪过一个念头：也许是旧衣服。

　　我按下快门的时候，也同时看清了他手中是一架乳白色的旧电话，我想这有什么可高兴的呢？同时也马上意识到这个流浪者一定是有精神上的问题，可是他笑得不是没有道理的，他把电话拿出来之后，放在旁边一个垃圾插的盖上，"喂"，他的声音之大，足以让街对面的人听得清清楚楚，我注意到身边还有几个行人也站着听，"是啊，我是史密斯，我好久没有听到你的声音了。你在天堂的日子肯定比我好过多了，我只能嫉妒你，哦，上帝，我的被子太薄了，云比它厚多了。"我注意到他戴着一顶黑色的破呢帽子，一身也是黑色的破衣服，与他作为一个黑人的形象成为纽约社会问题的一部分，我当时没有去想关于这个问题的敏感的细节，作为历史造成的那些值得讨论的人类生存状态，到底包括了多少文化因素及人吃人的技术问题。"哈哈"，他好像听到了什么好消息似池地笑了两声，"你毕竟不知道什么叫做房租，不过我可以告诉你，我叫史密斯，我在纽约。什么，你不知道纽约，这太使人扫兴了、你开这样的玩笑，让我这个纽约人多么伤心啊，也是，你知道我的电话号码就是证明了你知道纽约。听到这儿，我飞快地闪过：垃圾桶里的电话线是与上帝相通的！他不但有思维逻辑，而且联想也不差，失业救济金？他把头抬向天空问道，"你也知道失业救济金？太好玩了，看来我读的书真的不够，我真的不知道你也知道失业救济金，这事儿肯定是书里讲的吧，早知道的话，我就不退学去打工了，我才不在乎什么明天不明天的事情，还是多讲讲失业救济全的事，每个月我能领多少呢？对了，你交不交税？交给谁，是美国还是加拿大？交给克林领吗？（克林顿是此时的美国总统。）"他为自己的讲话哈哈地笑了一通，还夹杂着几声咳嗽，那咳喉声听上去是有病情的。他接着说："贫穷是我的上帝，贫穷是我的上帝，贫穷是我的上帝。是的，有空多来电话。"这时候他注意到街对面的我和其他几个行人在听他说话，他仍然很高兴地说："我有朋友，很多朋友，他们问你好，并且希望你有空来纽约玩。衣服？衣服我不要了，天堂的衣服肯定很贵的，你来的时候就给我带几个天使来吧，当然我喜欢姑娘，结婚请你喝酒，对啊，天上的香槟酒我还没喝过，你也没喝过我们的香槟酒，没关系，我不会醉的，好吧，好吧，你也多保重了。"他笑着把话筒挂上了之后，又低头想着什么，他开始按动想起来的号码。

"喂，儿子啊，是我，我，我当然是你爸爸，你以为是谁？别开玩笑了，我太太就在旁边，"他说着就把电话筒伸出，对着街对面的我们，"说啊，说啊，那是我的儿子，他想跟我的太太讲话，多可笑，他根本不知道我是谁，告诉他，我是谁，不知道我的人都是我的儿子，因为我不知道我的太太是谁。"他说这些话的时候我放下了举着的相机，我不知道他会不会因为我在拍摄他而被激怒。"你，"他指着我叫，"你过到我这边来，快点，快点。"我想这下惹麻烦了，心想是不是应该马上溜之大吉，身边的那几个行人也已经开始散去，"嗨，别走，给我根香烟，我允许你照相了。"我很犹豫地望着他，心里多少有点想继续看他的表演，最后我硬着头皮走过去给了他一支烟，并燃着打火机为他点了烟，我闻到一股酸臭味从他的身上散发出来，但他脸上的表情使我感到些微的放松，因为那是一张有幽默感的脸，事实也是如此。他对我说："这样你就可以少抽一支，肺就少掉一支烟的污染。"我对他说："你是一个表演艺术家。"我真的有这样的想法。"是啊，你应该买票，你能不能给我一块钱？"我马上知道自己说错了话，不给的话，也许会引起不必要的麻烦，于是就给了他一块钱，给完钱我就马上跑回街的对面，我知道对这样的人还是躲远点为妙，他看着站回到对街的我，脸上有一丝表情，那种表情好像在说；富人是怕穷人的。这使我马上想起以前在中国时经历过的文化大革命。他先想到上帝再想到儿子，这里包含着他生活里的某些重要的信息。如果我是一个西方的心理学家，肯定会分析出不少有关他的情况，可我只是个从中国来的新移民，对宗教和传宗接代的看法是有许多差别的，如果按照我们中国大陆人的观念来分析，那么他应该是出生在一个信仰宗教并且重男轻女的家庭，或者往深一点分析，他最后的希望是建立在这两个基础上的。当然我还可以说他是有儿子的，只是儿子已经死了，而且因儿子的死把他刺激成现在这种有点失常的精神状态，所以他想儿子也应该从天堂给他来电话的，或者他给天堂打电话肯定能找到儿子的，他给儿子打的是什么号码呢？我想起一个诗人写的一首诗里讲到上帝的电话号码，讲如何能给上帝打对方付款的电话，而且假设上帝是同意用钱来计算劳动价值的，那么这个号码无论是几位数都应该是 9，99，999，9999，99999，……，也就是任何位数的最大值。当时我想如果上帝和人一样在兜里揣个钱包，真是很有点幽默的，想必那个诗人正是这个用意吧。我这时忽然笑出声亲，因为想起了一个朋友开玩笑讲的故事；一个叫摩理的美国教授，他是教哲学的，人一贯很矜持，有一天他在街头邂逅了一个过去的学生，他一直是很欣赏这个学生的，于是就邀入咖啡馆一道喝一杯。他们谈得很开心，还讨论了一些哲学问题，分手前互留了地址电话，付款的时候学生坚持由他付，并说下次轮到教授付。教授回家之后的第二天想起有一个哲学问题的细节还可以与那个学生在电话里说说，就按照留条上的电话号码打了过去，接通以后，对方说的话使他马上就把电电话挂断了，他肯定自己按错了，就重拨一次，但还是刚才的接话者，这次他多听了两秒钟之后挂断了。他脸上有些发烧也有些恼怒，但又无奈地笑了起来，学生给他留的是要收费的性爱电话。他后来想起曾与学生在咖啡馆里谈到过佛罗伊德关于性转移的论点，是不是学生以此来提醒或证明什么论点呢，但他更倾向这是一个即兴的恶作剧，他想自己是很了解这个学生的，他缓过劲来之后感叹道；生意真是一条无孔不入的虫。单身汉的一时无法解决的性骚动，另一方面是爱滋病的流行，使许多本来召妓的人改用打这种电话来抚慰性的骚动，有些人就是一边听着一边进行手淫的。这种电话的一般价格是每分钟二至五元左右，是通过电话公司记录打电话的人的电话号码而记帐的，当然其中的一部分利润是电话公司分享的。我听到这个玩笑的时候，真的能想象出那个极为矜持的哲学教授听到这种突然的声音时脸上的表情会是多么有趣，他当时的心理活动也一定很有意思的。那个学生有意刺激教授也可以有他的哲学道理。而听故事的人都笑得很开心。

史密斯又开始按电话，我想这电话线在他心里不知道是连着非洲还是连着人类的内心，种族和个人生活中的位置肯定还是后者更重要，尤其在美国，世界的联合国，个人的问题是常人的第一问题。我的思路走远了一点，马上停住去继续看他，这时的他，把话简放在右耳上，专心致志地在听对方的话，他就在那里听着，达十分钟之久，我拍了几张之后，才又感到了天气的寒冷，看看他，穿得并不多，但没有一点感到寒冷的样子，我才又想起他也许神经是有一定的问题，他终于把话简放下了，谁知道他听到了些什么，我很想知道，当然只是想想而已，我是绝对不敢去问他的。他突然想起还有旁边的一个垃圾桶没有被翻看过，就开始翻了起来，显然他已经不再激动了，不再为电话的事牵动情绪了。我放下照相机,心想还会有什么可拍的东西。

他又笑了起来,我当然想看看他又找到了什么东西,这次他捡出一顶红色的帽子,很明显是女式的,但他好像想也不想地就把头上的黑帽子摘下来扔进垃圾桶,把那顶红色的戴在头上,戴之前还端详一下正反的方向,并且拍了拍上面的污垢。我也觉得他顿时比刚才亮眼了一些,于是马上端起相机按了几下快门。我想这是一次很好的收获,拍到这个极其难以遇到的场景,心里感到一种愉快,但这种愉快有隐隐约约地有点不舒服的东西,我想那是反省造成的,是一种极其自然的可被容许的虚伪。我想起摄影师和画家常常有这样的议论:被破坏的东西,比如烧过的房子、刚交战完毕的战场、废墟等都很入照,那种强烈的对比,使画面比正常的甚至美好的事物更具有吸引力,刚才我拍照时,其实大部分的时间都在考虑如何调节和变换角度光圈等摄影技巧的问题,是在一种工作过程的乐趣之中。我不但拍了他的特写镜头,也拍了广角的整个环境的镜头,当然也没忘掉拍出电话上没有外接线的局部细节。尤其他戴上红色帽子之后,画面上那片红色特别突出,我已经能想象出照片洗印出来之后的效果,为此我的收获感被满足了寒冷的天气也被轻视了。但我也是有遗憾的,我遗憾的是自己没带摄像机,不然的话,这简直就是一个小型的电视剧,而且还能录下他的话,我不无遗憾地摇了几下头。

他又开始拨电话,拨了一个,摇摇头,再拨一个又摇摇头,我心想那现象是占线。第三个拨通了。他说:"嘿,玛利雅,我在这儿呢,过来吧,我也不知道这条街叫什么名字,反正我在这儿,你过来就是了,我请客。别担心,我的甜心。嘿,你与哪个母狗养的在睡觉?我他妈的。"他把电话狠狠地挂上了,那种气愤的样子肯定是对方激怒了他,过去曾发生过类似的爱情遭遇。但他马上又没事人似地拨起了另一个电话号码。这个电话成了他的玩具,我这样想。又拨通了,他顺手拉住一个从他身边路过的老年人,硬把话筒塞进老人的手中,而且说:"这是找你的电话。"老人的态度是把电话筒放回到电话机身上,扭头就走开了。是啊,我感叹纽约人早已练出了如何对待这类人，那就是别搭话，并且马上离开。那老人干脆利落的反应使我对纽约产生一番并不是尊敬的尊敬。

我想他这样是会没完没了地玩下去的，而我也该走了。但我又想看看他如何处理那架电话机，我对自己说再等两分钟，如果他还不离开那两个垃圾桶的话，我就回家了。他突然抬头看见我还在对街看他，就做了一个很不友好的手势，我当然不会跟他计较，纽约人都知道尽量地不惹这类无家可归的流浪者，他们之中的许多人都有暴力倾向。所以我反而掏出烟盒向他晃了晃，意思是问他要不要烟，他向我招手，我跑过去给了他之后又跑回来，他冲我用手比试拍照的样子，显然他是让我尽情地拍他。这一下他肯定把自己当作演员了，他进入了演戏的角色，这对我来说不是我想要的感觉，所以我就假装离去的样子走了几步，我想看他何处理电话机的。

他把电话机扔回了垃圾桶，戴着那顶红帽子沿着街角拐过去了。

1994. 1. 30.

度 假

水、天、沙滩以及一栋孤零零的小楼，小楼后面是不到一人高的矮树林和连绵的小山丘，其它就什么也看不到了。到这儿的第一天晚上，我就在想斯平时在这里度周末也是一个人从纽约开车三个小时，然后寂寞地度上两天的。当然，我首先要领悟到斯是有钱人，不然肯定买不起这块濒临大西洋的乐园。

斯是我在纽约的好朋友，他虽然有一些中国朋友，但与我在音乐上有共同爱好而经常一起听听音乐会，再加上性格上较为合拍，生活上也就能互相踩出共同的节奏。他把他在五年前买下的度假屋钥匙交给我，让我有空就可以去玩玩，他则离开纽约前往香港，他要在那里工作八个月。

从纽约市穿过荷兰隧道我开车进入新洋西州的公园大道、以每小时 60 英里速度走了近三个小时，出了高速公路后拐上林荫小道，再拐上私家车道，把车一停就先换上游泳裤钻入海水降温。

回到小楼把带来的食品塞进冰箱，在靠近窗口的沙发上一坐，从面临大海的落地窗看着外面水天连成一片的景色，很快进入了瞌睡。我梦见的东西不多，醒来之后已经傍晚，八月中旬的落日被几丝云挡成一片红光，我想起梦见的一些紫色的光环，光环是可以用手摸的，好像是塑料做的。这次我来这儿可以与自己幽会三天，来之前我就想好了谁也不告诉，而且到了这儿也决不给任何人打电话，我要好好地体验一下自我，纽约城里繁忙的生活使我对这次度假充满了期望。

在落地窗前坐到外面什么也看不见了，我才开灯从冰箱里找出一些食品，很仔细地做了二盘菜，一边喝着葡萄酒一边细嚼慢咽。我想外星人会不会也是这样吃饭的，也许他们是喝一种燃料？我这样想是因为刚才坐在那里望着窗外沙滩和蓝天连成一片时想过宇宙在天外会有些什么活动。另外我也想过太阳是不是外星人造出来的卫星,以便养活他们培植的地球人。我们看不见外星人可能是他们又在其它地方培植了更高级的东西,所以,地球人就作为他们初级的产品而放弃了。放弃之后等太阳这颗卫星耗尽能源,地球人也就完了。那么,地球人要尽自己的能力在太阳消失之前发射另一颗太阳作为光源才行,我狠狠地喝了一口葡萄酒,好像这些都是事实。我把最后一些菜很快吃完,披上一件衣服就又去了沙滩,漆黑一片的沙滩,我选了一块礁石一坐,这才发现月光其实还很亮,浪涛声哗哗作响。也许是从哪本书上学来的吧,我开始思念故乡,我已离开故乡中国六年了。我努力思索哪一本书上有人提起过离开故乡六年之后在沙滩上的感觉,结果想不起来。

我想起当年在北京逛长城的情节,那一次也是一个人去的,在一次失恋后。我沿着长城走了很远,远远地离开旅游的人群,一个人坐在那里看绿色的山岭和灰色带子般的长城,那时觉得自己是确确实实地坐在那里了,不像女朋友,那种互相依赖的情感随时都会被社会或家庭变动甚至工作和健康变动所影响,我坐在那里找到了失恋的真正原因,她因为社会变动而找到了中国的一个最新的出口,那就是回到她以前的情人那里,他的许多亲戚全在香港,他可以把她作为太太带到香港去,她就是这样一个可以被人带走的希望。她不需要坐在长城的偏僻处想遭遇,因为她是主动的。而我坐在长城的偏僻处不到半小时也发现了自己也是主动的,因为长城虽伟大,但它一步也走不动了,而我随时可以站起来拍拍屁股地走人了。那时我偏偏又坐了二个多小时,为了让长城好好看看我,看我怎样把烟头一掐站起来退进旅游的人群,我退进去的时候有一种进攻的意识,不久之后,我在生活的人群中找到了一个愿意帮我出国留学的人。我现在坐在沙滩上学什么呢?六年来还是第一次真正地与地球的某一块地独处,方圆一英里之内都是属于我的,我知道斯买下的这块地是私有的,不然他不会买。

地球上有多少块这样的地是属于私人的啊,先是分成各洲、各国，后分成各民族各家庭，再分成家庭和个人，这就是财产，地球是一个大财产，属于人类还是属于外星人，看来是属于人类了，如果是属于外星人，他们现在也撒手不管了。但人类是满意自己成为主人的，许多人不满意自己也不满意作为同样是人的同胞，所以他们相信上帝和佛。所以，地球这份财产被他们划给上帝和佛·了，我觉得海浪声越来越大，如果我是一条鱼就能听出大海对上帝和佛抱以什么样的态度了，而现在我只能猜想，我猜想海水不断地想冲上岸来但又被水平线所局限，所以水平线是大海的脑力的极限，它想的事情都是在水平线以下的，只有潜水人员能去听出一些真实来。可惜的是大多数潜水员不是为了战争的缘故就是为了石油，要不就是为了寻找过去的沉宝，他们根本不想去听大海怎么说。

我感到困意与海风一道袭来，就很听话地走回小楼去，而且希望明天天一亮就上沙滩与清晨会面。

与清晨的会面并不理想，天阴得厉害，乌云好像要亲手摸湿我的头发，我记起有一年在上海外滩与一位也是为了躲雨的漂亮姑娘在一条弄堂拐角处躲雨时反而被楼上泼下来的一盆洗脸水浇透了，我记得浇透的是两个人，无所谓年青的一男一女，既然已浇透了就索性淋着雨各自赶路了。我现在希望乌云把它的洗脸水泼下来，越快越好，我真的很想走在上海的街上。乌云不理会我是怎么想的，洗脸水迟迟不泼下来，也许这一天它没脸可洗，一直到中午天还是乌云压顶但就是不下雨，弄得我感觉上去不了上海，只好去了纽约。纽约的地铁里我曾忘掉过很多次伞。下车时忘了拿，一钻出站才发现伞跟着地铁车走了。有一次碰到一个好心的人提醒我，但一钻出站发现雨停了，也不知道这算不算我这个人有些什么运气。我刚到纽约时所租的一个顶楼既便宜又漏雨，我向房东报怨，他派了一个人来修理了一下，但还是漏，最后房东说便宜没好货，反正这个楼目前正在登广告出售，他也不想花钱多修，让我搬走算了。房东还说他自己因为失业所以生活上也乌云压顶，只好卖楼度难关。关于乌云压顶的事还有很多，但最压的还是我自己的一件事，那是一个秋天，我刚从纽约一所英语学校毕业，心想英语问题基本解决，其它就看自己的能力了，我就很自信地冲进一家广告设计公司，带着自己的一些作品的照片找工作，老板是香港人，一口极流利的英语和广东话，但不会说国语，我们就用英语交谈，他好像对我的英语比对我的设计作品更感兴趣，他说大陆来的人能讲这么好的英语的人并不多见。他录用了我，试用期三个月，三个月之内要设计至少五件令他满意的广告作品。第一件是设计一家火腿公司的广告，我设计的稿子是这样的：一个很深的猪蹄印和一个很浅的鞋印，旁白是"美满的味道令您的咀嚼充满肌肉感！"老板很欣赏，接下来的几件也使他拍过我至少三次肩膀。同公司的一个张小姐是刚从纽约波来特美术学院设计系毕业的，她为此对我的设计才能多少有些妒嫉。但老板欣赏我，她也没办法。有一次她接了一个活，是设计运动鞋的广告，因为任务紧，就私下打电话到我家里，问我能不能帮她想个主意，我这个人吃软不吃硬，虽然我感到她对我不礼貌，但一旦她好言好语求上门来，也就一口答应了。我赶了个通宵，设计了一双绘有脚神经的鞋，使鞋具有生命感，并在公司外面的一家咖啡馆里交给了她。当然获得了老板的称赞。可是第二天我被老板叫去说我被辞掉了，原因很简单：经济不景气，公司必须把四个设计师裁掉一个，我是最新来的（才五个月），当然应该裁我。当晚公司的另一个设计师打电话告诉我为什么被裁掉的原因。原来老板看见我与张小姐在咖啡馆里喝咖啡，出咖啡馆之前张小姐作为谢意，吻了我一下，不是在颊上，是在嘴上，老板正巧在买咖啡，张小姐和我都没看见他，而张小姐是老板私下通床的情妇！我的那个设计师朋友早就知道，只是还没熟到把这类公司里的事告诉我，而我也没查觉到。设计师朋友前一天听到老板在公司的地下室询问张小姐，而张小姐不但没说我帮她忙，反而说我在企图勾引她！我挂上电话后气愤地给老板打电话说明原因，但老板不相信，他说要证实之后再说。张小姐当然否认了我替她作过什么设计，我显得反而更坏了，因为情妇的话在老板需要她的时候永远是真实可信的！此事对我的乌云压顶之感并非它本身，而是我认识到一个普遍的真理：美国这个国家虽然是民主的，但每一家私人公司都可以是一个独裁王国，老板就是国王，他想怎样就怎样，因为他的独裁是受国家的民主法律所保护的。人性的乌云在人与太阳之间，从人性往上是阳光是民主，人性往下是乌云压顶，老板是操纵乌云的人。所以美国有那么多操纵乌云的人建立了自己可以压顶的王国。

　　中午飘了几滴雨之后乌云走开了，也许去别的上空度假了。我坐在沙滩上接受阳光的抚摸，突然一只狗出现在沙滩上，它一身乌黑，很好奇地望着我，其实应该是我很好奇地望着它，因为这儿毕竟是我的地盘才对。它离我二十多米远的地方站住，用后腿坐下，一会看我一会看看大海，或许它是附近人家养的狗，因为它显得有一定的教养，身上闪着光，显然保养得不错，决不是野狗。它很想看我游泳吧，正好我也想游了，于是我指指大海，它一动也不动地看着我，我一边回头看它一边冲向大海，当我游出几十米之后，回头看见它跑到我的躺椅上去了，还是那个坐姿地看着我。我开始喜欢它了。我又游了十分钟左右，它还在躺椅上看我。我登岸向它走去，它灵活地一跃把躺椅让出来跑到十几米远的地方又坐下了，看着我用毛巾擦完身上的水珠，看着我躺下去。我开始叫它，它抖了抖身上沾的沙子，一路小跑地钻入沙滩后面的矮树林不见了。我心想这儿的狗也是独来独往地不打扰别人的隐私权，这也许是一条附近人家带来度假的狗，主人也许也像我一样一个人躺在沙滩上晒太阳，而他的狗就自由自在地闯入别人领地，以为不向别人吠叫就是最友好的教养了。不过，这条狗使我高兴了一番，它的出现使我加深了度假的感觉，原因很简单，它是唯一见到过我在这里度假的观众，如果有什么吃的东西在身旁，也许它会与我多接触一会。我的一个朋友曾经在超级市场买了几个便宜的罐头，越吃越香还介绍给另一个朋友，另一个朋友一听就知道是狗食罐头。后来那个朋友再也不吃了，但也没感到什么丢丑，他总是对一些新从大陆来的朋友说他刚来时曾吃狗食罐头的事情，并告诉他们去超级市场买罐头时要看清楚，还总结地说狗食罐头是挺香的，只是材料都不是上等的，所以还是别吃为妙。这个朋友是很朴实的，我一直很喜欢他，他后来找了个女朋友，女朋友说他朴实到吃狗食罐头还引以为荣，就嫁给了他了。我在为他做婚礼伴郎时还曾想过是否也应该去吃一个狗食罐头。

晚上睡觉时梦到了那条狗，只是它在我梦中与我住在一起，这与狗罐头也许没有什么关系，总之婚姻是婚姻，婚姻的幻想另有体形的，我倒是很想再见到那狗，因为它看上去很有个性，但后来就再也没见到它，也许它意识到这儿不是它主人的领地，或者它的主人已带它回城了。

我开始喜欢这种美国式的度假了，以前总以为一连几天面对沙滩是多么单调，而我们中国人的习惯是度假要比平时更累才对，玩得越累，看的东西越多才叫度假，才叫有收获。但我也想中国人也许因为没有私人领地这么一种财产，才没有这类的度假吧，一旦土地可以买卖，我想青岛那边的许多海滩也会有私人的钥匙了，我曾在青岛的海里游过泳，夏日之际的海滩人满为患，水中像煮饺子一样拥挤热闹，当然这也是一种游乐气氛，但一个人占领一片海滩的气氛也应该尝一尝，尝一尝自己这个孤独的饺子里到底是什么样的馅。

狗知道

我在纽约的一个美国邻居突然抽中一个大奖：五千美金和二张香港——纽约来回机票及一个星期免费旅游。他名叫戴维，戴维于是就和她的女朋友安妮一道准备享受这趟旅游。他把他唯一的一个麻烦留给了我——管理他那条杂种的但看上去比纯种狗还强壮凶悍的狗，这条狗的名字叫苹果。苹果是条公狗，戴维说最好每天牵它出去遛两次，每次半小时。戴维说要为此付我一些工资，我说免了，我说你就把你的汽车钥匙留下来，有时我可能开车带苹果去郊外玩玩。戴维把他的车钥匙连同门钥匙一起留下来就走了。

当天晚上（戴维是上午走的）我就牵着苹果上街，它好像特别高兴由一个新朋友与它共行，它用劲往前走的架势好像它是在牵着我，我从中国来美国的三年以来还是第一次遛狗。那种悠闲的感觉好像一股清泉流过手指直达心灵，那根牵狗绳凝聚着狗和我的力度使生活更容易掌握。苹果突然慢慢地松下步子，马路对面另外一只狗也在往这边看，苹果使劲把我往马路对面拉，我把它硬拖住，然后往前走，苹果抬头看看我，我没理它，反正是男女间的事。

我以前看一些美国人在街上遛狗时并没有过多的想法，习以为常，遛狗的人在纽约太多了。现在我也成了遛狗的一员，而且体会到一种狗与人互相影响的生活关系，我当天晚上就发誓再也不吃狗肉了，我在中国时吃过几次。我还想着周末时开车带苹果去长岛的富贵区转一转，因为我来美三年一直在纽约市，没有去过什么地方，而且我也没有汽车，也就是说我一下子有了两样从来没有的东西：狗和汽车。我还想一定要拍些照片：开着车牵着狗，再穿得漂亮些。把这些照片寄给国内的朋友们，他们准以为我发了大财，我洋洋得意地几乎睡不着地睡去了。

第二天一早我就开了一个狗食罐头给苹果，它吃了一半，我牵住它出了大门，我想这一次带它走另一条路，于是绕过昨天的路另走一条，苹果好像认识这条路，我一想也是，它已被戴维遛过数千次了，周围没有它不认识的！这时苹果站在一家卖酒的店铺前看那些酒瓶子，我平时也喜欢喝酒，所以就站住看那些酒，有些酒我从来没有尝过，尤其有一种酒用很小的深蓝瓷瓶装的，要卖八十几美金，这是我从来也没有尝过的。原因很简单：穷学生买不起。另外还有一种酒，就是众所周知"XO"也是没有尝过的，有一次在一个私人晚会上，酒橱里有一瓶"XO"，我硬着头皮向倒酒的朋友说可以不可以来一杯"XO"？结果回答这是一瓶未开封的有纪念意义的酒，主人是不允许喝的。那次晚会结束前我才从一个朋友嘴中了解到这瓶"XO"已经放在那里几十年了，是主人的伯父死后留给主人的唯一财产，主人的伯父三十二岁就酗酒去世了。我和苹果站在这家酒铺前的时间不短了，苹果也没嚷嚷要走，我这才发现它比我还认真地看着排列得很艺术性的酒的橱窗。我心想苹果也许能懂几个英文字吧。回家后我就去上学，放学回来又做功课吃饭，然后又遛了苹果一圈，苹果在街上撒尿拉屎好像比其它的狗文雅。尤其是拉屎时，它先发出一种哼声，与平时的叫声完全不同，是专门告诉主人准备拉屎了，然后我就把准备好的报纸放在它的屁股底下，它才开始拉。拉完我就把报纸一卷扔进附近的垃圾筒。我心想戴维把它训练得不赖。在纽约，如果遛狗者的狗在街上拉完屎，遛狗者必须把这堆屎用纸包上扔进垃圾筒，如果不处理，被警察看见是要罚款的。苹果是不见报纸铺在屁股底下不拉屎，真是条懂得干净也懂得法律的狗。我临睡前边看电视边喝一小杯酒，苹果蹲在旁边很乖地看着我，当我把杯子放下后，它把头探到杯子上方嗅着，然后舔着酒喝，我马上把杯子抢过来，到厨房倒了一杯水给它，但它嗅了嗅就一口不喝地走开了。我突然想起早上我和苹果一道看酒的橱窗，于是，我把一点酒掺进水中，我渗的是伏特加，放在碗中，苹果几口就舔光了。然后又抬头望着我，显然是还想要。我暗暗笑道戴维一定经常给这条狗喝酒！我又想会不会这条狗喝完会撒酒疯呢？万一喝醉了就咬人怎么办？我就不再给他喝酒，而是看我的电视。

但是我忘了我刚才给苹果在厨房掺水时把那瓶伏特加开着盖留在厨房了。看完电视偶然走到厨房，苹果已把瓶子放倒，我说放倒是因为我没有听见瓶子倒下的声音，苹果已在那儿喝舔了很久，我摸摸地上，流在地上的酒几乎没有了，苹果这时候也不看我，我把瓶子抓到手中，原来剩的大概四分之一瓶伏特加，如今只剩下瓶底一点没有倒出来了。我有点害怕地看着苹果，它好像还正常。苹果站起来跟着我走到客厅里。我一直盯着它，它好像知道它要干什么似的走到电话机旁，电话是按键式的，苹果把听筒用嘴叼起来，伸出那条左前腿开始一个一个地按，我紧张地看着它按了七下后叼着听筒我。我马上接过来，电话是打通的，那边的电话铃在响就是没人接，突然那边的电话自助回答机工作了，我听见的声音像是戴维的女朋友安妮，于是我为了确定一下，把电话挂上，从戴维家里找到安妮的电话打了一遍，同一个录音！所以，苹果刚才按了七下是按了安妮的电话。是戴维训练的？！可是戴维是不是发现苹果爱喝酒呢？而我又想起中国文人的一些饮酒写诗的故事，我想会不会苹果在喝完酒之后思路会变得敏捷呢？我把电话放下并且让苹果再去打。果然苹果又去打了一下，又是七个数字，七个数字是本区的，我想又是安妮的，我拿起来听，那边一个男人的声音在回答，我马上问他是不是戴维的朋友，对方说是戴维的哥哥。我明白了，就解释了一番苹果打电话的事情的。他不信，他说以前从来没有听戴维说过。我很纳闷地挂上电话。坐在沙发里沉思这件事情。苹果一脸聪明地望着我。我真爱它！我去厨房的冰箱里找了一节热狗香肠喂了苹果。苹果又跑到刚才它弄倒伏特加的地上舔喝。我用手一摸，还剩下一点在大理石的地面上，它把它们三下五除二地舔了干净。当我们再次回到客厅时，苹果又去打了电话，这一次又是打给安妮的，我从它的爪子的动作中看出是，8735326，这是安妮的！我这次准备对安妮的电话回答机说几句等她和戴维从香港回来时要告诉她一个秘密。突然，安妮真的回答了！我惊讶地问安妮什么时候从香港回来的？可是安妮说她肯定没跟戴维去香港！我愣在那里，思路很快告诉我戴维是否与另一个女朋友去了香港？而不是安妮！我与安妮支吾了几句，反正这事是败露了，但不是我的错，戴维也没叮嘱我，戴维对我说是与安妮一道去的。虽然我以前只见过两次安妮，但她是戴维正式的女朋友毫无疑问，为什么现在事情是这样的呢？苹果把此事给败露了！聪明的苹果呀！我突然发现自己太笨，为什么忘了问安妮知道不知道这条狗会打电话？！我于是又拨了电话给安妮问她知道不知道这条狗会打电话？安妮说从来没听说过。我又问知不知道这条狗喜欢喝酒？安妮说她也不知道。安妮问我戴维离开时说是与她一起走的之外还说了什么？我说没有其它的话。安妮很气愤地说戴维是个骗子。

戴维是不是骗子对我来说并不是稀奇，社会上的男女朋友之间发生的事都差不多，但是狗爱喝酒，而且酒后打电话不正像中国诗人李白酒后能吟诗吗？当然我绝不是说人与狗无差别，而是从生理上讲酒所起的作用对动物和人都有它激发灵感的一面。我当然也要让戴维知道这个败露的事是苹果干的。

戴维回来后知道此事只是耸耸肩说他与他的新的女朋友在这次旅游后决定订婚，至于安妮，就吹了。戴维不相信苹果能打电话，因为戴维不知道它有这才能。戴维也不知道苹果会喝酒。也就是说苹果的才智是偶然被我在无意中用酒引发出来的。所以，我要做的是证明苹果的才能。我把苹果叫到电话机旁边，苹果毫无反应，我就把苹果叫到厨房让它喝一些伏特加，然后苹果就真的打通了电话，使戴维惊讶不已，但苹果只会打两个号码，一个是安妮的，一个是戴维的哥哥吉姆的。我说肯定是戴维平时经常打这两个电话，苹果看在眼里记住了，并且现代电话都是按键式的，容易模仿，如果的指拨式的，那么，再喝酒苹果也是无能为力的——身体结构受限制！但它脑子里肯定是懂得的。所以，我对戴维说也许此事并不那么简单，也许苹果喜欢安妮，而且知道你与另外一个女朋友出去了并且瞒着安妮，所以苹果就想出这个主意让我来泄露出这个秘密！戴维根本不信我说的话，他摇摇头把苹果牵上街进行他度假后第一次遛狗。

鞭炮响起时

在纽约市曼哈顿的下东城找到一间统仓之后，我每个月就更加要努力挣钱来对付昂贵的房租，纽约曼哈顿的吸引力尤其使艺术家——创业阶段的艺术家——感到非要在这里亲临艺术的地震，才能感到生活的刺激。1989 年的秋天，我在卖掉几件自己的雕塑作品之后，有时间缓一口气地一连两个月在我的统仓里悠闲地创作和生活，而不必像不景气的时候每星期三天外出做工挣钱了。有一天我突然发现我们楼房对面的那座楼经常有几声鞭炮，每次都只有五六响，不多，几乎每天都有三四次，有时候半夜里也会有几响。我想到底是哪个孩子那么喜欢鞭炮而每次只放几只。决不多放，像上瘾一样，像酒鬼、烟鬼，吸毒者一样。自从我注意到这种鞭炮声之后，我就常常站在我的窗台上往对面的街上及窗口里张望，企图发现谁在玩这种我小时候特别喜欢的东西。我记得小时候我住在上海时，每次过年我都把大人给我的所有压岁钱用来买各种各样的鞭炮，但是我那时放鞭炮每次都是把买来的生部一次放光才过瘾，与对面楼房里那个人的玩法决不一样，我的性格是图痛快的那种性格，我还记得我当时放鞭炮特别喜欢把鞭炮点着后马上在鞭炮上捂上一个空的小铁罐，鞭炮闷声闷气地把小空罐震起来，然后掉在水泥地上，还有一次我曾失误地被鞭炮把手掌炸了一条裂缝直流血。但我还是继续玩鞭炮，那种兴趣如今我想并不是荡然无存了，而是生活的内容变了，再加上年龄的关系就疏远了这种娱乐，我还曾恶作剧地把鞭炮的引线加长，悄悄地放在朋友家门口点燃因为引线长所以我有时间两手插进兜里好像只是个过路者那样到远一些的街角去看鞭炮放响后的情景，那时候我朋友被鞭炮声惊吓得从家门口走出来，发现什么人也没有，而我远远地笑得弯了腰。

我终于发现对面楼里放鞭炮的人是住在 3 楼左边的一位中年妇女，她就在窗台上用抽着的香烟点着几枚鞭炮后就关窗进屋了。我想她是那种怪人，纽约有许多怪习气的人，这一点大家都这样说。我还发现她放鞭炮并没有固定时间。当我特意买了一小型望远镜之后，我发现她放鞭炮好像在例行公事，脸上一点表情也没有，我想她也许是有什么生活经历上的理由，比如是纪念某个亲近的人，可是按常规放鞭炮的含意是驱邪避魔，或者庆祝节日或家里的喜事。她放鞭炮肯定是有其理由的，最起码是一种怪癖，她看上去 40 岁左右，头发略呈棕色，像是染过的，高高的鼻梁以及灰色的大眼睛，皮肤是介于白人与南美洲人之间，很难判断他是西班牙人还是其他国家的人，也许我刚从中国来美国 3 年，还分不清什么具体的人种。后来我想反正纽约有世界各地的人，也有许多混血儿，总称纽约人就行了。她那种漫不经心地点燃儿响鞭炮后就转身隐入屋内的样子在我脑海挥之不去。我想这个形象这辈子将跟着我了，每当有鞭炮响起，我肯定会想起她来。

终于有一次我发现她和另一个男人在窗台上一起点燃鞭炮，确切地讲是那个看上去像是标准白人的男人站在她旁边看她用香烟点燃鞭炮，他也和她一样点鞭炮时毫无表情，点完之后他们转身隐入屋内，只留下对面的我想着心事。我瞎猜一通，但都是无法证实的猜想而已。我记得我小时候在上海农村看农人的孩子把一串鞭炮系在狗尾巴上，鞭炮点着之后，狗就在农田被尾巴上的鞭炮声惊得飞快奔跑。这种恶作剧也曾同样在猪的尾巴上炮制，但猪好像更懂得鞭炮，当鞭炮响起，猪挪了挪它的身子，然后几乎是坐下来一打滚，鞭炮就灭了，好像大人知道你小孩在干什么似的样子，猪那时在我的心目中是太严肃了一点，自从我看到她身旁有一个男人一起放鞭炮后，我对她的神秘感就少了许多，因为她不只是一个人拥有自己的秘密，她自己作为一个神秘世界的形象不再存在于我的想象中，她最起码与那个男人同时享有她为什么每天都要放几次鞭炮的秘密，因为故事和文学的影响，我对此事总是想入非非地瞎猜一些情节，其中两个我猜想的情节是这样的：第一个是最简单而流行的，她婚后的第二天，与丈夫一道去亚洲度蜜月，结果回纽约时只有她一个人、因为她丈夫崇拜印度的宗教而执意留在那里，并且答应她两个月之后再回家，结果至今未回。她曾去过印度寻找丈夫也是空手而归，从此她就精神不正常地放鞭炮，因为们结婚那天，她丈夫曾点烧过一串鞭炮。第二个猜想更加复杂而奇异。她是一个极其愤世嫉俗的女子，而且是哈佛大学毕业的博士，她专门研究国家的民族结构意识以及家庭的关系，但世界上不停地侵略性的战争以及内战使她内心充满人性的矛盾，每当她看一篇小说或报纸的新闻的时候，如果内容中有什么人或事是她反对或仇恨的，她就跑到窗口放它几响鞭炮当作枪声把地所恨的事与物枪毙。

我当然知道自己的许多猜想只是表现了我自己的生活经验和对世界的看法，所以，我也渐渐地被她的鞭炮声激发起猜想乐趣，我所有的猜想使我自己的想象力也开始增强，在将近一个多月的时间里，我对自己作为一个艺术家的信心也增强了许多。我常常对自己不着边际但又在文学上符合逻辑的猜想暗暗发笑。我也甚至有过去拜访她的想法，后来又放弃了，因为如果这是她的一个怪癖，那么她决不会允许其他人去参与的，那是她自己的世界里的一件大事，是她精神上的一根支柱。

这篇故事的读者当然知道接下来还会有情节的发展，读者一定猜到了我写这篇东西并不是仅仅为了说明纽约这个奇特的城市有各种各样怪异的人士，所以按照写小说的习惯标准我不再大谈自己的感受和猜想，我必须满足读者，而更要满足自己的发现以及能与大家分享的乐趣和责任。

我终于发现了她为什么要放鞭炮的事实之后，我没有告诉我的许多朋友，我告诉的第一个人是我的一个也是艺术家的邻居，他是一个很勤奋的画家，他画画已有20年的历史，他是出生在美国的纽约客，他一边画画，一边在一所大学教西洋绘画史。那天我对他说你是否也经常听到对面楼房时常放鞭炮的声音，他说是的，并说有什么奇怪的。我让他与我一道在我的家里喝酒聊了一些关于什么画廊最近在举行值得一看的展览，并且聊酒的种类等等。大约有两个小时，鞭炮没有响起，他也准备回他自己的屋里去继续画画。就在他从椅子上站起与我道别时鞭炮响起了，我马上拉他冲到窗口处，告诉他 3 楼的那个窗口是放鞭炮的地方。然后我让他看街角上有个人站在那里，我说那个站着的人在等人，我打开窗户再让他稍稍探出头去，看我们这个楼的大门，不一会儿就有一个人走出我们这个楼与那个街角上站着的人会合，并且一起走开了。我说你都看到了吧，他说那又怎么样，我马上拖着他下楼，我说你跟着我去看个究竟。我们尾随着那两个人，远远地我们看到他们在一个拐角处聊天，神情很警惕，但他们的右手的几个快速的动作，以及动作之后马上互相离去的情景使我的这个老纽约的朋友马上懂得了他们在做什么；他问我每次鞭炮之后都这样吗？我说是的，每次都是这样的。他说他已经完全知道这是一个什么样的过程了，他说在纽约扫毒之风越来越紧的时候，这些贩子以及上瘾者也有他们自己想出来的保险措施。他说肯定是买者先打电话给对面楼里的那个女人，那女人用鞭炮通知手上有货的我们楼里的同伙，这个同伙再去交易。我的这个朋友很好奇地问我是怎样发现的，我说我注意这件事已有一个月。曾有过一次，我发现一个男人也在那个女人身旁出现了几秒钟，而那个男人有一次被我在自己的楼梯上碰见了，于是我就发现了这个秘密。但我的朋友很严肃地对我说，你不要惹麻烦不要去看他们，一旦被他们知道你注意……他没说完，只是把食指竖在嘴唇上，我已经懂了，而且我也不再去发挥鞭炮响起时的各种想象力了。

趣味的抽象

　　一个靠卖画生存的画家，总会在其卖画的经历中有那么一两次最值得回味的过程，我靠卖画生存已有十年以上的经历，当然有那么几次卖画过程的故事可以说说。也许不少人已经听说过自己买自己的画的故事，比如我就听说过不止一次。其中一次是这样的：有一个画家在他的个人展览上为了表示他的画不仅能办成展览而且卖的也不错，他让自己的一个兄弟假装买主去画廊交涉，在其中意的几幅画下面贴上预定的标记，画展结束后当然是一个电话告诉画廊不买了。另外我也听说画廊为了做生意在他们办的展览里挑一两张最不可能卖出的画贴上已售出的标记。总之，商场如战场，孙子兵法的各种招数都能找出典故，而我遇到的一次也并不例外，只是看我在下面如何描写了。

　　在中国，送画的风气颇浓，某个朋友向我要画，我会视其的友好程度毫不吝啬地送他一张。但在美国，或在整个西方，这种风气相对来讲要淡得多。按西方人的观念，所有的劳动都是要付报酬的，画家的画更是劳动的产品，是不可以或者说不轻易送给人的。我到纽约居住的第三年遇到了一个美国人，他叫汤姆，我们成了朋友，不到一年我们就成了最好的朋友。他有一个公司，是和中国做进出口的生意，但因为种种情况和运气也不顺，所以几乎赚不了什么钱。他有时也帮我推销我的画，我们达成协议，凡是他帮我推销的画，每一张他可以取百分之十的红利。他是一个不太成功的推销者，在一年多的时间里他只帮我卖掉一张半，那半张是卖给他的一个叔叔，那张画他叔叔当时只付了一半的钱，后来又不想买了，因为他叔叔买画后不久就离婚，因为他看上了一个年轻的女人，迫不及待地离婚后家产的大部分都分给妻子和儿女了，所以他不想付那一半的钱，于是把那张画退回来换张我认为值那一半价钱的随便什么画都行，我就挑了另外一张给了汤姆的叔叔。这半张画不是我要说的我最值得回味的卖画过程。

汤姆有一天打电话给我说他的一个朋友看过我以前的一次画展，印象很深，现在他买了房子，准备买一两幅画挂在家里，所以他想看看我的画，因为他认为我的画在色调上很适合他新房子的特色。说实在的，我的抽象画与现代建筑真的有许多共通的性质，为了使我的画更具抽象性，我把可视出意义的签名都签在画的背面，这样一来画的抽象语言完全绝对地抽象了。约好来看画的那天，我突然接到一个朋友住医院的电话，就通知汤姆把我准备卖的几张画由他拿到他朋友处，而我则直奔医院去探望我这个突然因疾病而准备去世的朋友，他也许是得了艾滋病，也许是酒精中毒，要不就是自杀未遂。

汤姆的这个朋友名叫朋斯，他选中了其中的一幅，剩下的由汤姆退回来，我给了汤姆十分之一的售价，还请汤姆吃了一顿他最喜欢的希腊饭，因为汤姆有一半的希腊血统，也因为汤姆把我的画价拉高了一倍。朋斯是否发了大财，我问汤姆。汤姆说朋斯最近一年做股票的灵感极好，几次大进大出都赚了钱。

两星期后汤姆说朋斯请我和他去做客，朋斯的新居已经完全布置完毕，我和汤姆如约到了朋斯的家。朋斯很幽默地领我去他的书房看我的那张画，我一看就知道朋斯把画挂错了，不是挂倒了，而是把原来竖着挂的变成横着挂了，我当时因为礼貌关系就没吱声，反正我的画是色彩的抽象画，怎么挂都行，只要拥有者看着舒服就行了。朋斯还请了其他几位朋友，其中一个人知道我是这张画的作者就与我在这间书房里攀谈起来，其他人都走到客厅或卧室去品味朋斯的这所豪华的新房子。和我攀谈的人名叫大卫，他问了我关于中国画家在纽约的情况，最后就开始评论起墙上的那幅画，他把脸侧过来看，并说这幅画好像竖着挂更好看，我当时还没想说穿这幅画本来就应该竖着挂的，只是说抽象画可以从四个方向看，具象的画就只能有一个方向，为此抽象画在某种程度上给了艺术更多的自由。这时朋斯走进来，大卫就对朋斯说他认为这幅画竖过来挂也许更有另一番味道，并

153

问朋斯有没有试过。朋斯狡猾地回答说这样挂最适合他的对物质结构的理解，并且说一张钞票从任何一个角度看都是钱。我们都笑了。

朋斯是个既幽默又仔细的人，几分钟后，他悄悄把我拉到一旁问我这幅画到底是哪一个方向挂的，或者说我画的时候是按哪个方向来完成的。我学着他的思维逻辑对他说，我是按照我的方向完成的，而你可以按你的方向去挂，这并不存在任何矛盾，他笑了笑说希望知道我的世界是哪一个方向的。到了这时，我只好告诉他是竖着完成的。我说完后并没像预期那样看到他有一丝的遗憾，他反而变得更高兴而幽默了，他一把抓住在旁边喝酒的汤姆，告诉汤姆说我替他算了一卦，算出他眼光不同，所以做生意会比常人有更多的机会。汤姆莫名其妙地看着我，我则会意地与朋斯一起笑了起来。朋斯话题一转说应该谢谢汤姆，因为汤姆推荐的这幅画特别合乎他的口味。

朋斯不久又把我叫到一边，问我这幅画的签名是否在背面，是按哪个方向签的。我说是竖着签的，他就把我拉回书房，其他人此时都在客厅里听音乐喝咖啡，他把书房门一关，把画取下来，让我横着再签一个名，我照办了。他打开书房门之前又想起了什么，又把画摘下来让我再在另两个方向也签上名，这样四个方向都有签名了。

那天告别前朋斯又让汤姆转交给我一个信封，我当着汤姆的面打开，里面是一张一百元钱的钞票，而信封的四个方向正是朋斯的四个签名。汤姆莫名其妙地问我怎么回事，我把经过告诉了汤姆，又按比例掏出十元钱给了他，汤姆不要，我硬是塞进他的口袋，并说钱也是抽象的，看你如何用它。这幅画的买卖过程就此完成，朋斯第一次付了一千五百元，加上这一百元，一共一千六百元，也许朋斯把它当做四幅画买下了，这种幽默则不是每个人都有的，也许朋斯另有其它逻辑，我就不太清楚了。

鸽子的故事

离路边不远的地方是涂上黑漆的铁栏杆，铁栏杆围住了一片绿草地和几株看上去很健康的树。绿草地后面是教堂，教堂很庄严，大门的木质看上去很好，可以联想到皮裙子或皮夹克的质感，但不是那种穿在姑娘或小伙子身上时的那种感觉，而是挂在橱窗里由塑料模特儿穿着的质感。一群鸽子在草地上啄食着他们认为可以啄食的东西，这些鸽子很自由自在地迈着不屑于飞翔的脚步，他们的羽毛光滑而洁净，……。

我站在栏杆外面的路口等我的可能成爲女朋友的朋友，她明显地迟到了，我可能会有更多的时间去观察鸽子。

在教堂的墙角处，有一个石槽，里面的水倒映着天空的蓝色，一只鸽子在啄食这片天空的蓝色，它索性一跃入了石槽，水刚好到它的肚皮，它嬉耍水，蓝天闪著银光时隐时现，草地上一只雄鸽在发出呼噜声地追求着一只瘦小但昂首阔步的雌鸽，我想到我在等的那个朋友的大个头和丰满劲，不由得笑了起来。因爲反而是我显得瘦小。

这群鸽子一共十一只，大概是三雄五雌，另外有三只看不出雌雄，因爲他们还小。我擡头看看路口的路牌，路牌上写着十二街，我心里想：「十一只鸽子加上我也是十二」「十二象征着什么？十二？不对，我的约会地点是十一街！」我马上从十二街街口眺望十一街街口，那里什么人也没有，几个行人匆匆过马路之外，街边好像也有一群鸽子。我慢慢踱步十一街，没有我要等的那个人。我又踱步回到十二街，为的是再看看那一片绿草地、教堂，和鸽子所形成的和平安详的景色。

一个岁数大约在四十左右的妇女从教堂的里面出来，她拿着一个纸袋直接走到草地中央，把纸袋里的东西倒在草地上。然后看也不看地扭身进了教堂。鸽子中有几只慢慢踱步过去啄食几口，那是些黄颜色的，大概是麦粒什么的，但大多数鸽子好像还很饱，没有什么兴趣啄食。我又扭头往十一街走去。

这一次我在十一街还是没有看到我要等的朋友，不知道为什么我想道：「也许是她的公司老板让她去买麦粒餵公司台阶上的那群鸽子，所以耽误了时间。」她在纽约一家会计公司工作，公司坐落在中城公园大道上，有着很大的一片台阶和一片鸽子。

十一街街口很脏，不像有着教堂的十二街街口那样干干净净，十一街街口有两个电话亭，其中一个电话被人揪断了，听筒没有了。另外一个电话有人在用，我突然注意到十一街街口也有一群鸽子，但也比十二街栏杆里的那群鸽子要脏，而且样子也瘦弱，甚至其中有两只看上去负病在身，一拐一拐地迈着不得不迈的步子。好像是因为实在飞不动了，只好靠步行的样子。同样的是，它们也在啄食，可是地上是水泥，看不出有什么东西，它们之中没有呼噜着的雄鸽，难道全是雌鸽吗？当然不是！

它们为什么不去十二街街口的那片绿草地，为什么？要知道，只隔着一个街口呀！

我不由得又一次踱到十二街街口，我数了数草地上的鸽子，仍然是十一只！我更感到他们的健康和无忧无虑，他们的步伐铿锵有力，他们的羽毛光亮而洁净……

再踱回到十一街。这里的鸽子有廿多只，每一个都脏而且瘦弱，他们依旧在找不到什么食物的水泥柏油路面上啄食着什么，好像只要保持啄食的动作就能安慰自己，或者给胃制造一个「正在吃着」的假象。它们爲什么不去十二街？我试着驱赶它们，当然是往十二街那个方向。可是它们好像知道十二街那边有什么东西似的，但它们不去，被我驱赶飞去的鸽子又落在了十一街街口那个马路那一边。我简直有点奇怪了，我差不多想问它们，你们是十一街的公民吗？你们非要住在这儿吗？十二街那边的教堂草绿草地上还有许多食物呢！快去呀！笨蛋！

我又一次踱到十二街。我抬头望望教堂的尖顶，又望望绿草地，那群富足的鸽子现在使我想起那个喂它们的妇女了，难道她仅仅以喂着十一只鸽子为荣吗？她知道不知道，仅仅隔着几十米的另一个街口的一群又脏又饿的鸽子，根本不知道这儿有吃的？

或许，鸽子们不可能打电话通知，它们没有通讯系统？总之，这个事实将一直折磨着我——也许鸽子也有种族、部落甚至不同的赞助人，就像这个纽约城里成千上万的大大小小的公司一样……。

1988 年 7 月写于纽约曼哈顿

我和我的"妓女"

　　那是在夏威夷"哈娜露露岛"的"维姬姬"旅游区发生的事。"维姬姬"旅游区有许多旅馆，我住在其中的一家，一共五天，在那里放松一下在纽约造成的紧张情绪，顺便也试验一下在新环境中有什么新的创作感觉。那里有许多日本游客，除了那夏威夷的热带气候与异国情调之外，也因为从日本坐飞机直达夏威夷是很方便的。

　　我在夏威夷时一个字也没写，很舒适地享受着阳光和海水。那是二月份，二月份的纽约天寒地冻，我从旅馆里给在纽约的朋友打电话说我正在替他们提前办理春天来纽约的签证，他们很羡慕。

　　五天结束得比想象中要快，我收拾行李回了纽约。我还是没有什么想写的东西。可是，我当时不知道两个月后的今天有一件事逐渐显影并且不断放大起来，我知道不写就对不起自己了。

　　维姬姬旅游区一入夜，街头就更热闹了，白天在海边游泳晒日光浴的人就都挤进街道，挤进各种餐馆酒吧。我独自一人在街道上走的时候并不很孤独，但总遗憾身旁没有一个女友在一起，一群大约三四个妓女正在街口拦住两个日本男旅客讨论生意，我路过的时候听见其中一个白人妓女正在用日本话流利地说着什么。我心想她们很专业。又是两个妓女迎面过来，其中一个朝我挤了一下眼，我发现她是一个也就二十岁出头长得很迷人的白人姑娘，穿戴也不是像其它妓女那么暴露型的。正当我一愣的时候，她已挎起我的手臂用日语说了一个词，我摇摇头说我不懂日语，于是她改用英语问我要不要一个幽会。我望着她的略施化妆过的美丽的脸，很不情愿地摇了摇头。我此时还看见一些过路的游客正在看着我和她，当然过路人可能希望看到我和她达成交易地拐弯走到那个不知在哪的场所去。我很没经验地把她的手拉开，又坚决地摇了摇头，我离开她独自坚决地往前走去。可是我走了几步又往回走，并且走到马路对面往回走，我是想看看有没有人被她作为客人拉走，尤其想看到是什么样的人会被她拉走。我故意在暗处走，我看见她正与一个日本人谈，但那日本人甩手走开了。她接着又拦住了两个日本男人，这一次谈得比较久，其中的一个人显然有兴趣，因为他把一只手搭在她肩上说话，我想这个日本人是个老手，他的动作那么自然。我暗暗埋怨自己当时太紧张，不然就可以随便聊聊，或请她吃个晚餐什么的，也许这样就能了解一些情况作为写作的素材，我也想到了艾滋病，但也许她们有什么好的防范措施。我越看他们聊得起劲就越涌起一股勇气，我想如果她这一次没有拉住客人，我就去请她跟我走，我会过去挽住她的臂膀把她带到一家比较僻静的餐馆里去吃晚餐，我当时还没有吃晚餐。于是我就走得更靠拢他们一些，这时那两个日本人离开她了，但其中一个走了没几步又跑回到她身旁说了些什么，她摇摇头，用手拢了一下她那咖啡色的头发，并且努了一下嘴角走开了。好了，我可以行动了，我鼓励我自己穿过马路向她走去。她真的很漂亮，她猛然回头看见了我，可是她并没有什么示意地把眼光滑开到一旁去了，她是没认出我呢还是认出我是曾拒绝过她的人，我想她肯定认出我了，她也肯定我身上也没什么油水可捞的，所以她才不在乎又看见了我。这样一想的过程中，我的勇气也突然消逝得干干净净。我站在那里掏出一支烟点上，她又往前走去了。我很甘心地慢慢地尾随着她。我为自己找各种理由来说服我自己再次鼓起勇气来。我活到三十几岁还从来没有接触过一次妓女，妓女的存在对我一直没有什么影响，但这一次好像很不同，我虽然也想起一些小说里对某些妓女正面同情的描写，但我认为这些描写都不是从妓女本人的观念来进行的，什么是她们本人的生活观念呢，我认为十八世纪、十九世纪、二十世纪的妓女肯定有一部份人有着一个共同的观念，这个观念含有性解放的意义。我当时再次走向她，我一边走一边想，为什么如此年轻漂亮的女郎在这二十几分钟里竟没有一人愿意跟她离开这街区去到另一场所共度好事的呢。就说我吧，我再一次与她擦肩而过，我仍然什么话也没说出来。这时候我肚子已经很饿了，我决定放弃带她走的想法。我又往回走拐进一家僻静的餐馆，当招待女郎问我几个人进餐时，我突然神使鬼差地说了两个人，于是我被安排在一张两人进餐的桌子上，招待女郎往桌子上放了两副刀叉。我随口要了一瓶葡萄酒和两个杯子，当然是我一个人开始喝了起来，并且把菜单捧在手中看看。我已开始假设她坐在我对面，我抬头看了看她的眼睛，透明并且发出微蓝的色调，但也含有一丝做作。这时候招待女郎又过来问我是否要先点菜，我说可以，并且解释说我的朋友可能会来晚一些。我在另一个空杯里也倒上了酒，两个杯子我轮流喝，我想我第一句话应该问她是不是另有职业，她回答说她还在上大学，在夏威夷大学。我很不好意思地问她干了多长时间这种工作，她说已经有两年了，白天上课，晚上一般每星期出来干三四天。我又喝了一大口应该属于她的那个杯子里的酒，我看见她看看餐馆里周围的其它桌子后很小心地把她那咖啡色的头发摘了下来，露出一头金黄色的短发，这时候的她看上去更像一个学生。我马上明白她这样化妆上街肯定是为了预防碰到认识的同学，摘了假发之后的她，比先前更自然地开始问起我的情况来了，我在一一作答之后，她说她还没有碰到过中国人，她提起了1989年6月4日的事情以及东欧的事，她的祖先是从波兰来的移民。女招待端来了我的菜，很同情地看了一下那个依然空着的座位，我回头望望餐馆门口，冲着女招待苦笑了一下。我端起她的杯子一饮而尽并马上再斟满。我问她为什么要干这种工作，她说为了交学费和生活。我问她有没有试过其它工作，她说试过，但她又说其它工作用课余时间去做不但累而且挣得钱也不够。我说许多我认识的美国朋友是贷款上大学的，毕业之后找到工作再慢慢偿还。她说她有选择怎样挣钱的自由，并说她自己的天生形象和条件很适合做现在这种工作，并且也使对方有满足感。我很不好意思地提起艾滋病，她说她有一定的防范措施，而且她专挑东方人，因为东方人患艾滋病的人很少很少。她还补充说明任何一种工作都有不利的因素，这一行也一样。她的口气好像把妓女这一行当作其它行业一样来谈，那种自信使我不得不问她有没有爱情，有没有男朋友。她说目前没有，半年前有过一个，但因为这个男朋友有一次在谈到妓女这一行业时暴露出痛恨和看不起妓女后她离开了他，虽然她一直没有说起过自己在暗中干着这一工作。我问她有没有什么客人曾引起她燃起爱情的。她点点头，并说几乎没有客人为她而燃起爱情的，这是关键所在，因为人们都不会在与妓女干完事之后还想把她娶作妻子的。我说一些小说里，包括中国的欧洲的美国的都曾描写过娶妓女为妻的事。她说这种偶然是不应该以此来抱什么希望的。她说事实上正因为男人长久以来可以没有爱情就和女人睡觉已成惯例，所以女人没有爱情也可以与男人睡觉并且还要收钱是对历史不公平的弥补做法。我又要了一瓶酒，女招待更加同情地瞟了一眼依然空着的座位。我又问她有爱情做爱与没有爱情做爱对她有什么不同的经验。她几乎是拒绝回答，说这是男人提出的问题，她说她事实上把这一工作当作临时挣钱的过渡期，一旦毕业，就找个工作，找个男朋友。她问我有没有女朋友，我让她猜，她说应该有的。我问她做了这种工作后，哪怕是阶段性的，会不会从此对男人有不同的看法了。她的回答使我后来也想过不少次，她回答说这种看法不是比平常更真实吗。真的，我们怎样来回答这个问题呢，一个平常的女人和一个妓女所意识到的男人哪一个更真实呢，哪一个更是男人的本质呢。我问她对我有什么看法，她说到目前为止，她认为我还是比较客观地在用感性和理性进行谈话，但再过一会儿，酒喝得多了之后可能会有另一番行为吧。我笑了，并问她警察在街上管不管她们，因为她们一眼就被看出来是在拉客。她说警察也是一种工作，他们必须按照他们的工作条例去做。我说什么是妓女的条例呢。她说挣钱，用我们的劳动。我说你把此称为劳动吗。她点点头，并补充着说她认为这是一种劳动，有些人不同意是因为他们担心她以后无法再过正常人的爱情家庭生活，但是这是她自己的生活，她自己有把握并且可以把性和爱情分开来，为什么别人要替她担心呢。我好像上了一课，但又不甘心地问她是否认为做爱和耳朵要听好听的音乐、嘴想吃好吃的东西以及眼睛想看漂亮的色彩是一样的器官的天生要求，而且这一点男女都一样。她说差不多，并说妓女的产生是因为男人有这种需要，而妓女有没有这性需要并不重要，但男人要付钱，各有所得。她突然很兴致地谈起那些有婚外情的女人，她说她们有了婚外情之后与丈夫的做爱是不收钱的妓女行为。这一说使我又喝了一大口酒，而且把她酒杯里的酒也喝了一大口。我问她是否男人在看待妓女的问题上有许多传统上的对女人的不公平，她肯定地点点头。那么，我问她女人在看待妓女的问题上又怎样呢。她说不管女人是如何看待这个问题，做妓女的只能是女人，这是一项女人才能做的工作，而且女人如果反对妓女，是因为本质上是反对男人把妓女看作妓女，许多男人虽然找的是女朋友，但他心里知道不久将弃她而去，这也是找妓女的心理，总之，男人会常常认为妓女不经过追逐就得手了就不如因一段追逐而得手愉快自豪，我说但不是所有的男人都把女人当猎物的。当然，她说和不是每一女人都是妓女、不是每一个男人都找妓女是一样的道理。她发现我已喝多了，就悄悄地戴起她的假发，她问我住在哪里，我说我知道怎么走，我们来到街上，街上依然是极其热闹地男男女女地拥来拥去，我发现自己原来是一个人，就趁着醉意晃晃荡荡地晃回旅馆，进房之后倒头便睡。

"爱"的代价

纽约的中文报纸看完后满手都是黑色的"新闻",据说这个印刷油墨的问题在本世纪很难有被解决的希望。但小王是一个刚到美国两个月的中国留学生,他翻报纸翻得满手黑却不是为了什么新闻,而是他被朋友的朋友从落脚处赶出来了,他在那落脚处大大方方地脱了鞋舒服了两个月没付过房租和电费。现在,朋友的朋友限他三天搬出去,因为朋友的朋友的另一个朋友又要从大陆出来留学了。小王的朋友虽然还在大陆,但是却调兵遣将地给许多朋友安排国际性"免费落脚处"。真够神通的!

小王在限期的第一天发现朋友的朋友把有电话机的那间小客厅用锁锁上了。小王就换了一些二角五分的硬币在街角的硬币电话机上打电话找房子。他按照中文报纸上的广告打了几十个电话,因为他想找一个住处离他将要上学的那个学校近一些,并且越便宜越好。结果终于找到了一个较理想的地方。房东是台湾来的,人比较和气,娶了位从大陆来留学的漂亮太太,太太不再留学,在家裡烧饭带孩子。当小王告诉朋友的朋友已经找到房子并把地址抄给他的时候,朋友的朋友很吃惊地说,这位漂亮太太原先是他的女朋友,后来嫁给了一张台湾来的绿卡。

这下不要紧,小王住进新住处之后,朋友的朋友就经常来电话,谈话中当然是不时地问问那位太太的事情。当小王告诉他那位太太与小王眉来眼去的时候,朋友的朋友就极力怂恿小王主动进攻,并且说这位太太肯定不爱她的台湾先生。其实小王只是逗逗他而已。

过了几天,朋友的朋友又打来电话,他直截丁当地告诉小王他已经把那位太太与小王的暗地里的恋爱告诉那位台湾先生了。小王吓了一跳。但小王马上就清楚朋友的朋友想搅乱这位太太的生活来报她甩了他的一箭之仇。

小王就找了个机会趁台湾先生不在家的时候找这位太大谈了此事。太太说她先生并没有质问过她这件事，或者是台湾先生得知消息后想慢慢地暗中观察？总之，太太说她过去的那位男朋友太无耻了，造这种谣来陷害小王。小王拍着胸脯说他不能为此就搬走，而是应该大大方方地住下来，万一台湾先生来质问，就有理说理，不怕的。

就这样过了一个多月，一天，小王从学校回家后又把一份中文报纸翻得满手黑，也不是为了看家乡的新闻，而是想找工作挣钱，虽然外国留学生在美国做工是不合法的，但中国餐馆等一些工作还是可以找到的，只是报酬低一些而已。小王去了几个地方都被拒绝了。他在一家中国餐馆旁边看见一家介绍保母的中国人公司，就闯了进去，边闯边想，如果给有钱人管管孩子也许工资挺高。一进去不得了，他看见台湾先生正与朋友的朋友聊天，小王惊得马上躲到一边，幸好还有几个找工作的人在等。小王偷偷地观察他们俩，很明显地他们都是这个公司的人，在一排办公桌里面。小王看着朋友的朋友对台湾先生点头哈腰的样子就清楚台湾先生是老板，而朋友的朋友在为台湾先生工作。

小王溜出那家公司后，心还在跳。小王想了一会，就悟出其中道理来了。小王就按照自己的经验把整个故事设想了一遍：太太和朋友的朋友都是大陆来的留学生。他们的岁数都不小了，三十一、二岁。所以上学校读硕士博士或学士都感吃力，经济上也不行。太大有机会被台湾先生看中，台湾先生有钱，结果，太太与朋友的朋友在商议之后用假结婚来达到办绿卡的目的，当然台湾先生是不知道的。太太在结婚后又介绍朋友的朋友去台湾先生的公司工作。而台湾先生一直蒙在鼓里。但后来太太有了台湾先生的孩子，这孩子使朋友的朋友吃不准是谁的，而大太如今的意思是不要着急离婚，但朋友的朋友就开始怀疑各种情形，精神有点变态。而今后将如何发展，也使小王的故事不知如何结局。小王漫步在大街上，他自问生活的目的和条件的创造是怎样的一回事。但他很茫然。总之这件事弄得小王心里很不好受，因为他略有些偏向于朋友的朋友和那位太太的处境，因为都是大陆出来的，而且年龄都在三十几岁，在外面不好混。

又过了几个月，小王也渐渐地不再多想这件事，因为他自己也面临了许许多多的在美国打基础的问题，他找了一份晚上看守仓库的工作，老板说这样就不必怕移民局的人来查是否雇佣黑工的人了，因为晚上很少来查，万一来查也只是一个朋友在公司里睡觉而已，是抓不住把柄的，但工资极低。这天小王没有及时起床，因为前一晚与公司的老板喝酒醉了，所以没去上班。他听到朋友的朋友在隔壁与太太说话，朋友的朋友说台湾先生真是活雷锋是共产主义战士，那种舍己救人的精神使他永世不忘。原因是台湾先生答应去大陆娶朋友的朋友的妹妹为妻并把其带来美国，朋友的朋友说台湾先生自从与太太结婚之后从来没有同房过，使他佩服得五体投地，而且离婚后也让朋友的朋友马上与太太结婚得到绿卡，只是碍于太仓促而故意拖下来的，但过几个月也该可以了。所以，现在的情形是：台湾先生在与太太假结婚并离婚后已经准备再帮朋友的朋友的妹妹假结婚。而朋友的朋友与太太准备过几个月结婚，太太已有绿卡，而孩子也是朋友的朋友与太太生出来的，因为他相信台湾先生完全出于帮助从来没有同居过。而朋友的朋友吓唬小王是想赶小王搬出去，后来看小王并不太碍事就算了。小王真的长了见识，感慨万分地检讨着什么是更优越的社会制度，他发现自己的知识很难回答这个问题，但隐隐约约的地感到都不是那么对劲，他认为都不够自然，太机械化了。

（现在，我讲一下这篇故事的情况，我名叫严力，是大陆来的自费留学生，小王是我到美国后在一个晚会上结识的，他知道我写些东西，就把这个故事讲给我听，他说可以写篇东西投给《美国文摘》，因为他觉得这种事情很适合写成小说，我拍着胸脯对地说三天就可以写出来。在我写到结尾时，小王突然来找我，神色紧张，他告诉我新的发展。）

小王的一个大陆朋友来信说把一本字典寄到朋友的朋友的住处去了，因为小王没有把新地址告诉这个朋友。所以，小就去朋友的朋友家去取，那天正好是有事路过，就事先没有打电话。小王敲门，没人答应，小王有钥匙在身，因为他搬走后钥匙一时没找到，后来找到了也就没还。而且，小王和朋友的朋友见面次数极少。小王想开门进去，如果有信件就可以取了就走，留个条。小王为了谨慎起见，又按了按铃，还是没人答应。小王就开门进去，他愣在那裡，因为他看见台湾先生和朋友的朋友正赤身裸体地睡在一张床上，朋友的朋友极严肃地说他只有一个要求，要求小王无论如何别把此事告诉太太。他把小王的钥匙收下，把小王推出门外，隔着门轻轻说了一句："爱是有代价的！"

血液的行为

李竹被定为地主是在 1966 年末，造反派从本镇另一个地主方贵生家里抄出来的材料上发现，四十年前李竹的爷爷卖了一大片地给方家之后才变穷的，也就是说李竹家在卖地之前是一个不大不小的地主，五十年代没有被发现肯定是一个疏忽或者里面另有隐情，于是调查这个隐情就成为造反派几个小伙子们的专职工作。李竹被他们关在镇上的小学校里，因为学生都不上课了。李竹虽然知道四十多年前自己家里的情况还不错，但并不证明这就应该成为被批斗的对象，所以他极力为自己辩护，理由是现在他的家可以说是一贫如洗，一个成分的虚幻的东西又怎么能说明他剥削其他人呢？不管他想得通还是想不通，在他被关了半年多之后就已经丧失了为自己辩护的勇气，他作为一个被挖掘出来的地主更要接受批判和劳动改造。接下来的五年他和他的家人在镇上受尽了磨难，到了 1972 年，李竹的一个远房亲戚当上了乡镇干部，因为这种关系李竹终于被认为是一个已经被改造好了的地主而成为一个普通的镇民。但是他已经在精神上彻底被扭曲了，他认为自己的地主成分以后什么时候还会被人重新提出来进行批判的，成分的压力从此不可能离开他了，他还认为自己身上流动的就是地主的血，这是他在小学校的隔离时期造反派领导不断向他重复的两句话："你爷爷的地主血液在你的身上是不可能被换掉的。""我们造反派身上的贫农的血也将永远是属于我们自己的，这就是为什么我们与你们这样的人是截然不同的两种人。"

正是因为李竹的精神状态出了毛病之后，他的儿子李大前抓住了一个进修赤脚医生的机会，在那位远房亲戚的暗中帮忙下到城里进修了两年。李大前是一个孝子，也因为李竹就这么一个儿子，其他两个都是女儿，而且都已经嫁到别的镇上去了，李大前的媳妇照顾着李竹的吃穿住行，一般来讲李竹的精神状态并不那么糟糕，但发作起来就会从家里跑到不知什么地方去，几天以后才会回来，当然有时候是家人把他从山里找回来的。李大前学成赤脚医生后对李竹确实有不少帮助，再加上镇里人都来找他看病，与镇上民众的关系也为之改善许多。所以整个情况的好转促使李竹的情绪也渐渐好了起来，加上孙子的出生更使他有了一个说话的对象，不管这个孙子还不能与他对话，但最起码李竹可以把心里的话向这个孙子倾诉，由此获得了一种平衡。

到了1986年，李竹的孙子李雄已经开始上初中了，他获得了到附近城里去上中学的机会，这当然也是因为李雄的父亲李大前已经是镇上唯一一家医院的副院长，李大前的想法是以后要让李雄出国留学，所以一定要让他上好一些的学校。李竹则有点不习惯孙子忽然离家到城里去上学，闹了一些情绪。李大前怎么劝也没用，孙子离开后的两个星期里他几乎不吃什么东西，最后李大前就用当年他因为地主身分被关在小学校的事情来说服他，并说李雄只有出国才能真正摆脱地主身分的纠缠，而想出国就必须上好的学校，而本镇中学的师资力量又太差。这一番劝说居然特别管用，也就说明李竹还有着极浓的地主身分的心理扭曲。

之后每次李雄放假回来李大前都会听见李竹对孙子进行出国留学的目的是为了彻底摆脱地主身分的说教，当然大家都明白李竹的这种表现是一种病，虽是一种病但也说明了当年造反派是如何折磨他的。他一说起在小学校里被关的半年多和后来在镇上劳动改造的日子时就满脸红光，这种红光是一种对健康不利的激动，每当李大前发现这种情况就会想办法打断他的话，把话题引导到另一个方向去，大前太了解他父亲的病情了。

1992年李雄考上了上海的一所大学，就在他读大学二年级的时候，他爷爷李竹得了一种坏血病，而治疗的方法是要经常换血，好在大前这时候已经是正院长了，不至于为了看病而倾家荡产。李竹在病床前对儿子大前说看来这次终于有机会把身上地主的血换掉了，你千万要找贫农的血给我换上，千万别疏忽了。以后每次换血的时候大前都来监督，他不是怕手下的医生输错血，而是怕自己的父亲对医生说要换贫农的血，这种事情传出去不好听。所以每次换血前大前都会趴在父亲的耳边说："你放心吧，这是贫农的血。"

　　不久李雄放暑假回来了，在病床前李竹对孙子袒露了自己现在的心情很好，因为终于可以把身上地主的血换掉了。他还说早知道可以换血，1966 年前就把它换了就不会受这么多的苦了。他建议孙子如果大学毕业后没有办成出国留学的话，就去把血换掉。孙子知道他这是病话，但还是回答说现在不是要换上贫农的血了，要能换的话就换成资本家的血，因为时代不同了。李竹一听他要换上资本家的血就大声叫道："不行！万万不行，这是在找苦吃啊！你不能这样，不能这样，你一定要换上贫农的！"李雄只好马上哄他说："对对对，我一定换上贫农的。"李竹听孙子这么一说才缓过一口气来，他说我再换两次就可以换彻底了，目前为止已经换了十八次了，你爹说一共要换二十次才能把身上的地主的血全部换掉。李雄就只好顺着他的话说一些不让他激动的事情，他和大前都清楚这种病要不是有院长儿子的作用早就放弃治疗了。而目前的形势也不乐观，大前悄悄对儿子说最多再耗上一两个星期。

　　事实上又耗了五天，李竹就结束了他七十五岁的一生。在他临死前大前为他换了第二十次血，当时他用一种极为满意的口气对大前说："你也应该考虑换掉你身上的血，你是院长，换血是应该很容易的事情，但这种事情我也知道不能宣扬，如果大家全换了血，这个世界就没有差别了，人人都可以当院长，所以不要给太多的人换血，为了保住你的院长位置也不应该给别人换血，我是没有什么遗憾的了，唯一是希望小雄能顺利出国留学，在出国之前你替他把血换成贫农的，这样就万无一失了。"大前知道自己只有点头作为回答，父亲是一个病人，一个马上就要离开人世的人。他哭了，因为他记起了当年和父亲一起被造反派欺辱的岁月，父亲的病就是被欺辱的后遗症。

　　李雄是和他妈妈一起与爷爷度过最后一次会面的，那是在第二十次输血之前，李竹拉着孙子的手说："人都免不了一死，能完成心愿再死也算是不冤了，我过去所受的苦虽然很刻骨铭心，但现在想起来，它使我有机会认识到换血的重要性，现在可好了，我到另一个世界去是以贫农的身分去的，当然我是不会像当年整我的那些贫农一样去整地主或富农，我没有这种兴趣，我认为血源是重要的，但好的血源并不证明就应该整别人，好的血源应该做更好的事情，你们就等着我的好消息吧，我到了那个世界一定干出一些好的事情出来，在这个世界我就是因为没有好的血源也就没有机会作好事情，因为他们不让咱们做，因为只有成分好的人才有机会当官做好事。"他还对李雄说："你妈妈真的不容易，她出身贫农却跟着咱们家受地主的待遇，她没有抱怨过，还因为她是贫农出身而帮我们躲过几次危机，这我以前给你讲过，你千万要对你父母好，将来有机会出国就把你父母接出去，我听说国外什么都好，但不管是好到什么程度我希望你们将来来另一个世界找我的时候都是贫农的血源，小雄换了血后，你的孩子也就是贫农出身了，这是不会改变的了。"此话之后他就昏过去了，醒来后换了第二十次血。

李雄和爷爷的感情是很深的，所以他回到学校后有一段时间很是闷闷不乐。他知道换血之说没有什么根据，但爷爷毕竟满意地走了，这种满意就是换血带给他的。他虽然记不住文革期间自己有多少苦难，因为他是1974年出生的。但是爷爷的病情间接地让他领受了那种恐怖，所以说他因为爷爷的后遗症而经历了文革。他与其他同学的不同也就在此。他有时候会突然感到心里很空，感到爷爷的命运笼罩在他的头顶，这种时候他就会变得无比沉默，并且一头扎进书籍和功课中，每每这样的状态他反尔功课完成得又快又好，一段时间下来，他遇到难一些的功课就会情不自禁地让自己进入对爷爷的怀念之中，然后就进入了做功课的状态。

他以优异的成绩在1996年毕业了，同时他也考取了托福，就在他犹豫是读硕士还是联系国外奖学金的时候，他父亲的一个病人的亲戚从美国回来听说他成绩优秀就主动愿意帮他出国，也算是对他父亲治好了他亲戚之病的谢意。出国前李大前对儿子说："你还是很幸运的，没有遇到文革的耽误，比你大五岁十岁的几代人都被文革耽误了，你要好好读书，将来我和你妈也想到国外看看，你在国外毕业后找个工作，再找个老婆，肯定会很幸福的，我们这边你就不要担心了，现在电脑这么流行，你再加一把劲，肯定会有经济效益的，中国将来也会有你施展的天地，到时候你想在哪儿干都是会不错的。"李雄的妈妈则说："老婆最好还是找中国人，我听说外国女人很自由化，不稳定。"大前在旁边听到后插话说："你现在还没有女朋友吧，要不要在你走前找一个，这样我们也放心。"李雄则说临时找一个有什么意思，这样不是更麻烦吗？明明知道自己要走了，还找一个人来牵挂真是太傻了。他说得不无道理，父母也就没有再接着说这个话题。

纽约呈现在李雄眼中的时候是夜晚，他在飞机靠窗的座位上发现灯光确实壮观，但他早就做好了思想上吃苦的准备，他知道暗淡的生活即将开始，这是因为当他还是在中国的时候就已经了解了许多关于纽约的事情。但是他也知道这里的规则比较清楚，只要能在比较有名的大学学一个比较热门的专业就可以找到一个工资不错的工作，然后就是日复一日地"享受"和平的生活，这当然不包括感情上的问题，感情上的问题谁也无法预测，再有钱的人也难保不受感情的折磨。他想到这儿自己笑出了声音。但是钱绝对是最关键的，他想首先要从经济上站住脚。

学校的生活很快就开始了，英文并没有给他太多的麻烦，他认为自己是有语言天才的，还认为只要自己努力就没有什么办不到的事情。事实上他并不是太顺利，原因是他开始恋爱了，对方是一个出生在美国的华裔，刚开始接触的时候就显出了许多文化和经历上的差距，这虽然是他的第一次恋爱，但他在中国时顺利的学校生活令他第一次有了挫折感，虽然不是学业上的，但它也是发生在学校里的事情。

第一次与珍妮做爱的时候他就知道她已经是老手了，虽然他和她都是二十三岁，是她教会了他如何做爱，所以他并没有因为她不是处女而感到沮丧，反尔有一种庆幸，因为他想如果过不久与她分手的话就不会有太多的遗憾。但当珍妮表现出来的态度比他更不在乎的时候他有了挫折感。珍妮还与另外一个美国同学约会，她的理由是青春并不是一次只开一朵花。她的意思是她可以同时与几个男人交往，几朵花同时开。所以不管李雄多么现代，在开放的中国多了解西方，他也难以接受这样的一个处境，于是他开始了举措。他首先向她重复了自己的要求：只与他一个人在感情上交往。她当然没有放在心上。他接着真的不再去找她，她的邀请他也不接受。分手的日子大约过了两个月之后她来到了他的住处，而他声称自己正要出门办事，就匆匆离开了，珍妮在他的身后喊道："你有种的话就找一个美国女人让我看看！"

他果然找到了一个长得很迷人的美国同学，并且带着她去参加一个珍妮也在场的聚会，他扬扬得意地与新女友南茜高声聊天并笑得很开怀。珍妮当然明白他在玩什么游戏，就走到李雄面前把手搭在他肩上说我答应你的要求。他愣了一下，因为没有想到她会来这一手，但他马上就知道她是在报复他，是临时的，不是她真实的意思。他就把她的手从自己的肩上轻轻地拿下来，并说我一点也不明白你在说什么："不过我可以向你介绍一下我的女朋友南茜。"珍妮看了一下南茜伸出的手对李雄说："我还以为你除了我就找不到其他的女人了，原来这里是一个能把我从你手里救出来的人！所以我要表示感谢。"说完向南茜点了一下头就走开了。李雄心里清楚这个回合是自己赢了，感到的满足使他多喝了几杯，结果是一离开聚会的地方就醉在路边的草地上了。南茜是一个比较内向的女孩，不知道怎样对待一个倒在路边的人，她想了想之后决定把他留在那里慢慢缓气吧，而她则回家睡觉去了，她毕竟刚结识他不久，而且连发生性关系的时间还没有过。

当他醒来独自回家的时候发现珍妮坐在他的宿舍门口，这时候已经是半夜两点多了，他心里有一丝奇特的移动，他知道那是什么。她说看来你是把全部体力都交给南茜了，你是不是把她当作我来干的。如果是这样的话我就原谅你了。他这次没有拒绝她跟他进了房间，他先进了厕所忙了一阵，出来后发现她已经帮他倒了一杯苏打水，他默默地一口喝了下去，这时候一个奇怪的念头出现在他的脑袋里：她的血是什么成分的呢，美国有没有贫农呢，或者是种马的血？她确实有一种性的号召力，可惜他没有和其他女孩子发生过关系，也就说不上对比。

他们疯狂地做爱。他感到自己做得特别好，也是因为她表现出从未有过的激动。之后她怀疑地问他你与那个美国女孩混到这么晚难道没有做事情吗？他说你认为我做完了就不能再做吗？她说这是男人的生理局限性，不是你想做就能做的，我看你是没有把她搞到手。他说所以就发泄到你的身上了是吧？她笑着说咱们别兜圈子了，我们之间很在乎对方，我说不出你到底为什么吸引了我，反正我想今后不会有其他男人来破坏你对我的感觉。他哈哈笑了起来，又突然停下来说我爷爷生病的时候不懂血型是什么东西，所以他选择了输贫农的血。珍妮没有听懂他在说什么就让他再说一遍，他没有重复而是另起一个话题，他问她如果可以选择换血，她希望换成什么样的血，她毫不犹豫地说换成歌星麦当娜的血。她反问他会换成什么样的，他说我希望不是血，也许是汽油吧。她又问他刚才说到他爷爷的什么事情。他说没什么，只是我爷爷愿意当什么财产也没有的人。她摇摇头表示不相信世界上还有情愿当穷人的人。他说你们这种生活在美国的人不知道理想的力量在被扭曲的时候会让人性有多少作恶的机会，穷人意味着不必担心有什么东西会失去的那种自由，这种自由藐视一切财产，从而破坏财产，还原到自然的动物与动物搏斗的乐趣中去，这是已经存在的文明所不敢想象的。她听得一头雾水，但也知道他是在说关于中国以前发生的事情，但她虽是中国血统，但她的母语是英文，所以她的语言历史背景是西方的，语言的表达背景当然也是西方的。

关于李雄的经济情况基本上就像各种有关中国留学生在美国的生活，他在一家干洗店打工，老板是美国人。同时他还帮助一个汉学家教授翻译一些中文的东西。珍妮则是用贷款上学的，准备毕业后找到工作慢慢还，所以她只是用周末的时间在一个杂货店挣一些零花钱。

李雄遇到一个玩股票的美国人戴维，受他的影响也想买一些冷门股来发财，可惜的是没有几个月就亏掉了。李雄认识到必须更加投入才可能摸到股票的筋脉，他拜一个同学的父亲为师，每个星期免费为他打工两个半天，他想在掌握一些技巧之后自己开一个代理股票的办公室，也就是用别人钱去赌。

有一天珍妮拿来一些大麻，他们悠闲地边聊边吸，对他来说是第一次抽，珍妮在观察他的反应，结果是他很伤感地大谈他小时候的事情。他说你对中国是太不了解了，不过你不能算是中国人，你使用的母语是英文，你只能算作英文人，美国人也不算，为什么呢？因为你在家的环境是中国式的，你只是第二代移民，反正还在成为美国人的途中。我爷爷在我很小的时候就说我是地主出身，我当时只有五岁，我说地主是有土地的人，我爷爷说不是，为什么呢？因为现在追究的是过去有过土地的人，比如一百年五十年前有过土地的人就被称为地主，意思是说不管你现在有没有土地，你要背着你祖先的历史生活，我当时并不明白这么多东西，我只知道和邻居家的孩子打架时我爷爷不让我还手，因为我们家是地主出身，而这个邻居的出身是贫农，贫农出身的人可以打地主出身的人，当时我就认为贫农一定是皇帝的亲戚，可是看看我们家邻居的样子并不像，有一次我憋急了，当邻居家的孩子又把垃圾故意扔在我家门口附近的时候，我就狠狠得揍了他，他比我大几个月，但个头还比我小一些。揍完后我很得意，因为那孩子没敢哭出声来，但没想到他是憋到他父亲下班回来才发作，也就是说我下午揍了他，四个小时以后他突然对着他父亲哭了起来，我爷爷被叫过去告了一状，无非是我们家出身是地主，他们家孩子就敢往我们家门口扔垃圾，但那时候已经是 1979 年了，我爷爷真笨，居然回来把我打了一顿，我当然是咬牙一声不吭，我不出声我爷爷就打得越狠，打着打着爷爷对我说："小祖宗啊，你就大声哭几下吧，只要让邻居听到我在教训你就行了。但我就是一声不吭，爷爷的火气也上来了，他顺手拿起桌子上的一本精装的毛语录砸在我拉住桌子腿的手上，我没有松手，他又砸了一下，我浑身一抖感到全身出汗，而且情不自禁地把手捂在了胸前，但是我没有哭，我逃到门外去了，我一跑出门外，就感到胜利了，因为邻居没有听到我爷爷教训我的声音！我跑到一个与我家关系很好的叔叔家，想在那儿躲一躲再说，没想到我的手开始肿了，叔叔这才知道我是被爷爷打了，他就把我送到我父亲所在的医院，查验结果是骨裂，裹了石膏，像个伤兵，可是我从父亲的态度上知道他是支持我的，也就是说他认为是邻居家的孩子不应该扔垃圾纸片在我家的门口，但我父亲很认真地对我说："我支持你，但你不许哭，爷爷的神经受过刺激，别让他太内疚，反正你回家后不要宣扬你的受伤。"我跟父亲回家后，爷爷还在生气，说我太倔了，我就对着他把裹了石膏的手举了两下，同时我的泪水就开始在眼眶里面晃荡，想到父亲的嘱咐，我就强忍住了。爷爷就问是怎么弄成这样的，父亲说可能是你打得太重了一些，不过一个星期就可以拆掉石膏了，小孩子长得快，问题不大。我爷爷楞在那里的时候我很得意，因为他知道自己做错了。可是他表达认错的方式太过分了，他抓住我的手跪在我面前，是妈妈把他拉起来的，我这才像邻居家的孩子一样，憋到这时候才哇哇地哭了起来。

珍妮搂住了李雄，因为这种讲述再加上大麻的作用把气氛弄得更哀伤。珍妮说我虽然不知道中国到底发生过什么，从道听途说那里所得到的感觉是中国和苏联都被奇异的理想推到了一种疯狂的状态之中，不管怎么样，现在看起来都已经过去了。李雄显得很累地躺在珍妮的怀里，已经进入了似睡非睡的状态。

吸大麻变成了他们在一起经常要做的事情，一次他们开始探讨上大学的意义，珍妮认为这是现代社会的游戏规则，也就是说每个人要学一门技术并用这个技术去谋生，最后的结果大都是用技术和时间以及体力换取金钱，再用金钱去买所有被标了价格的商品，有什么东西没有被标过价格呢？她问道。李雄的回答是突口而出的："我！我还没有被标价！"她说你正走在被标价的途中，因为你一拿到美国的学位，你就会寻找那个有年薪的工作，那个年薪就是你的价格。李雄说那么创造发明呢？她说创造发明一旦完成，就马上会被标价的，这是毫无疑问的。李雄说假设一个大学生毕业后找到一个年薪五万的工作，假设他一干就是四十年，后面二十年的年薪是六万吧，那么二十年一共是两百二十万，可是有些做房地产和股票的人用两三年就挣到了这笔钱，之中的差别就太大了。她说这毕竟是少之又少的人才这么幸运。李雄说既然上大学的目的就是为了找到一个工作，那么为什么我们不自己就成立一个公司，从现在就开始，大学也可以不上了。珍妮说自己的公司一旦倒闭就什么也没有了，这就是自己当老板和别人当老板的差别，那些大公司已经积累了大量的资金，有时候的不景气照样能停过来，小公司就不行了，一阵不景气的微风就可能把它吹倒，所以要找一个大公司去工作才会有更长久的保证。他说这么说世界永远在大公司的控制之下了。她说一般情况就是这样的，这就是常理。他叹了一口气说我不想上学了，我明天就去开自己的公司！珍妮说听上去很激动人心，但你有多少钱来开公司呢？他说不需要太多的钱，因为是去融资，是用别人的钱来作股票，我现在已经学到一些操作的方法，真的，我认为既然所有的方向都指向金钱，那么方法和方法之间是平等的，不上学并没有什么不好。她说但是你在美国的身分是学生签证，你没有工作的许可。他说这还不简单吗，我现在学习股票的那家公司就可以雇佣我，或者咱俩去办个结婚证明。她说你真的想退学了？他说我已经想过很长的时间了，就这么定了，是你和我去办个结婚手续还是我让公司雇佣我？她说我要考虑一下。

失败了，半年不到李雄就失败了，退学之后他工作很努力，也从别人的手里融到了一些钱，但股票市场风雨难测，加上有些人很快就撤资了，他坚持了一阵之后知道很难再有起色，除非另起一行干别的。他对珍妮谈了自己半年来的体会，还讲了一个在中国时的故事，他说当时是 1992 年，有一个大学里的同学叫路，路的家在 1949 年以前是资本家，1992 年政府把以前没收的资产和房地产退回给他家，所以他一下子就变成了富翁，许多人都羡慕他，可是他们家族在文革期间因为是资本家出身，受到了许多冲击，家族里面一共死了三个人，两个是受不了折磨自杀的，一个是被红卫兵打死的，这就是代价，而当时他们已经没有任何财产了，只是因为过去有过财产，而且那时候也不知道到了 1992 年政府会把财产退还给他们，所以说财产对他们家来说既坏又好，或从另一个角度讲凡财产都是要付出代价的。珍妮说那是在中国，而且是在那种特殊的时期，现在是在美国，你到底想说的是什么？他说我什么也不想说，我只是认为财产在我的概念里面和我爷爷出身是地主有关，我爷爷的爷爷把地卖了之后已经是穷人了，而我爷爷的出身还是地主，不过大约是在 1980 年我爷爷的出身改定为富农也是奇怪的，因为不能从地主一下子变为贫农，只能先变成富农，富农就是家里情况比贫农好一些的人家，其实早在 1949 年前我爷爷的处境和贫农就没有什么两样了，所以我想说的是挑拨人与人之间的斗争用财产多少的差别来进行是最可靠的，甚至只是一个概念上的出身就行，而在美国我也发现有些大公司其实已经难以运转下去了，但靠它的名声就可以让银行或个人来注入资金地起死回生，因为这家公司的出身是"大"公司不是"小"公司，这个"大"，就是地主，这个"小"就是贫农。珍妮似懂非懂地说你别绕圈子了，你往下怎么办呢？李雄说其实我不是已经开始了吗？！我已经参与了一家与中国做生意的贸易公司的运作，由我来进行与国内商家的联系，我已经找到了一个以前大学里面的同学，他现在在国内做生意做得很大，我想是很有前景的。

那你喜欢我什么呢？珍妮这样问他已经有好几次了，因为每次他也没有回答得很具体。这一次他准备仔细回答，他整理了一下脑袋里面的思绪说道："先从美国，不，先从纽约说起吧，纽约有这么多的中国人，这些面孔对我来说是一种亲戚和血源的关系，美国人的游戏规则里绝对含有着它的文化因素，这样就有了隔阂，所以我面对一个美国女孩子的时候，我面对的是一个从形象到习惯都不一样的世界，但是让我面对一个同样也是从中国出来的人，我会带着伤痕来看待，我会想到她从我这儿得不到她想得到的东西，或者说因为我们都是从中国来的，所带的东西是一样的，互相解决不了什么问题，纽约就像一个集市，我们带着同样的货物都是为了换回美金，我们之间没有办法交换。也许这样说得比较露骨但必须这样才能说得清楚。于是我就认为出生在美国的中国人最适合我，因为形象上有了血源的亲近感，然后内心又没有在中国生活过的创伤感，你虽然不太会写中文，但会说，你的第一语言是英文，中文是你的第二语言，对我来说中文是我的第一语言，英文是第二语言，你就可以看出我们在这几个方面的互补关系，另外你教会了我如何做爱，还教会了我许多英文里面的东西，而我则教会了你许多中文里面的东西，当然你的漂亮也是我为之倾心的。"珍妮表示满意地点点头。他说其实我不太愿意这样逻辑性地进行分析，听上去像在作一桩生意，缺少了浪漫，你不觉得我刚才好像是在作报告，在总结公司几年来的业绩。珍妮说我从你的这个报告中更多地了解了你，你是一个会归纳事物的人才，在其他方面你也表现出来过，现在我就更加坚信了，你想我为什么喜欢你吗？他说你喜欢我是因为我野心勃勃。不，她说我喜欢你是因为你虽然在中国受过不少苦，但从来没有因为自己是中国人而感到自卑，我遇到过不少从中国出来的很自卑的中国人，他们有的说到了美国基本上不与中国人来往，因为中国人素质太低，所以有些这样的人就故意不说中文了，他们以为满口英文就可以脱离他（她）的中国背景了，还有一些人在许多场合都表示出对中国人的蔑视，这些人真的太肤浅了，你就不一样，你没有这种包袱，让我这个不是中国人的中国人感到平等。他说还有别的吗？她说当然，你的这种状态使美国女孩子也愿意与你交朋友，她们平时据我了解根本不考虑中国男人的，但是她们喜欢你，让我产生嫉妒感。另外你一直不让我在你冒险的生意上投入资金，虽然你的理由是万一输了我会对你失去信心，其实我觉得你是另有考虑，你考虑的是不要因为这点钱影响我的情绪，你是有设计的一个人，你跟我在一起是用两个人的未来来考虑步骤的，我说得对吗？他默默地点点头。他说如果那个公司不雇佣我的话你会因为我要有身分可以做生意而与我结婚吗？她说我想我会的，其实婚后不就是咱们现在这样过日子吗？

　　一年很快就又过去了，李雄的生意并没有什么起色，他被原来在中国时的同学欺骗了，货物发过去后，余下的一半货金再也没有汇过来，而且那边公司的电话也停掉了。李雄对珍妮说这个人野心太小，为了十万美金就把公司也关了，因为他如果再等半年，也许因为我的信任，他可以卷走更多的钱。这十万美金我东凑西拼也把一半的责任解决了，我现在又要从零开始了。珍妮说问题没有这么简单，你在这家美国公司留下了不好的记录，在同一个生意的领域里面会传来传去的，你的声誉就损失了很多，另外你还是太讲义气，做生意不是用感情去润滑的，是规则和合同，这些都必须在成交前搞清楚。你反正不够专业，也许这也是你的中国背景造成的，需要一段时间去清洗掉。

但是他又一次失败了。

抽大麻是不能解决的，珍妮虽然也与他一起抽，但她提醒他要振作起来。他又狠狠地吸了一口，并且紧闭住嘴地把烟咽进肚里，久久地才张嘴呼吸。他说我爷爷把血换成贫农的，会不会影响我的运气呢？她说你爷爷其实并没有真换，只是一种意愿和说法。他说我爷爷也让我换，我要换的话，必须换成哪个大富翁的才行。她说你是一个热心肠的人，也许可以做点其他的事情，不一定非要做生意。他说我退学就是为了做生意，怎么能不做呢？她说你就是把血换成酒精也还是没有用的，血液和性格决定了一个人的大部分行为。他站起来倒了一杯威士忌，也给她倒了一杯。又卷了一支大麻烟，默默的抽着喝着。珍妮知道自己因为他这两年来的生意上的失败也很沮丧，但又帮不上忙，因为她离毕业还有一年多，也就开始与他一起胡说八道起来。她说自己之所以出生在美国是因为她的父亲在英国读书的时候梦见将来的妻子是一个美籍华人，她说她身上的血液成分是奶酪和土豆组成的，她说她的梦想是要抱着帝国大厦睡觉。李雄就插嘴说她这是性幻想，是希望自己能怀上一座大楼，把它生下来以后就可以解决在纽约的住房问题。他又为她和自己倒了酒，摇摇欲坠地靠在墙脚对她说我一定要解决换血的问题，我爷爷的下意识肯定是来自上苍的指令，我爷爷说在另一个世界等我们，在我们去之前要把血换好，不然会受欺负的。她说你不觉得今天的大麻比以前的厉害吗？他说我没有感觉，只是感到自己能和一些很远的信息联系起来了，其中最主要的是能和我爷爷的内心有了对话的可能，以前我总认为他是一个病人，所以对他的所作所为毫不在乎，但今天我忽然领悟了其中的许多东西，中国人所谓的难得糊涂也许就是这么一个状态。她说你联系这些东西对你的生意不会有好处的，你应该有所选择地去联系信息，也许那些发了财的商人都有这种特异功能，而我好像没有这种特异功能，抽大麻之后你总是比我更能进入情绪。他说也不一定，也许你自己没有领悟到的东西会在第二天第三天才出现在你的脑袋里，我现在真的很舒服，我能感到我爷爷的呼吸，能感到他为我盖被子的时候总要说上一句"身体暖了恶梦就进不来了"的气氛，我能感到他在期待我换上贫农的血，但是现在时代变了，我要换的不再是贫农的而是亿万富翁的血，或者是天才的血。她说到哪儿去找亿万富翁的血呢？我从小就做梦可以住到纽约的长岛，那里有童话的气氛，一幢独立的小楼和周围的树林，尤其在圣诞节的时候，那种气氛至今都像一阵挥之不去的云雾。他说你这是不想长大的愿望，不算是发财的愿望。她说如果有了这些东西不就证明已经发财了吗？他说我们是要找到发财的能力，因为我们还要享受发财的经过！她说人家比尔盖兹几年就把他的电脑公司发展成世界最大的电脑公司，这不是侥幸的事情。他说那可口可乐公司就用一张配方就成为了世界最大的公司，几乎人人都喝可口可乐，人人的血液里都有可口可乐，对了，必须让可口可乐像血液一样流动在血管里面才能做一个成功的商人，因为几乎没有一家公司可以与可口可乐公司抗衡！对了，我爷爷肯定同意我把血液换成可口可乐的，你说呢？珍妮没有回答，他知道她已经睡着了。他很兴奋地自言自语着："可口可乐，我终于找到你了，你在我血管中一旦流动起来，什么样的生意我不能做成呢？我不再讲义气和使用感情，我将一帆风顺地把生意做起来！"他摇摇晃晃地走到冰箱那儿，拉开冰箱的门，发现里面有一立升的大瓶可口可乐，他笑了起来，声音大极了，但还是没有把珍妮吵醒。他把可口可乐拿在胸前，然后坐在沙发上想怎么才能让它流动在血液里面，他记得父亲怎样用针管给病人输血，但这是可口可乐，是应该用杯子来装的，但如何进入血管呢？他笑了，因为他听见爷爷在他耳边说："那就用针管吧！"他知道隔壁就有一个药品店，那里有一次性的针管。他跑出去买了两个回来，一个是抽血用的，一个是注射可乐的。当他真的拿起针管的时候，他犹豫了一下，但扎进去的时候没有疼痛的感觉，他高兴了，他知道这是爷爷在帮他的忙，他顺利地抽出了三管血，又顺利地输入了三管可乐，他对自己说："今天就先这样，这种激动人心的时刻要让珍妮亲眼看一看。"他去喊珍妮，她迷开一只眼睛说我的头很晕，让我再睡一会儿吧。他就松手把她放下了。他想不要太着急，反正用一个星期的时间来换也不长，当年爷爷换血的时候，前后输了二十次。他倒头睡去了。

他是被珍妮喊起来的，她说水池里面有黑色的东西。他说那是我的血，血冷了以后是黑色的。她说为什么是你的血？他说我们不是说了要把我身上的血换成可乐吗，这样就会在商场上战无不胜。她惊叫起来说你真的把可乐输进血管啦？他说那还有假吗？说着就撩起袖管给她看手臂上的针眼。她楞在那里不知道说什么了，因为他看上去没有任何异样，精神也不错。但她还是又问了一遍："你输了多少可乐？"他说三管，以后每天输几管，估计两个星期后就差不多了，到那时候您就看我如何在商场上驾驶云雾吧，你的长岛之梦都不算什么大事情了。

过了大约十几个小时，他对她说你也不必去读书了，这两个星期就陪着我，看我把血换完。现在是第二次。他边说边清理用过的针管。她说再去买两个新的吧。他说不需要，洗一洗就行了，况且咱们现在也没有什么钱了。她说我真的很害怕，我像是在梦里。他说你不是在梦里，是在一个新的纪元面前，你知道吗，这是我爷爷进入了我的灵魂，他在帮助我们，你放心吧，我爷爷这辈子没有享过福，我爸爸也没有，现在是我的机会了，中国人说话："上几辈子积的福轮到这辈子了。"他操作起来的时候珍妮闭起了眼睛，他大喊你给我睁开眼睛！她睁开了，也被看到的事实信服了，她看见血被抽出来，又看着可乐被输了进去。

两个星期就这样过去了，珍妮说你准备怎么开始你的生意呢？他说首先是要一笔资金。她通过这两个星期惊心动魄的换血行为之后，已经相信李雄会成功的了，所以她早在几天前就把自己在银行里面的钱全取出来了，一共是一千三百二十五块，她把它塞到他的手里。他说我要从股票开始，他拿起电话打给以前那个与他一起做过股票的朋友："请告诉我香港股市最近升得最快和跌得最快的是哪两种股票。""请把今天新上市的美国股票告诉我。""把中国最近准备上市的重庆市的股票告诉我。""我一会儿再给你电话。"当他再打电话过去的时候他是把所有手中的钱买了中国重庆市上市的电话公司的 B 股股票。然后他对珍妮说这要一个月或两个月以后才能见分晓，现在我们去把我的那辆破车卖掉，用这些钱去装修你舅舅开在下城的那家咖啡馆，算是我们的投资。

珍妮的舅舅一直对自己开的这家咖啡馆没有信心，所以已经有十年总是处在不死不活的状态中，当他们拿着卖车后得到的两千五百块出现在她舅舅面前时，舅舅感动地说你们真的愿意让这个咖啡馆开得兴旺吗？李雄说那当然，我知道你给咖啡馆起的名字是你死去的妻子的名字，我们想把它开好，所以我们认为必须重新装修一下，我们两个准备买些材料，然后自己动手来装修它，大概需要一个多星期，我们的条件是盈利的百分之二十归我们。舅舅笑着说如果能盈利，我可以给你们百分之五十，因为我最近五年几乎是在赔钱开的，其实就是为了纪念我死去的妻子，我曾发誓把这家以她名字开的咖啡馆营业到我死去为止，现在你们愿意接手的话，我愿意每星期来两天，其他时间让你们管，你们只要不向我再要钱就行，所有赚的钱全归你们。这好像是天上掉下来的馅饼，把李雄和珍妮乐坏了，他们说好明天开始进行装修。

他们这才意识到其实这个机会一直就在那里，以前为什么没有想到呢？为什么在李雄换好血之后就想起来了，唯一的解释就是可乐起了作用。珍妮对他说我真害怕你变得六亲不认，别的人你可以不认，但我你可不能也像可乐似地只为了盈利啊。李雄说你别担心，我事先已经想到可能会有这个后遗症，所以我已经在输血完成之前写了一个关于我所有财产的分配方法，其中一半是你的，而且写好如果没有你的签名我是不能修改的。你可以向吉姆律师去询问，但到目前为止我觉得对你还是充满了信心的，看来可乐只在生意的领域里起作用，但愿真的是如此。

咖啡馆被装修成美国电影里常常出现的监狱里食堂的样子，这个主意当然是李雄的可乐血液所产生的，新的广告词是这样的："进过监狱的可以到这儿来回味，没有进过的可以来尝尝"同时也用大盆子和大勺子来服务简单的饭菜。这当然在餐饮业成为了一个头条的新闻，尤其是游客，所以在重新开张的一个星期后只能接受预约，结果预约的队伍排到了两个月以后……

半年后重庆市电话系统的股票已经翻了几十倍，而咖啡馆则每天盈利一万块左右，因为他们还并吞了隔壁的一家家具店，使这个咖啡馆变成了纽约市最大的几家之一。各种报导接二连三地出现在各种报纸和刊物上，电视台也特别推出过几次专题的报导。而那些曾经进过监狱的人更是拉着朋友们来回味自己当时在监狱时的感觉，这些以前的犯人还提出一些更好的建议来使这个咖啡馆更加完美，所以说它受到了各界人士的爱护，许多其他城市的餐馆也向他们提出用他们的名字开分馆，所以光是同意以他们咖啡馆名字开的分店就使他们盈利了几百万，而且还只是刚开始，接下来的盈利分成就更是源源不断了，他们签了六十多个城市出让名字的分店，几乎美国的每个州都有了分店。无怪乎纽约时报的记者在一个报导上说："……它虽然不是快餐店，但它的气势比快餐店高级多了，它可以算作美国文化在世纪末的几大特点之一。"

于是有人要为他们写创业成功的传记，他们拒绝了，道理很简单，他们怕掀起一个全球性的把血换成可口可乐的高潮。珍妮则认为可以让人来写，只要隐瞒换血的情节就行了。但是李雄不同意，他认为这样也许会得罪给他灵感的爷爷，爷爷从来不隐瞒他想换血的意愿，所以他也不应该隐瞒，而目前最好的办法是什么也不说。

有一天李雄被邀请为一家新落成的文化俱乐部剪彩，当然是希望他能赞助一些资金，他大笔一挥就开了一张五万美金的赞助支票。剪彩后有一些文艺活动助兴，其中有一位诗人的朗诵给了他极其深刻的触动，因为那首被题为"纽约"的诗中有这么两句诗："纽约在世界的心脏里洗血，把血洗成流向地球各地的可口可乐！"他牢牢地记住了这两句诗，也记住了那个诗人的名字。他回家后把这两句诗念

给珍妮听，她以为这是他想出来的句子，当她知道是别人的诗句时，
就说看来这个意识也有他人在感悟，这个世界真需要一些冷酷的东
西来让它运转。他说我今天不是情绪一来才开了一张五万美金的支
票，而是我认为文化圈里面有一些奇怪的人，这些人不那么热衷于金
钱，而是热衷于揭发别人和自己，有一些观念的东西我认为是另一个
世界才需要的东西，比如这个诗人，他看上去很自信，但又指出这种
金钱世界的威力，他既然知道这个威力，为什么还要写诗呢？他应该
去挣钱才对，也就是说他想批判这种金钱的现象吗？但是这个世界
可能取消金钱的作用吗？金钱是一种最好的价值运转标准，我想不
出还会有什么更好的东西代替金钱来衡量劳动的价值，对了，我想把
这两句诗印在咱们餐馆的宣传品上，你觉得怎么样？珍妮想了想说
可能不太合适，因为这有点像替可乐公司做广告，另外这和你的餐馆
有什么关系呢？李雄说关系很简单，那是我自己心里的意愿，它和我
身上的可乐有关系，再加上我遇到这个能和我不谋而合的人，证明了
他有什么地方与我是一样的。她说你可以去做，但首先你要获得这个
诗人的同意。他说那当然，我会让秘书去找到他的。

　　诗人名叫维尔钦，他走进李雄办公室的那一瞬间，李雄的脑子里
闪出一个与这个诗人玩玩游戏的想法，他对维尔钦说我想把你关于
洗血的诗句印在我的一些宣传品上，但是我不知道这样的话我应该
付你多少钱？维尔钦耸耸肩膀说您看着办，我也没有遇到过这种事
情，不知道应该是怎么个做法。李雄就假装很认真地说我可以给你五
十块美金。维尔钦的脸上毫无表情地说可以，反正诗写出来是让大家
看的，这五十块钱你不给我也没关系，因为我也从来没想过要用诗来
挣钱。李雄就很有兴趣地问你用什么来养活你自己呢？诗人回答说
我在一家复印店工作，业余时间写诗，而这个工作也仅仅是为了保证
我能继续写诗，如果我有钱我会专业地进行写诗，其他什么也不做，
我写诗已经十几年了。李雄问出过诗集吗？诗人说出过两本。那么卖
诗集能挣钱吗？诗人说我已经告诉过你写诗不可能挣钱，是为了表
达自己对世界和人类社会的看法。那么你的关于纽约在世界心脏洗
血的观念能具体解释一下吗？诗人眼光里显出一丝兴奋地说这就是

说生意是不讲感情的，生意需要的是产品，产品是没有感情的物质，如果说产品具有感情，那是人为移入的，比如你与你家里的一个台灯有感情，是因为你使用了很长的时间，习惯了它，换一个的话会觉得不适应，所以我认为这个世界以它越来越多的商业行为影响了人们更少的感情行为，所以说如果能把产生感情的血液换成可口可乐，人类就会少一些麻烦和自相矛盾。李雄听到换血这个词的时候感到被刺了一下，心想这个诗人也有这个想法，他对诗人说那到底能不能把血换成可口可乐呢？诗人笑了起来说你觉得可行吗？李雄说我认为可以试试。诗人继续笑着说你可以当诗人！李雄说我就是诗人，是行为上的诗人。接着他话锋一转地说你既然说我不付你钱也可以用你的这两句诗，那么你能不能在一个这样的合同上签字？诗人耸耸肩说当然可以。说着就从自己的口袋里面掏出一枝笔准备签字。李雄走到隔壁嘱咐秘书马上打出一份合同。他回来对诗人说我没有不付钱的习惯，这样吧，下个月我公司总盈利的百分之十归你，就一个月，我也说不清楚是多少钱，到时候我秘书会通知你来取支票，另外我愿意和你交个朋友，每个星期五晚上我都会在下城百老汇我的那个餐馆吃饭，你随时可以来和我一起吃饭聊天。诗人说如果你下个月没有盈利，反尔亏了的话，我是否要负担亏损的百分之十？李雄哈哈大笑了起来说你不知道最近我的生意有多好吗？你没有看报纸上经常有介绍吗？诗人摇摇头说我真的不知道。李雄叹了一口气说到底是诗人，诗能让人保持一些非主流的东西，所以诗人绝不会成为流行的。诗人说你不是要把我的诗句变成流行的吗？我真担心我的诗会影响你的生意。李雄说我是商人，是不会干亏本买卖的，为什么我不能利用诗来帮助我的生意呢？诗人说诗是很难被商业利用的，综观大部分的文学艺术，已经被商业全部利用起来了，我不认为那是坏事情，但诗确实难住了商人，同时也难住了诗人自己，我不认为诗人就不喜欢钱，但是不知道为什么，诗就是不能卖钱，可是许多人很固执地认为诗是人类不可缺少的精神，你看诺贝尔文学奖，半数以上是奖给诗人的。李雄说我要试试，最起码你的这两句诗要和我的商业连在一起了。秘书进来把打好的合同交给他，他看了一遍后就在一式两份上都签了字，然后交给诗人签，诗人看都不看地就签了。李雄把其中的一份给了诗人，然后是握手告别。

李雄把与诗人的会面经过转述给珍妮听，她听的很有兴趣，她说诗人是一种偏激的人，他们把写诗当一个孩子来养，挣钱是为了能养活这个"孩子"。李雄则说我认为诗是一种文学里面的宗教，不然为什么这种平时不被人关心的东西却可以经常得到诺贝尔奖呢？珍妮说对啊，你一说到使我想起来了，为什么呢？它是宗教吗？他说既然这个诗人能有把血换成可口可乐的想法，就证明有冥冥之中的东西在召唤，就像我爷爷召唤我那样。你说我能算商人吗？我只不过是利用了一种别人还没有发现的方法打开了脑袋中的一把锁，然后我就能更快的发现商业机会里面可以开发的东西，我不受感情之血液的影响了，我觉得我只是一个发明者，不是商人。珍妮开玩笑地说你不是商人也不是发明者，你是诗人！他说我可不会写诗。她说你可以用行为写啊，你的换血行为就是维尔钦的诗句的行为，所以你是一个用行为写诗的人。他说这样也对，可是诗是挣不了什么钱的。她说你不是让维尔钦用两句诗就挣了最起码八万美金吗？咱们公司上个月的盈利是八十万不到一点，下个月起码是八十万到一百万，因为下个月有三家分店同时开张，会有更多的分成转如咱们的帐户，所以维尔钦可能会得到十万。他说这样的话维尔钦就要变成专业诗人了，因为他说他有了一些钱的话就会专门写诗不干其他的了，我倒愿意交他这个朋友。珍妮说你应该交这个朋友，因为只有他具有把血换成可口可了的想象，你们应该是有血缘关系的。他说你这么一说我倒是觉得可以让他为我们写传记，他会写得有声有色，因为他也有这种想法，你觉得呢？她说是可以考虑的，只不过一旦发表后就会有许多人也去换血，这个世界就乱了。他说已经发现的东西迟早要暴光的，只是早一点和晚一点的事情，我倒是有欲望想看看世人的反应，那一定会很有意思，我现在都能想象舆论为这一事件所进行的风卷云涌。她说还是应该再考虑一下，不必这么快就作决定。

李雄还是在两个星期后约了维尔钦，他对诗人说你有没有兴趣写我的传记？诗人说没有什么兴趣，因为有很多更好的专门写传记的作家，你为什么要找我呢？他说是有专业的作家想写，但是他们不一定能写好，其中的原因是很关键的，如果我说出了让你惊讶的事情，你会不会同意写呢？诗人说那要看是什么让我惊讶的事情了，这个世界上还会有什么值得惊讶的事情吗？李雄说一般来说是没有什么值得惊讶的事情了，能发生的都发生了，不过发生在我身上的事情就不同了，因为它以前从来也没有发生过，这一点我是可以向你保证的。诗人说那你就说来听一听。李雄说请原谅我这么拖拖拉拉，因为我真的很愿意由你来写，而且你也会觉得只有你才能写的好这个题材，我就告诉你吧，我是第一个把血换成可口可乐的人，我身上流动的是可口可乐！诗人摇着头表示不相信。李雄就把诗人领进一个密室，当着他的面抽出一管似血非血的东西，然后输进一管可乐。李雄还解释说我每个星期都要抽出几管血输入几管可乐。诗人惊讶地说那么就是说我的诗给了你这个灵感？李雄说在听到你的诗之前我就已经换好很长时间了，但你是我所知道的第一个也有这个想法的人，所以你就知道我为什么非找你写不可了，你现在觉得你想写吗？诗人点点头说那么也就是说换完可乐之后你真的在生意上得心应手了？李雄得意地说在短短的时间里我已经是千万富翁了，并且马上就会成为亿万富翁。

维尔钦用了将近两个星期的时间写成了二十万字的一本传记，李雄和珍妮读后仅仅让他修改了几个小错误之后就发表了，引起的轰动是巨大的，但质疑的文章也有很多，最激烈的一个社会批评家和两个医学院的研究室主任联名向法院控告李雄和维尔钦，理由是他们哗众取宠，而且会误导没有独立思考能力的青少年们去尝试换血而导致死亡等等。李雄和维尔钦在一次电视采访中是这样答辩的：我们不相信换血的事情是每个人都能做到的，可能只有少数的人有这种生理上的可能，最起码在李雄的身上实现了，它没有被排斥，如今他还每个星期换几管血，必要的时候可以公开进行，让公众能亲眼看到，另外，我们可以在这里读一段书中的描写：（李雄的爷爷就是一个相信能不按血型换血的人，他在1992年因为得了坏血病需要换血，在不断的治疗和换血的过程中运用他的意识把他身上地主的血换成贫农的血，因为他相信自己有这个意识上的能力，而这个能力显然也遗传到他孙子李雄的身上了，当然也完全有可能他会在另一个世界里帮助他的孙子顺利地进行换血的意愿。）我们在讲一个已经发生的事情，这当然需要研究，但如果把李雄囚禁到一个医学院去的话是需要他自己同意的，不然就是违反人权的，而李雄在这里表示他不会同意，他要享受自己的生活。

事情到了这个地步李雄愿意在电视上进行一次换血的操作，但最后没有实现是因为考虑到别人的效仿，因为此书发行的第一个星期里面就有几十个人试着自己换血而被送到医院去抢救。法院唯一的办法是让医院对李雄的血液进行一次化验，看看里面到底是什么成分。政府为此事件成立的一个调查小组认为所有的调查应该秘密进行，决不对外界报导，另外这本书也先压一压，停止销售。当李雄和珍妮以及维尔钦在一所秘密的诊所里面与调查人员一起等待血液化验的结果时，所有的人都表情极其严肃，只有珍妮和李雄很轻松地聊着公司里面的事情，化验人员把结果交给调查小组的组长时摇着脑袋说里面有许多可口可乐的成分。

而美国政府关于这个调查结果的批示是：与李雄和所有知情者定一个五年严守此一秘密的合同，给政府这段时间在医学上研究这一特殊的现象，五年以后可能会再签一个延长几年的合同。而此书只能用科幻小说的广告来推销。

但是李雄还是请了律师来为自己辩护，因为这样一来他会被认为是一个招摇撞骗的人，他的名誉损失将是无法弥补的，因为报纸和电视都有过大量的报导，不可能就这么被压住了，所以怎么来处理这个令政府头疼的事情呢？伤透了脑筋的有关人员提出了许多解决的方案都不理想。最后只有一个方案也许可行，政府官员单独找到了维尔钦。

官员说现在唯一的办法是你来承担这个事情的结局，办法是这样的：你因为写出了那两句诗之后希望能变成现实，其实你这时已经得了臆想症，你找到一个突然在商业上成功的人李雄来证明你的臆想可以变成事实，你利用李雄总想与众不同的心理来为他写传记，并说服了李雄同意用你的想象力来编造故事，因为这样就会与以往所有成功者的传记不同。

维尔钦说如果我同意会对我怎么样呢？官员说那就要你接受记者的采访来把这样的一个"事实"说出去，万一有人控告你，会以精神病患者的名义让你不会受到任何刑事上的处分。而经济上来说，会有人来买下你这本书的各种各样的版权。维尔钦说这样说来我的名誉就会有一些损失。官员说那你有什么要求？他想了想说我的要求是政府在纽约的时代广场租下一个大型广告牌，上面是那两句关于洗血的诗句，我的要求是租用一年。官员说这样不行，因为你没有那么多的钱，会引起各种猜测，把此事弄得更加复杂。诗人说如果李雄能掏这个钱，政府会不干涉吗？官员说给我们两天的时间，两天以后再讨论。

维尔钦当然把此事告诉了李雄，李雄说看来也只能这样了，既然政府出面了，而且也算为我们的处境有所考虑，我们还能怎么样呢，况且这个事情确实奇异，按常识来讲，大众也不太会相信我们，所以大众显然是会站在政府方面的。关于广告牌的租金我绝对能出，但我认为政府会不同意的，那么怎样才能使我们在这件事情上不那么委屈呢？诗人说确实有一些年青人受此书影响而试着换血被送到医院去抢救，这一点我有责任，所以我只好委屈一下了，常言道诗人是社会的良心，但你的事情又是真实的，所以在真实和救人之间我的良心就先救人了。真实的事情十年后还是真实的。

政府官员说广告牌的想法不可行，因为你的诗句可能会引起可口可乐公司的控告，因为他们会认为你是在诽谤可口可乐，官员还顺口背出了他的诗句："纽约在世界的心脏里洗血，把血洗成流向地球各地的可口可乐！"虽然说不上谁能赢，但肯定会引起许多不必要的麻烦和经济上的负担，你或者有其他什么想法吗？诗人说我已经烦了，让我继续写我的诗吧，我没有其他想法了。官员极其高兴地与他握了手。因为他们算是圆满地解决了这个事件。

1997.3.于纽约曼哈顿

一百美元

在街上演奏，招来一些过路客，也招来一些知音。当然，有人马上会想起招来一些收入，有些收入甚至令上班的人羡慕。老实说，我上街去吹笛子完全是受了挑拨——我的一个朋友张先生，他也是从中国来美国的留学生，他认为我的笛子应该在街上一边吹一边给过路人钱，因为吹得太难听，而不是过路人给我钱。我和张先合租一个公寓单元，天天受他的嘲讽。我又别无其它的爱好，所以，从中国带来的一根最普通的笛子成了我留学美国时最重要的消遣节目了。可是张先生非说那是应该倒给钱的一种音乐，如果我真敢上街像美国人那样演奏的话。

第一次上街演奏，我站在街边看准我准备要去的那个街角，心中设想着我站在那里时的模样。那模样很像一个音乐家，悠然自得，把满街的汽车当作牛羊一样看待……但是我又担心美国人不懂我吹的是笛子，这种笛子我从来没看见美国人用它来把自己培养成音乐家。我从斜挎在肩的书包里抽出这根笛子，笛膜很牢靠地粘在上面，半透明地呈现出一些幻想，我在准备创造我自身的历史，一个新的起点将要开始！冒险吧！哥们，我拍自己的肩膀。我鼓足了勇气向那个准备占领的街角挪过去。这时应该是下午 5 点。张先生说好了 6 点钟要来看我怎样倒给过路人钱。

现在我已很牢靠地站在应该站的街角上了——美国纽约市百老汇大街的下城的一个街角上。我松了一口气，把脚步又挪了几下，感到真的站牢了。我没有马上想到演奏，我想的是以前我在街上看美国人演奏的经验。我也想到了在地铁站里那些演奏者，其中许多人也是外国人，他们放在地上的一顶破帽子或者一只琴箱里被过路客放了不少硬币，偶尔也有不少纸币。我今天准备的是用一张美国花旗银行的广告叠成的纸盒子，看上去还挺有艺术味的。这也算是我观察美国生活的一种灵感来源吧。

5点20分，确切地说是公元1988年7月1日下午5时20分我把我的嘴向笛孔凑上去，双手的架势很紧张，我的呼吸更紧张，这时候纽约百老汇街头的人来人往以及车辆拥挤的景象很难被当作是放牧牛羊。我不得不面对现实——目前需要的是勇气！这到底是不是有点丢面子我已弄不清楚了，我只感到一种对我自己性格的挑战！为什么那么多不同国家的人都能很自然地在街头演奏，甚至不把过路人以及围观者放在眼里而很享受地演奏着自己的音乐？为什么我那么紧张？我想起中国的一句老话：街头卖唱的！这多少带点儿辛酸味和所谓旧社会的味道。我的嘴唇发干，我舔了又舔，手腕上的表已指在5点23分了，我的嘴已经在笛孔上待了3分钟之久而没有吹奏，我一闭眼，连着吹了几个单音试试音调，同时把手指起落一番活跃一下。我眯开一点眼，发现有三两个人已站在离我三、四米远的地方等候了。我马上把眼又闭上，开始吹我的拿手好曲——《十五的月亮》。然后又吹了《深深的海洋》和《社会主义好》。当我吹到十五的月亮结尾的时候，我的眼睛已经睁开了。但不是看观众，而是看月亮还没出来的晴空。那时候正巧有一架直升飞机在高空飞过，一个这样的念头闪过——那驾驶员扔出一枚硬币，很准地落在我摆在地上的纸盒里！吹到《社会主义好》的时候，我已完全放松下来了。甚至脚也开始打起节拍来了。有几个围观的人还鼓了掌，不过，我真的已经汗流满面，我用纸擦汗又擦手心、笛子，我缓了一口气又吹了几首，这时候，我发现世界与我的音乐节奏一致了，不像半小时以前那种混乱状态了。有几枚硬币落在纸盒里叮当有声，我听起来比我的笛声好听，我想张先生也应该听到了，尽管他还没出现，有一个观众过来与我聊天，聊了几句发现我的英语语法一会跳远一会跳高就放弃了与我长聊的打算，但他从口袋里摸出一张5元的纸币，他的手在空中停顿了有五分之一秒的时间，以示他对我的欣赏与支持，然后放进了我的纸盒。我发现我的纸盒正好有一行英文字："lt　is　your bank……Citibank！"我暗暗乐了，里面已经有些钱了，现在是 5 点 45 分，张先生还没到。"它是你的银行——花旗银行！"纸盒子上的英文字译成中文后也许更有味。我又开始吹我刚才吹过的那几首曲。眼前已看不到刚才的观众，站在四周的七八个人全是新的过路客。6 点钟过了 4 分钟时张先生到了，他在围观的几个人旁边冲着我笑，这种笑是认输的笑，因为他很清楚地看到了我脚下纸盒里的一堆钱。第一次收获差不多是 40 元，准确地讲是 39 元 8 角 5 分，我吹奏了不到 3 个小时。我收拾起纸盒离开街角时是 8 点零 7 分。我请张先生吃了肯塔基炸鸡。我和他都觉得这天的炸鸡特别香。后来我几乎每个星期都上街吹奏三四次，没有什么特别的故事发生。但有一件事我必须用它来作为结尾，因为不讲这件事，我的这个故事的名字就表现不出来了。

那是发生在我第 7 次上街吹奏，我的一个观众很热情地在我吹了几支曲子后上来与我交谈。他看上去四十几岁，标准的商人打扮，一身整洁浅色的西服，领带是斜条的，拎着一个公文包。一股淡淡的香水味从他身上飘出。他掏出一张 100 美元的纸币递给我，而不是放在地上的纸盒里，他指着那个用银行广告叠的纸盒说他喜欢这个主意，这是个绝妙的主意！他另外又从口袋里掏出几张一元的纸币和几个硬币投进纸盒，很欣赏地看着他的钱在纸盒里的模样，他一句也没提到要对我的音乐怎么样，他临走时给我一张名片并且说他希望我一直使用这纸盒在街上吹奏，我感动地说着谢谢。他走远了。我端详这张名片，上面的头衔是：花旗银行副总经理。

婚礼

那是一张婚礼的请帖，我发现地点是在纽约市的画廊区。新郎是一位从中国来的画家苏发，而新娘也是一位中国人，叫陆莲子。苏发与我是在纽约认识的，交往很频繁，但没有发现过他身边曾有这么一个可以与其成婚的陆莲子，这一点使我很吃惊。上个星期我还与苏发一道喝酒打牌，而现在突然收到他于两个星期后结婚的请帖。我脑中浮现出苏发那种神秘的表情，他的眼睛比一般人眨得快也更加频繁，正像常人说的那种鬼点子很多的眨法。我只在牌桌上听他讲起他妈妈最近几天将从北京来纽约探亲，探她这个六年多没见面的儿子。牌桌上有人说这个儿子探不探不重要，因为他太怪异了。这点我同意，苏发原先是画抽象画的，到了美国后搞起观念艺术来了，他比较有名的一件观念作品是为报纸改日期，他把去年的日期贴在今年的，还把将来的也用上了，结果许多内容变成以前或以后发生的，而我印象比较深的是冬天的日期但内容是夏天的热浪袭人，几位老人因太热引起中暑而去世了。苏发还搞了其它一些观念作品使他给人的印象很前卫也很怪异。不过他在街上为人画肖像挣钱时倒是画得很写实逼真。我打电话给他询问从哪儿跑出来的这么一个新娘。他哈哈大笑地说是上帝安排的机遇，是在一家咖啡馆遇到的，也是画画的同行，而且也是从北京来的。他说这叫真正的一见钟情，躲也躲不掉的生活作品。我仔细询问了陆莲子的情况，得到的印象是蛮不错的，她才二十三岁，比苏发小十四岁，是国内新起的一批前卫画家中受人注意的一位。来美国才一年多，她在国内就听说过苏发，所以俩人一搭就热，真是躲也躲不掉。我想起苏发曾经在纽约追逐一位跳舞的女子，两年多下来最后还是没成的浪漫故事。苏发说他妈妈已经到了，而他又闪

193

电式地准备结婚，他妈妈一定太高兴了。苏发说他妈妈的嘴要不是有两只耳朵挡着，不然真要裂到后脑勺去了。我的另几位画友也打电话向我表示对苏发的艳遇及马上决定结婚感到新奇和吃惊，而我很自然地把自己的看法说了出来，那就是苏发在纽约六年多来没有过一位真正的女朋友，而他已经三十七岁了，也该是时候了，不然也太不走运了吧，而且他又那么能说会道，一副老纽约的样子肯定把那位叫陆莲子的同行唬得一愣一愣的，再加上他长得也不错，又开一辆兜风的二手跑车，以前没有碰到合适的女孩子肯定是情运还没有到，而如今一到就不可收拾了，所以非结婚不可，而且上帝还在这个时候让他妈妈远赴重洋来探亲，赶上这个独身儿子的婚礼，看来今年苏发的运是转到了最佳时刻。另外，苏发把婚礼安排在画廊里是因为他正好也安排了一个展览，还有什么事能比这个发生得更好的吗？我很羡慕苏发，这是多么戏剧性的时刻啊，人的一生中如果有这么一次也可以很欣慰了。与我自己的遭遇相比，唉，我结过两次，离过两次，每一次都只维持了不到两年，现在还有一个孩子要与第一位妻子共同抚养。我画的画也没有画廊可以展出，更是不好卖，只好每天打工，周末上街画肖像，唉，人比人气死人。不过，苏发的这种时来运转我想也会轮到我的，我比苏发小四岁，我希望四年中也会有这么一次，但我不会像他那样马上就结婚，我被前两次的婚姻搞怕了，也怀疑自己虽然结过两次婚，但对女孩子还是不够了解。在苏发婚礼前几天我打电话给他，问他是否要帮忙，他谢绝了。我特意去买了一件礼物，准备去参加婚礼时奉上。

婚礼是下午五点开始，至九点。我因为是他的好朋友，就在四点多一点到了那家画廊，苏发与画廊的两位工作人员已经布置完了。又是展厅又是礼堂的气氛很浓，我发现所有的作品都是与爱情交往有关的。苏发搬出了他那看家本领，几幅放大的他与陆莲子的野外游玩的照片很是夺目，尤其照片上的日期分别是半年或三年前的，也就是说他照相时故意把相机上的日期拨到以前，这样就制造了他与陆莲子已相识了很久的假象。另外，他还把几封他与陆莲子的通信用镜框镶上，信上的日期有六年前的，还有三年后的。信中的内容也是乱搬的，搬得也很有意思。比如他对在国内的陆莲子说他很怀念北京的帝国大厦，因为从那上面可以看到她家阳台上晒着乳罩。他还说他对纽约的自行车人流感到新奇，所以决定去买一辆送给她在北京街上骑，那一定很时髦。

另外有两封信是讨论如何教育他们将来的两个孩子，而陆莲子认为双语教育很重要，谈到一定要让孩子在家说中文，在外说英文。苏发说应该每说一句话都用中文和英文说一遍，但又马上说这样也许太像口译员了，不过可以试试。我一边看一边笑。这时候苏发把刚进来的新娘介绍给我，我发现她长得很聪明，但不漂亮，她指指满墙的作品，告诉我那是她和苏发在不到一个星期中赶制出来的，主要的灵感是苏发的，她只是提供一些意见。我问她是否已决定将来要生两个孩子，她很爽快地点点头。这时候苏发的妈妈到了，我一看到苏发的妈妈穿一身牛仔服就知道这是苏发的主意，没想到这身牛仔服是陆莲子昨天带她去买的。特别使我惊讶的是陆连子穿的婚礼衣服是她自己用餐巾缝出来的，各种颜色的。我心想这两个真是天生的一对，他们天生就有玩艺术的天赋。这时候已经到了七、八十人，时间是五点整。仪式开始是由画廊老板致词，老板说他对这个展览与婚礼结合在一起感到兴奋，他说这是一个实际生活与艺术展览结合在一起的典范。最后他还感谢一家中文和一家英文电视台前来摄制这个完美的夜晚。苏发和陆莲子交换戒指的时候全体鼓掌了好几分钟，而苏发与陆莲子把各自的戒指又从手指上脱下来互换了好几次，最后还互相问哪一个是他或她的，逗得全场大笑。有人在喊接吻，苏发和陆莲子并不互相接吻，而是各人从口袋里取出一张纸，纸打开后上面写着一千个吻和小心艾滋病，然后由陆莲子把两张纸叠在一起放进一个事先写好地址的极大的信封里，信封上的地址是月球，而邮票是登月的图案。陆莲子用涂了鲜红唇膏的嘴吻了几下信封，造成了几个红色的唇印以示邮戳。然后在掌声中由陆莲子把这一硕大的信用图钉按在墙上，显然又是一件作品。接下来是介绍一些特殊来宾并且大开香槟酒，许多人都在看挂在那里的信，当然我们这些老朋友把礼物堆在一个角落之后就聊开了。这是一个极其成功而又奇特的婚礼。我抓了个空跑去与苏发的母亲聊天，她真的很是高兴，尤其这时候画廊已挤得水泄不通，两家电视台的人站在高凳上拍得极其起劲。我说她儿子很会表演，这种表演是观念艺术的一部份，她问我什么叫做观念艺术，我只好简单地说即是一种丰富人们思考方法的艺术，它不仅仅局限在视觉上。这时候中文电视台的摄相机过来了，采访者要让这位妈妈谈谈感受，我让到一边，听她如何回答，她说她此次是来探儿子，没想到还能碰上儿子的婚礼，尤其是她原先一点都不知道的情况下，使她兴奋之极，因为她一直在为儿子的婚事担心。她对自己儿子的评价是太任性而且分别六年多来一点也没变。她对陆莲子很满意，认为虽然才二十三岁但显得很成熟。采访者又问她希望有几个孙子孙女时，她很机灵地说应该去问那小俩口。于是摄相机就去追踪人堆里的苏发和陆莲子，这时候我注意到画廊门口有人在发放什么东西，就跑过去看。那是两个画廊的工作人员，其中一个问我是不是要离开，我看看表，才八点半，就说还不准备离开。他们说离去前才能发这封信，而且信封上写着必须在离开画廊半小时后才能拆开来看。我看看那一箱信，心想这也许又是一个什么怪招，反正离开后会真相大白的。我又跑去与苏发干杯庆祝。苏发与陆莲子正与几个人在聊为什么这个展览只办一个晚上，有人建议可以再进行一、两个晚上，而苏发说这是一次性处理的。第二次是无法进行的。为什么呢？没有回答，陆莲子只说马上就会明白的。天下没有不散的宴席，我告别后拿了一封在门口发给每一个离去者的信，在坐上地铁后迫不及待地拆封打开。几行字凸现在眼前：

　　亲爱的朋友：
　　这是一次为婚礼而设计的婚礼，我们的作品。婚礼的两个人没有以前也没有以后，一切开始在画廊里，一切又都结束在画廊里，没有实际生活的延伸。是一场今晚五点至九点的表演。谢谢大家的参与。
　　　　　　　　　　　　　　　　　　　　苏发、陆莲子
　　　　　　　　　　　　　　　　　一九九二年七月于纽约

我打电话给苏发是第二天的事,他说一切都结束了。我问他真的与陆莲子不会结婚吗?他说当然不会,这是一个展览,这个展览的主题必须由一男一女来完成。我说陆莲子不错,也许以后会产生什么也说不定。苏发说不可能,陆莲子早已结婚,而且说好是共同设计此一展览。我说那么你妈妈也是事先知道的了,也就是说她也参与了表演。他说她也只到最后拆信时才知道,多少有点生气。不过,这是一种新的经验,使她多少有点线索去感受什么叫做观念艺术了。我很是感叹地想象着他妈妈在不知道真相之前是如何地高兴,而在真相大白后又是如何地哭笑不得。苏发这小子真的是有点走火入魔,玩笑开到他妈妈头上去了。我说我能与你妈妈聊两句吗?他说可以。他妈妈显然已从震惊中缓过来了,她说这种事只有在美国这种社会里才会发生,她认为画廊老板以及苏发和陆莲子都有点不正常,不过,她说整个婚礼过程倒是挺感人的。

以后的几天我一直在注意报纸和电视台如何报导这个事情,当我看到后,认为他们对这个观念艺术的表演的分析不那么准确,我总觉得这个表演引起了我思维上的一些东西。它们是些什么我暂时还归纳不出来。反正那是些深度上的东西和破坏性的,都可以用艺术形式来表达,而某些创新的形式正是人类为了迎合自己新的历史时期而产生的,二十世纪与十九世纪不同,二十世纪上半叶与下半叶也不同,甚至一九九二年与一九九一年不同,……总之,在这里我也顺便请那些没有在那天参加婚礼的人按我所描述的去亲临其境地想象一番,也许会悟出一些我还无法归纳成文字的感受,如果谁有兴趣,我们还可以约上苏发和陆莲子一起见见面。我的名字和地址如下:

Wedding1992

P.O.Box418

NewYork,NewYork10013

U.S.A

谢谢!

石雕的故事

最早的梦总是最清晰，我的可以被称为人生之梦的第一次是很久很久以前，但我对它有不少次脑袋里面的复习，所以它是不会褪色的，反尔更加色彩化了。随着历史事件的沉积，当时的梦想也不过是很简单的事情：我想有一台照相机。

照相机其实已经不是这个梦想的主体部分了，因为我为什么想得到它是最关键的，如果没有那个原因我就不会想到照相机。那是在公元 1965 年冬天的时候，我住在上海，我还不十分懂得什么叫预兆，尤其是政治预兆，所以文化大革命是怎样发生的我也就无从谈起。我住的地方是一个庭院式的小楼，庭院很大，庭院前面靠近大门的地方有一个人物的石雕，后面靠近小楼的地方也有一个，它们的形象虽然很接近，但不一样的是性别，世界上有男女两性，所以有了这两种性别的石雕，如果性别有四种或五种，那么就要有四个或五个才能以示区别。既然是两个，也就简单多了，事实上两个已经很复杂了，它有写不完的故事，而且每天还在发生新的故事。

有一天早上，天气很冷，从我睡觉的房间看出去发现庭院好像被冻小了，也许是热胀冷缩的原因吧，庭院大门也被冻小了，但门框却没小，所以几乎能看见风像人一样从门缝处往里钻，先进脑袋后进身体，我当时就想笑我自己，因为事实上风是翻过围墙进来的。我想起昨天傍晚舅舅给我照相时把我的围巾放在前面那个男石雕的脖子上忘了拿回来了。昨天舅舅很高兴地给我照相是因为要把照片寄给我的在其他城市工作的父母，我的父母为什么不在上海工作是很容易解释清楚的，那就是为了理想也为了工资。但工资和理想难道在上海就不能完成了吗？最好的解释是有人安排了谁应该在哪儿工作和居住，这就是权力，我父母没有安排自己的权力，他们是生出来就没有还是后来失去的？我那个时候不会提出这种问题，而现在也已经不觉得这是个问题，因为一台机器上的两个不同的零件不会互相提出为什么你被安装在那里我被安装在这里的问题。我离开房间去拿围巾的时候，发现我的围巾在小楼门口的女石雕的脖子上，但昨天明明是被我放在庭院前面的男石雕的脖子上的，用我小小年纪的记忆力按医学原理来讲是不会错的，但想象力呢？我想象这是谁把它拿过来的，最简单的就是问一问这个小楼里所有的人，结果谁也没有见到过我的围巾，舅舅说如果谁看见了你的围巾是会拿进房间的，不会从一个石雕放到另一个石雕的身上去，他还说这是最简单的逻辑。

晚上奶奶说明天的气温还会下降，让我上学时要多穿衣服。睡觉前我又想起了围巾的事情，用我有限的想象力想到也许是男石雕让给女石雕戴了，可是石雕是不会动的，它怎么可能从庭院前面走到庭院后面来呢，但我还是不能没有解释，我就又把围巾放到庭院前面的男石雕的脖子上才回来睡觉。第二天早上我从窗口看出去，围巾又被戴在了窗口下面的女石雕的脖子上了，我知道自己发现了一个奇迹，于是也没有对奶奶和舅舅讲，我想晚上再把围巾放到男石雕的脖子上，然后不睡觉地守在窗口看看到底是如何发生的。

这晚我很激动，关了灯后就守在窗口一动不动地望着庭院前面的戴着围巾的男石雕。街上的路灯可以照到庭院里，所以庭院里有什么动静是很容易看到的。我大约守了有两个小时后就在窗口处睡着了，醒来时男石雕脖子上的围巾已经到了女石雕的脖子上。我只好上床睡觉。但我做了一个梦，梦中奶奶对我说男人要有男人的样，如果只有一条围巾就要把围巾让给女的，你是男的，以后要让着女孩子，因为你的力气比她们大。我醒来后就想象出晚上我在窗口处睡着的时候，是男石雕走到女石雕的身边把围巾给了她，但是石雕能走吗？而且我从来没有看见过会走的石雕。当我又一次守在窗口的时候，我极力克制自己不能睡觉，我用一枚大头针扎自己的手指，我终于看见男石雕走动起来了，更加惊讶的是女石雕也走动起来了，他们的动作有点像多少年后我在美国看见的机器人，他们相会在庭院的中间，男石雕把手抬起来，取下围巾给女石雕戴，但女的把他的手推开，意思是让他戴，这时候北风刮得围巾乱抖，我在窗口真的很担心万一没有拿住被刮掉怎么办。男石雕确实比女石雕有力气，他推开女石雕的手，最后还是把围巾戴在了她的脖子上。女石雕往前面走去，她让男石雕到后面去，我看懂了她的意思，她是说既然让她戴上围巾，那么就让她站在风比较大的庭院前面，我心中暗暗希望男石雕别同意这个主意，因为他们对调位置的话，会被我家的人发现，我希望他们的这个秘密不被其他人发现，一旦被发现我也不知道会有什么样的后果，总之我在给男石雕使劲，想让他别同意对调位置。果然他拉住了她，并把她推向庭院后面的方向，她并不马上往回走，而是把围巾取下来给他戴，意思是很清楚的：谁在风大的地方就让谁戴。我马上想到自己还有一条围巾，可以明天给他们，这样就没有这种让人掉泪的谦让了。不过我还是提醒自己每天早上要在其他人没有看见石雕上的围巾之前把围巾拿掉，而在睡觉之前再去给他们戴上。

　　第二天我在睡觉前悄悄给他们一人一条地戴好，我也想知道这样的话他们晚上还会不会走动，因为不需要谦让围巾了。事实上他们还是走动的，因为我给女石雕的那条比男的长一些，也厚一些，结果这个晚上她坚持换了一下围巾，因为他站在风口处，所以要戴长一点和厚一点的。后来的几个晚上他们也会走到一起说点什么，虽然我听不见，我就想到了一个主意。我对奶奶和舅舅说为什么不把两个石雕放在一起，而是分开放。奶奶说他们能保护咱们家，前面是一道防线，后面还是一道防线，是可以辟邪的。我说这样不合理，如果邪能把前面的男石雕打败，就更能打败后面的女石雕，因为男的比女的力气大，如果他们在一起就有更大的力气。此话把奶奶问住了，舅舅说这很有道理。于是就把女石雕挪到前面和男石雕放在一起了，挪的时候我最激动，我时不时地观察石雕的表情，希望能悄悄看见他们对我的微笑，我虽然没有看见，但看见奶奶和舅舅以及家里的其他人都为我这个主意高兴我就已经很满足了。挪完后的当天晚上我就后悔了，因为把他们放在一起就意味着他们不需要走动了，但我也不可能再把他们分开，因为这是我的主意，我受的教育是不应该推翻自己的，尤其是被认为是好的主意。我扒在窗口看他们一动不动地在一起，我心里真的很矛盾，我多么想再看见他们走动啊。不过我想到自己的父母远在另一个城市的时候就觉得自己做对了，因为不知是什么原因使我和父母拉开了地理上的距离，照奶奶的说法是工作的需要，我觉得这个需要很残忍，所以我安排了石雕的团圆，如果还有一个小石雕的话，我也会把他或她与他们放在一起的。

可惜的是好景不长，1966年的夏天，一群戴着红卫兵袖章的人冲进我家，除了把我家翻了个天翻地覆，还把石雕的头都敲掉了，他们说所有迷信的东西全要毁掉，我与石雕一起拍的照片和底片也被与其他被认为该烧的东西一起在庭院里烧掉了，红卫兵走后我就去把石雕的头再放上去，可是男的那个头已经被敲成十几块，我想起舅舅曾经摔伤了脚所用过的绷带，就花了好几个小时用绷带把它们包好，终于放回到他们的肩膀上去了，然后我就去找舅舅，我说与石雕一起拍的照片全烧光了，我刚才把他们的头包好放回去了，咱们再拍一次吧。舅舅哭丧着脸说你到房间里看看。我看见照相机的样子并不比石雕的遭遇好多少，而且绷带也帮不了忙，它的"眼睛"已经碎掉了，它被舅舅放在床头边上，显然已经在舅舅的手中被悼念过一阵了。舅舅说因为是苏联产的。我心里多么盼望能有照相机把我和受伤的石雕一起照下来啊，我正在犹豫要不要把我看到的石雕曾有过的行为告诉舅舅，他突然想起了什么重要的事情，一步就往庭院里奔去，我也跟在后面，他看见了我包好的石雕的头，冲过去就把它们拿了下来，他说你不能这样做，这会给全家惹祸的，万一让红卫兵看见了，这就是一种反抗他们的行为，他边说边把绷带拆下来，他说幸好没有外人看见，他嘱咐我再也不能这样做了，得到我的点头之后他才松了一口气，他说以后会再买一个国产的相机给我拍照。我说以后就不能和石雕一起拍照了。他说没关系，咱们可以拍其他的风景。我说石雕打不过红卫兵，是无法辟邪的。舅舅很认真地对我说这种话千万不能再对任何人说，因为我们是成分不好的人家，是要被专政的，专政就是要把我们关起来的，现在还没有关是因为他们没有找到定罪的材料，所以今后千万千万不能多说话。我的眼泪在眼眶里面只停留了不该停留的一秒钟就流了出来，我站在没有头的石雕面前，在心里对他们说相机已经坏了，而且有相机的话也不能和他们一起拍照了。

1996. 2. 纽约

我和一星

　　我知道人们对未来有各种各样虚构的权力，比如 2010 年据说可以到月球上度假或到火星上去举行婚礼，这是有科学依据的推测，但也可以把它当作已经发生的事情写在书本里面。但是，对过去的虚构在文学上更加流行，至少在中国是这样的，比如各种各样演义帝王宫廷生活以及争斗的小说、电视剧不断出笼。而美国好像最多的是关于美国西部牛仔时期的英雄才有类似的虚构。显然历史的长短是一个原因，中国可供虚构的历史太多了，美国只有几百年，而且记录得相当完整。对了，记录是很重要的，同样是近几百年的历史，中国的就有不少版本，这样也让文学人士有更多的空间进行虚构。这样的话，作为一个中国历史旁观者的老外来看，就会感到无所适从了，先不说老外，就是中国人本身也对历史失去了兴趣，道理很简单，有很多历史处在不确定之中，尤其是许多细节性的东西，被许多大词一遮而过，历史的趣味性就此完全丧失了。我写这篇东西并不想那么严肃认真地来分析，我只是想写我的一个朋友，写写他的过去和他虚构事物的本领，来表达我对他的欣赏。

　　他叫一星。据说他父母 1949 年结婚第三天时有人给他父亲送来一张去香港的船票，因为找不到第二张船票，于是就放弃了去香港，留在大陆后陆续生了他姐姐、哥哥和他。于是，文革之后中国普遍存在着的虚构是这样的：假如 49 年我爷爷或我父母或我的什么离开了大陆，就是另外一个故事了，早就发了。

　　时间到了 1981 年的上海，一星三十岁，我和他已经认识了十几年，但他从来没有这样虚构过他的父母，他是另一种虚构，他对我说："只当我父母是 1950 年从香港回到祖国来的。"他就是这样一个人，不写作，但有作家的思考，不过说他有作家的思考也不对，因为有太多的作家把写作当作一种拿工资的工作。1985年一星得到了一次去香港的机会，他工作单位的领导想培养他，三个名额有他一个，是去考查。一星说所谓考查就是单位的奖励，让你见见世面，回来要更加听领导的话，我正想辞职呢，如果去了，回来就难以启口了，还有一种就是在香港叛逃不回来了。他想了两天后对领导说我要是觉得香港好，能不能就不回来了？领导说这怎么行，你不回来的话，我的官也别当了，你真有这个想法？一星说就是因为你看得起我，我才对你说的。领导于是就把名额给了另一个人。领导后来私下对他说你够讲义气的，当时你去了并且留在那里，我是毫无办法的，我这个职位也就要让出来了。所以啊，一星接着他的话说我现在想辞职，你看在我那个面子上，批准吧？！

1981年的时候几乎没有听说过谁敢辞职，尤其是一个市区里面的大机关。领导楞了一下说理由是什么？一星慢悠悠地说我想做生意，现在已经有人自己做生意了，我也想试一试。领导说还没有先例，我去打听一下再回答你。

后来他成为他们单位第一个辞职下海的人，他对我说就当我去了香港回来了，变了一个人，学到了自由市场的经验，准备干一番。我说你要干什么呢？他说开个小餐馆，民以食为天，肯定赚钱的。那时候我还没有跟上他的想法，我认为他就是太浪漫了。

可是一年下来，他与一个街道中年妇女合伙开的小餐馆居然赚了不少钱，但是树大招风，结果在卫生方面被人刁难了几次，虽然还是扛下来了，但他已经丧失了兴趣，就把他的股份让给了另一个人。我还记得那是1983年初的一天，我坐在他最后一天当老板的餐馆里喝酒，他对我说我不会后悔当初辞职的，现在我手里有一万块钱，这年头有几个人有，按照一个月一百块的工资，这里是一百个月的工资，与大多数人比，我就是香港了，可是话又说回来，当时我接受领导的培养，也许现在不是处长也是科长了，权力也是钱吗。

我对一星说你就是你，当时你父母反对你辞职，你就说过自己当老板也是可以辞职的，现在中了那句话了，接下来你打算做什么？一星说老实告诉你吧，先享受享受，最多给我父母和姐姐买个彩电，其他的，咱们几个哥们以后每个星期聚几次，都由我来请客。

时间到了 1985 年，一星已经迷上看书有两年了，主要是文学类的，但他的结论却是这样的：文学太好玩了，几十几百年的事情一本书或几句话就讲完了。我问他是否也想写一写？他摇头说应该是让生活按照小说的进度去过，那才浪漫呢。

1986 年我说想出国，他说别多想，努力出去吧，但一定要替我路过香港。后来我还真的在去美国留学时特意路过了香港。我在 1987 年从美国给他的信中提到我在香港时，曾经想到他如果住在香港的什么地方就可以找他聚聚了。他回信说假设你在香港找到了那个叫一星的人，但他已经变了，你们只是很肤浅地吃了一顿饭，你好我好地闲聊了几句而已，所以说历史可能就是这样的，我们有巩固我们感情的环境，对环境不一样的人我一直持怀疑的态度。

一星说的不错，我在美国的环境将改变我，问题是改变了之后我们还会是朋友吗？这是我 1994 年出国后第一次回国前所想的问题。

一星来机场接我时，带了一束鲜花，我说咱们还用来这一套吗？他说我吃不准你往哪个方向变，反正礼多没人怪。这时候的一星是在一个贸易公司里当策划，拿着个手机。我说你又赚大钱了，现在还有一百个月的工资请客吃饭吗？他笑着说假设我还是这样，你从美国回来还不惭愧吗？所以为了不让你们这类人太没面子，我现在压缩了我的存货，我现在起码有一个月的钱请你们美国吃一顿。

我说请整个美国？你真的发了？他说美国也是有代表的，你代表美国就行了，然后你回去写一篇报导，就说我把你像美国总统那样招待了一通。他知道我在美国一家杂志做事，就这样发挥了一下。我说挺想你的。他又发挥着说，看来你在美国还学会了同性恋，不错不错，慢慢向家乡的父老们汇报汇报。

第一次回国的两个星期假期一晃就过去了，与一星聚了不少次，其中一次我一直回味无穷。那是在他家里，是他自己买的，是刚刚开发的名叫辛庄的住宅区。他还叫了几个我以前不认识的朋友。我们一起喝酒聊天，欣赏他收藏的当代较前卫的艺术品，从艺术品的表面看，中国和西方的已经很接近了，只是在题材上稍有差异。另外有一点不同的是，他收藏的四五十件作品大多数是艺术家送的，在西方是完全不可能的。一星说这就是证明了中国人还不会做生意，但是也证明了中国有很多像我这样的"客户"，谢谢你提醒我，以后我不管给多少都买他们的。后来我们谈到了电影，一星接着一个朋友所说的媚俗的话题说，事实上真正的意思不是媚俗，而是聪明的人用媚俗的方式赚钱，目的是钱，结果呢，媚俗和钱也都不是问题，而问题是人类把智力用在什么地方，现在是一种全球性的恶性循环，那就是用智力去赚钱！为什么说恶性循环呢？因为有钱就可以虚构一切知识并让它成为真实。他喝了一大口酒之后又说，所有的知识要转变为赚钱的知识，这是对知识的污辱，但已经进入轨道，视而不见是最聪明的。

他说的这么严肃，使在场的人都感到了一种压力。他却哈哈一笑说，别紧张，我是在虚构我面对的是美帝国主义，我想象我是在美国的哈佛大学发言。听他这么一讲，大家都用手指着我，好像我就代表了美国。我也笑着说一星现在越来越中国了，看来不出国还是有底气，不会被别人看作四不像。一星给我倒了一些酒说，你去美国等于文革时期的插队，去物质丰富的地方也是插队，因为把你从原来生活的环境里抽离出去，中断你一贯的思维和行为方式，从这个意义上讲不是一样的吗？你或许会用物质的丰富来安慰自己，但你已经孤独了！你不可能在新的环境中再年青一次。

我被他说到心里去了，我说好像出国几年的不是我而是你，你怎么能体会到呢？一星说这几天咱们天天在一起，使我能有条件把自己虚构到你的处境中，这几天我虚构在里面，真的很痛苦。说到这儿，他还假装抹着眼泪。我笑着说，你可以活在虚构中，我也可以活在虚构中，我在美国虚构中国的日子。一星说不对，虚构是为了结论，不能解决真实的生活，我的意思很明白，就是让你回来，我身上少了你感觉不对。

他最后一句话使我一惊，加上酒的缘故，我哭了。但是后来是他比我哭得更厉害。

生活的重心是那么容易转来转去的吗？虽然我们情同手足，我回了美国之后并没有策划回国，但是，我明确地知道自己迟早要回去的。

1999 年 12 月下旬我又回去了，在那里度过了迈入新世纪的除夕夜，当然经常和一星在一起，直到 2000 年的 2 月我才回了美国，在美国我前后写了两篇东西，并且传真给他，不久他来了一个传真："虚构万岁！不过文字是不能虚构的，你用的是中文，除此之外，你文章的结论是什么？"我回了一个传真："假如能把你和我虚构成同一个人，才是虚构真正的力量，那么这同一个人如今是在纽约还是上海？"他传过来的回答是："在中文里！"。

下面是我的两篇东西：

明天晚上有一个酒神仪式，你一定要来看看。我的朋友一星在电话里对我说的时候，我能感觉他为此很激动，好像等不到明天了。我说明天是三十一号。他说对啊，就是要在跨世纪的时候才叫仪式呢！我用挑逗的语气说你是不是搞错了，他们是不是在搞邪教活动？他一听就急了，不会的不会的，那可比这教那教要艺术多了，是在一个很大的地方，主办者爱喝酒，还有和酒有关的作品，晚饭之后开始，你就十点去，肯定很热闹的，你从美国回来，不知道咱们上海也有火的东西，观念艺术不一定比美国的差。

按照一星给我的地址，1999 年的 12 月 31 日晚上十点我准时去了，已经到了不少人，空间确实不小，五十多平方米的客厅里面除了作品外，一张桌子上放了一些食品和酒，剩下的就是一些椅子了。我被介绍给主人，他叫大宝，也是所有作品的创作者，他说先随便看看吧。

一张破旧的床垫子由四个酒瓶支撑着，垫子上放满了各种各样的开酒器具。另外一件作品是在一本马克思的资本论上挖进去一个瓶子的形状，里面放的是一瓶北京名酒二锅头，里面的酒已经被喝掉了一半。一星在旁边说现在这个时代应该放一瓶法国的 X.O.。我说还应该用尼采的书，里面放一瓶可口可乐，两书与两酒的对比也很有意思。最后一件作品是电脑合成的两张照片，一张是自由女神手中的火炬变成了一瓶酒，一张是上海东方明珠电视塔塔尖部位变成了一个酒杯。不少人在对作品进行议论，同时也在喝酒，喝各种各样的酒。

我多少有点遗憾地问一星，还有别的作品吗？一星说大宝主要是画抽象画的，这是为了新世纪的到来特别玩玩的，图个热闹。大宝过来劝我们多喝酒，他说他需要一些空酒瓶当场做一个作品，希望大家努力喝酒。

终于有一个空档的时间可以与一星聊聊天了，我和他有五年没有见面了，这次从美国回来也只是下飞机后与他及几个朋友一起吃了顿饭。我说前几天找你找不到，你去什么地方了？他说还不是忙着挣钱吗？我说你还单身过着，没有找到合适的？他说这年头还是单身比较容易，事实上也有女朋友，只不过大家都没有结婚的冲动，就拖着了。我说那么今天这么重要的日子你们也分开过？他皱皱眉头说她去打麻将了，麻将是很多人的精神鸦片，本来她说会来的，看来是离不开了，在麻将桌上跨入二十一世纪也算是一个纪念。我笑着说你还挺容忍的，这种态度是不错，但也确实证明你们两个好像已经没有激情了。他说还谈激情，所有的激情全冲着钱去了，这年头，钱才是动力。我说你没有什么钱，不是也活得很好吗？他说我是赚不到大钱，没办法才这样的。这时候又进来了一群人，离十二点还有四十分钟，进来的人里面有一个是我认识的，于是又寒喧了一番，并被拉去与一些朋友认识一下，就这样转来转去地喝酒打招呼。

大宝占据了房间的一个角落，开始在地上码放空酒瓶，有几个人在向他传递四处散落的瓶子，许多人在旁边想看出个明白。大宝一脸严肃地说酒神酒神李白是中国的酒神，据说酒后诗比尿还多。大家还是不明白，继续看着。他一行行地码放着，直到空酒瓶没有了。他说还不够，于是把桌子上的各种没喝完的酒也码放上去了。他拍拍手伸了个懒腰指着第一行的瓶子边数边说这是题目：气死李白的十四行诗。于是大家就往下数，确实是十四行。有人叫道"够绝的！"还有人把酒瓶的总数点了出来："一共是一百个，连题目一百个字，最后一行是一个字，这是个什么字？"最起码有四、五个人同时回答说："操！"，于是哄堂大笑。

十二点还差十秒的时候，全屋的人开始从十倒数，数到一的时候，又有几个人同时大叫："操！"，就这样在上海某间公寓的客厅里我和这些艺术家一起从二十世纪跨入了二十一世纪。我突然想到了一星的女朋友，想象她如果在十二点敲响的一刹那，摸到了牌，大喊一声："自摸！"会是多么地刺激。我把这个想法告诉了一星，他哈哈大笑，眼中闪现出一丝忧郁，我就没有再多说这个话题。接下来是把那个床垫的作品搬开，开始了跳舞。

我和一星来到街上已经是快两点了，街上还是有很多人，其中不少人在等出租车。一个老外喜气洋洋地抱着一个中国姑娘在我们旁边走过，一星对我说体力有限，他抱不了多久的。我说你还真够幽默的。他说别看老外喜气洋洋，上海姑娘斩老外可利害了，不过话也说回来，作为男人来讲，我还很同情他。我说此话怎么讲？他说这种愿打愿挨的事情如今早已多见不怪了，但是大家一起愉快的时候，付钱的还是男人。

我默默地揣摩着一星的内心，作为一个不到四十岁的中国人，在这个时代有什么样的特点呢？一星好像看出了我的想法，他说你在想什么？我说我在想你。他说有什么可以想的，用生命去换钱，再用换来的钱维持生命，美国人以及全球的人不都是这样吗？！我无话可说，极端一点地讲，确实就是这样的，他的宿命在这个竞争激烈的社会中，有着人口膨胀地球资源越来越贫乏的背景。他换了一个话题说美国到底怎么样，你在那里七、八年了，还想回来过日子吗？我说你问对了，就是因为各有利弊，我还在犹豫呢。他说你还是回来吧，我听一个出去的作家说，母语是一种不能替代的营养，讲母语多痛快啊，你没看到刚才的最后一行，就是那一个字，而且为什么不是五言七绝而是十四行，这是大趋势，人类的文化共享，有些东西不是靠翻译的，是撞击出来的。听着他的发挥，我有点陶醉，在美国很久没有听人这样絮叨了，母语在向我召唤，我觉得一星好像就代表了母语，因为我是和他（母语）从小一起长大的。

分手前我们又谈到了晚上的酒神艺术，一星说有一件事情你还不知道吧？大宝今晚的这个地方是花五百块租的，他没有钱，但为了这帮朋友高兴也为了自己的艺术骚动，这笔额外的支出是我和他一起从十二月二十五号到三十号，在一家大商场给人安装了六天的彩灯和擦洗橱窗的玻璃挣来的，五百付租金，五百买了酒，还是因为我认识其中的一个经理，才把这个活给了我们。一星的这番话让我又回味了过去在一起时的美好时光，我们看到的不是谁穷谁富，看到的是相互的真诚，看来一星没有变，而我呢？过几天我又要回美国了，操！

时间过的真快，转眼我们都是往五十去的人了。一星这样对我说的时候，眼睛里闪烁的却是二十几岁时的光芒。看来就在他说这番话的时候，已经想到了二十多年前的什么事情。

于是我就喝了一口杯中的酒，慢吞吞地说你想起了什么就快说。

他说你看这家餐馆，装潢得多么豪华，以前都是电影或书本里才有的，以前咱们体力充沛，酒也喝的多，现在都喝不动了。他这么一说，我就知道他想说的是当年钱不多的时候，把餐馆里的胡椒粉兑在白酒里面喝，达到过瘾的劲头。但他笑着说我不是指那件事，我想起刚刚知道有迪斯科的时候，你在家里对着镜子练习，一练就是一个小时，体力真好。

我说你一会儿说餐馆装潢豪华，一会儿说我体力好，到底要说什么？

一星说这还不明白吗？以前一切简陋，我们体力好，如今条件奢侈我们则体力下降了。举个简单的例子吧，还记得我和小燕在郊区树林里做爱，让你望风的事情吗？那是 1978 年，那时候的中国是什么形势啊，大白天我们这样做就是找刺激，你在外面抽烟，也就是半个多小时，我射了好几次。现在是二十一世纪了，反而不浪漫了。

我说小燕和你分手后再也没有见过吗？

他说你知道的，85 年分手之后就没见过，你 90 年去了国外后倒是听说她做生意发了，现在想想她以前也够前卫的，八十年代初她的迪斯科跳得多好，那时候有几个会跳的。

我说你还没有把话说完，有什么快说。

一星笑起来很年轻，他用年轻的笑感染我对他要讲的事情的兴趣，他也是用这种方式迷惑过不少女孩子。他说老实告诉你吧，现在的女孩子真的不如以前的浪漫，我为什么还是单身，就是因为找不到以前的那种感觉，半年前我和一个女孩子谈恋爱，其实不叫恋爱，叫找感觉，她只想去豪华的地方找，我们在宾馆开过几次房间，有一次我们去杭州玩，在北高峰的树林里，我想起和小燕的那次，于是和她亲热起来，并提议在那儿做爱，可是她说这地方多脏啊，怎么都不愿意，结果还是回了旅馆才使她有做爱的感觉，而且还说我干起来没有激情，说我岁数是不是太大了点，也许是老了，但我觉得原因是她不够浪漫。一星还总结地说我的意思就是，现在的人，生活的舞台越来越物质了，不豪华就不会生活了，不豪华也刺激不了感觉了，你说这有多累！

我说你也别太叫劲，她多大岁数了？

他说二十六岁。

我说二十六岁的话，也就是 74 年才出生，这代人和我们的时代经验完全不一样了，对他们来讲不需要精神幻想来体会愉快，一切都可以通过物质条件来表现，这是他们的经验。

一星说半年来我和她的关系也冷淡了，她原来以为我做房地产会发财，结果这一行越来越不景气，她还想让我出一笔钱让她出国去留学，这一去还能跟我在一起？我们心里都知道这是在互相挤榨，能挤多少是多少，然后遇到好一点的就跳槽。所以说还是单身算了，一旦结婚再离婚更麻烦。

我对一星说也许你可以找个与你年龄相差不太多的女子。

他说可能吗？四十岁上下的女人谁没孩子？有了孩子对我还能有多少关心，再加上这个孩子还不是我的，我还要培养对这个孩子的感情，我可受不了这个负担。就说没孩子吧，四十上下的女人也一定伤痕累累了，哪还会有情绪来浪漫的？

我说你的问题就是还在追求浪漫，什么年龄了还这样，真拿你没办法，虽然你性格长相都不错，再加上幽默感很强，但年轻的一代毕竟比你更有条件。一星又笑了，他这种笑就是故事，这一点我是太知道了。

　　他说想知道吧？告诉你二十一世纪的第一个星期我干了什么吧。我结了一次婚，但这是一个工作。我挣了五千美金，折合成人民币是四万多。

　　真的？我说这倒是让我大吃一惊，只听说过为了得到美国绿卡，中国人可以出上万美金，你作为一个中国公民，难倒还有人想通过结婚拿中国绿卡的？

　　一星说这是另外一回事情，一个法国人想出一个构思：拍两对中国人在二十一世纪初的结婚和离婚过程的片子，一对人离婚，另一对是结婚，就拍过程，不需要构思任何情节，记录中国人结婚和离婚需要的是什么样的手续。这个法国人找到了我的朋友大宝，你还记得迎接二十一世纪的除夕夜，我们不就是在大宝那儿过的吗？！当时我没有透露，是怕节外生枝，中国的事情你是知道的。大宝是有太太的，他和他太太办离婚，我是单身就正好找一个合作者办结婚，先到街道办事处开单身证明，然后取表格填表格等等全过程都录像了，整整折腾了一个多星期，唯一出了个差错是大宝离婚过程中，太太的一个朋友提醒她是不是大宝假戏真做而引起的，后来那个法国人出面解释清楚了，幸好那个法国人是个男的，不然说不定他太太还不配合呢。长话短说，法国人找到的投资基金会是美国的，这个策划给了他一笔预算，材料等操作过程用了不到五千，剩下的每人得到五千，这种事情一辈子也就遇到一次，是吧？！

　　我说记录中国二十一世纪初的结婚离婚的程序，不至于花这么多钱，肯定这个策划还有其他的说法。

　　一星说毕竟你是在美国住了十年，看来对美国人的想法有不少了解，让你说对了，法国人的这个策划是和观念艺术有关的，那就是：我们是为了钱而结婚离婚的。在录像开头的时候有这样的对话："让你们这样做，如果没有钱，你们愿意做吗？""不愿意！"。

　　我对一星说这个法国人是个观念艺术家？一星说是的，而且做的很成功，并且在美国、欧洲、非洲以及澳洲都同时录了这样的节目，也就是在五大洲各选了一个国家做。

我琢磨了一会儿说，这里还有一个角度，那就是暗示真实的结婚和离婚也都是为了金钱？！这个节目的策划还真有点意思。但是你们刚结婚能马上就离婚吗？或者还要维持一段时间才能离婚？你现在可是一个法律上的丈夫了。

一星说把它看成一个行为艺术还是很有意义的，刚才你不就领悟了其中的观念吗？这个观念也是我在录相之后领悟出来的。至于我的婚姻，过一段就离掉它，没有什么后遗症可担心的，与我合作的也是一个比较前卫的画家。

我说这个法国人会发表这个作品吗？

一星说当然会的，这是真实的，是社会的一个现状，你说是吧？不过也许我们看不到，也许只在美国发表吧？！不过我们会得到一个复制的录像带。

我点了点头说，目前纽约还挺流行观念和装置艺术的，一些基金会也支持这一类的艺术，其实这类艺术八十年代末在欧洲很流行，可是美国那时候正好是经济不景气的时候，那时候纽约苏荷画廊区关掉了将近一百多家画廊，直到九十年代中期，美国经济好了之后，才又回过头来搞这个中断了的艺术门类，所以说现代艺术的繁荣更依赖经济，这又是一个金钱的例子！

一星随着我的思路说确实是金钱，但是人家美国人花钱留下了作品和记录，你看我们这儿，钱都吃了、卡拉OK了，我不知道这是文化还是素质，但我知道人家知道怎样去赚别的国家的钱。

我问一星还有什么故事吗？

他摇了摇头说一时想不起来了，不过，中国到处是故事，你回来多去接触接触吧，一定会有收获的。最后他以总结的口气说：每个人和每个社会都有自己的价值观念，生活就是在实行这个观念，所以说，生活就是观念的艺术。我的观念是，生活中有很多东西不是钱能买到的，比如浪漫。

2000. 1.

www.ingramcontent.com/pod-product-compliance
Lightning Source LLC
Chambersburg PA
CBHW060358030726
47497CB00003B/762